ROSES AND THORNS

Roses And Thorns

PRISCILLA SALCEDO

For those of you who read *The Rose Colored Prince* and thought, *"Did that actually happen? I want to read more,"* this one is for you. Thank you for joining me on this journey. You are the real MVP.

CONTENTS

A letter to the Readers

D^{*ear Reader,*}

Welcome to the fuckery I call life. This is a story that will take you on a wild ride packed with hope, pain, happiness, a pinch of lust, and a whole lot of what the fuck did I just read? If that's what you were looking for, then congratulations, my friends—you've found the right place..

In case you weren't around for my last fiasco, let me fill you in. First off, welcome. Second, here's the short version: I learned that fairy tales are exactly that—tales. Fictional, sugar-coated lies designed to make you think life is a perfectly paved yellow brick road. Spoiler alert: it's not. The road is covered in thorns, potholes, and questionable decisions, and if you're anything like me, you probably forgot to pack shoes.

I'd like to say I've come a long way since then, but honestly? Who knows. Because you see, just when you think things can't possibly get any worse, the universe has a funny way of showing you not to tempt it with a good time. Cue this era of my life. Buckle up—are you ready?

Before we dive in, here's a friendly heads-up: You will be triggered. Consider this your warning.

Happy Reading,
Patricia

| 1 |

The Mirror of Truth

The world feels different now. *I feel different.* It's almost unbelievable to think there was a time when I would've given my last breath for someone who couldn't have given two shits about me.

Prince Charming? What a joke.

We've all been there—caught in a relationship that knocks the air from your lungs. The kind that's so toxic, it seeps into every corner of your soul, leaving you shattered and questioning if you'll ever piece yourself back together. But here's the thing: only a love like that can crack you open enough to see the truth of who you are. It's a mirror—one that reflects both the best and darkest parts of you. The pain cuts deep, forcing you to confront yourself, to wrestle with your values and dreams in ways you never imagined. It's transformative, yes—but only after it's stripped you down to nothing.

Toxic relationships have a way of peeling back the layers, stripping away every illusion until you're left staring at your raw, unfiltered self. It's in those moments of vulnerabil-

2

ity—when despair seems to have hollowed you out—that you begin to discover your strength. Your resilience. Your capacity to heal and grow. You learn, often painfully, where your limits lie—what you can endure, what you simply cannot, and what must change if you're ever to move forward. There's a brutal honesty in surviving such a relationship. It's a harsh, unrelenting teacher, but the lessons it imparts are invaluable. You come to realize that your happiness cannot hinge on another person's validation. You start to understand the sacredness of boundaries—how vital it is to honor your own needs, your own desires. And slowly, painfully, you emerge on the other side with a sharper, clearer understanding of who you are and what you truly deserve.

For me, seeing the worst parts of myself was both devastating and liberating. It was the wake-up call I didn't know I needed. I saw a version of myself I never wanted to meet again—a shadow of who I once was, riddled with anxiety, paranoia, and fear. I was someone who clung to chaos because it felt safer than the silence of letting go. Back then, I believed he was my entire world, and the thought of losing him felt like an unbearable void. I would've rather drowned in the turbulence of his life than face the quiet unknown of my own. But the truth is, I wasn't losing him—I was losing *me.*

I'm grateful for the single, fleeting moment of clarity that smacked me upside the head before I let the best years of my life swirl down the drain like leftover spaghetti. It's wild, isn't it? How a relationship can shape you—for better, worse, or, in my case, into someone you don't even recognize. Seriously, who was that woman? The one who sacrificed her joy, her well-being, and her *entire identity* just to cling to something that was ripping her apart like an old sweater snagged on a rusty nail.

But here's the thing: now I see it for what it was. That breaking point? It wasn't the end of the world; it was the beginning of mine. It was the grand kickoff to finding me. *Cue Christina Aguilera's "Fighter" blaring in the background because yes, this was my personal music video moment.*
"Makes me that much stronger, makes me work a little bit harder, makes me that much wiser, so thanks for making me a fighter."

I'm telling you, the dark period of my life didn't just knock me down—it threw me face-first into a mirror. It forced me to confront my deepest fears and insecurities, peeling back the layers of that nice, polished facade I'd been wearing like overpriced concealer meanwhile the person underneath was a mess. But you know what? In those depths of despair, I started to recognize my own value—a truth I'd been ignoring for *far* too long.

When I look back now, I can't help but cringe. Who was that woman constantly anxious, tip toeing on eggshells, and living in a perpetual state of "What if he gets mad?" That wasn't me. That was a diluted, stripped-down version of who I am. And I swore to myself I'd never let anyone, *anyone*, reduce me to that again.

That relationship? Oh, it dismantled me, all right—piece by painstaking piece. But funny thing about being taken apart: you get to see what parts actually need fixing. Turns out, self-worth was missing from my toolkit. And let's face it, without self-worth, you're willing to accept crumbs instead of demanding the whole damn cake. I had to let go of who I thought I needed to be for someone else, so I could finally discover the person I was meant to be for myself.

Were those years brutal? Hell yes. Did they feel like a waste at times? Of course. But here's the kicker—they weren't. They were an invaluable chapter of growth in my life. Painful? Absolutely. Necessary? More than I'll ever *really* want to admit. Now, I'm the one holding the pen, and I promise you this: This is *my* story and boy will this end differently than the last.

Reflecting on the lessons learned from four years of trauma, there are truths I'll never forget:

1. **You cannot fix or build someone into the partner you need.** If they aren't at your mental or emotional level, no amount of effort on your part will change that. Love doesn't thrive in one-sided labor; it grows in mutual effort.

2. **Reciprocation is non-negotiable.** Without it, there's no balance, no equality, and no true connection. A relationship without mutual investment isn't a relationship—it's an illusion.

3. **You are not your partner's therapist, doctor, or savior.** You are their partner, friend, and confidant, but it's not your responsibility to rescue them from themselves. Losing your identity to "save" someone else is the quickest way to lose yourself entirely.

4. **Did I mention reciprocation?** Yes, it's worth repeating because it's that important. Without mutual respect, care, and effort, no relationship can thrive.

Emerging from that toxic relationship felt like shedding old, suffocating skin. The process was painful, yes—but it was also necessary.—a period that taught me resilience, self-awareness, and, most importantly, the kind of love I deserve.

Now at 32, single, and living in a four-bedroom house with just my dogs, life doesn't look quite like the picture I painted for myself in my 30s. But truth be told, it's not as bad as it sounds. In fact, it's different in ways that have turned out to be strangely beautiful. Your thirties are an odd yet transformative period—a time when life demands that you shed old expectations and make peace with who you're becoming. By now, you've likely weeded out the people who no longer fit your life—or at least, you're working on it. Friendships that felt unshakable in your twenties have faded, and the ones that remain are rooted in genuine connection. Slowly but surely, you start to figure out who you are, or at the very least, who you're striving to be. The real challenge now is learning how to present that person to the world with confidence.

Dating in your thirties comes with its own unique set of complexities. On one hand, you're likely carrying less baggage and are more accomplished, self-assured, and clear on what you want. On the other hand, there's this looming societal pressure—a quiet but persistent question: "If you're still single, what's wrong with you?" It's maddening, really, the way the world seems to measure your worth by your relationship status. And yet, there's also something incredibly liberating about this stage of life. For the first time, you're free to define success and happiness on your own terms, without the weight of external expectations. You begin to understand that fulfillment isn't tied to a checklist of milestones—marriage, children, career achievements—but rather to the quiet, unshakable joy of living authentically. This time is an invitation to rediscover yourself. To ask the questions you avoided in your twenties and lean into the answers, no matter how uncomfortable they might be. It's a decade that offers the space for deeper self-discovery and an opportunity to build a life that genuinely feels like your own. So no, life at 32 may not look like the vision I had in my twenties. But it doesn't have to. Because even if it's not the picture-perfect dream I once imagined, it's real, it's raw, and it's mine. And there's something profoundly fulfilling about that.

How does a woman who's on call 24/7 meet someone new unless it's at work? The dating pool for transplant doctors, surgical techs, and nurses is about as promising as a dry sponge. Many live in different states from their spouses, while others are unhappily married or divorced, their relationships casualties of unrelenting work schedules. Not exactly the stuff of fairy tales. I remember during my clinical training, a surgeon pulled me aside one afternoon, her tone more serious than the lecture we'd just left. "Never date another transplant professional," she warned. "You'll never see each other, and when you do, you'll both be too exhausted to care. You might as well stay single." Her words have been living rent-free in my head ever since, lounging on the couch and helping themselves to all my snacks.

Now that I'm tentatively wading back into the dating pool, I hear her advice loud and clear. Still, I couldn't resist the siren call of online dating—because nothing screams "romance" like swiping through profiles during a lull between emergency calls. It's not ideal, but what other choice does a workaholic introvert with a knack for dodging social interaction at bars have? Tonight, though, I wasn't swiping. I was decompressing in the most cliché way possible: curled up on the couch with a glass of wine and my dogs, half-watching a cheesy romance movie. The kind where the male lead has an unnervingly perfect jawline, a penchant for dramatic monologues, and somehow always knows the right thing to say.

On screen, he was gazing deeply into the woman's eyes, his voice low and velvety. "You're the only thing that makes sense in my world," he declared.

I rolled my eyes so hard it was a miracle they didn't stick. "Oh, please," I muttered, taking a sip of wine. "You met her, what, three days ago? Calm down, Romeo."

The woman, of course, teared up on cue, her lips trembling as she whispered back, "I've never felt this way before."

"Yeah, because it's fiction," I quipped to no one in particular. My dogs, sprawled across the floor, didn't seem to care. "Try feeling that way after he forgets to take out the trash for the third week in a row."

The male lead pulled her into a sweeping kiss, the kind that defied physics and logic, and I let out a cynical laugh. "Sure. Kiss her like that after a 14-hour shift and see how it goes. Hint: it won't."

I reached for another sip of wine, sinking deeper into the couch. Watching these movies used to make me wistful, but now they just made me laugh. Love in the real world was messy, complicated, and often inconvenient. It didn't come with poetic declarations or perfectly timed rainstorms. It came with schedules that didn't align, arguments over whose turn it was to cook, and long stretches of loneliness when work took priority. But despite my cynicism, I couldn't help but feel a tiny flicker of something—hope, maybe?—buried deep beneath the sarcasm. Because as ridiculous as these movies were, the idea of finding someone who could make the chaos of my world feel a little less chaotic didn't seem so bad.

Against my better judgment, I opened the dating app and was immediately greeted by, "Girl, you must be tired because you've been running through my mind *all day long.*" I snorted, unable to hold back a chuckle as I scrolled through the endless parade of corny pick-up lines.

"I called the radio station to ask why you weren't on the top 10 hottest singles."

Points for creativity, I thought, though I couldn't help but roll my eyes. The lines were undeniably catchy, and while they weren't exactly dripping with sophistication, they were at least entertaining. A welcome distraction from the monotony of swiping left on profiles that all seemed to blur together. It didn't take long to conclude that my soulmate probably wasn't lurking in this virtual crowd. The app felt more like a never-ending carnival of recycled one-liners, awkward compliments, and well-meaning but misguided attempts at charm. Still, I couldn't bring myself to delete it just yet. As much as it felt like an exercise in futility, there was something oddly refreshing about it.

Because here's the thing: even if the matches weren't exactly stellar, the process itself wasn't a complete waste. Online dating was a kind of emotional cardio—a way to stretch my social muscles and put myself out there, no matter how cheesy the interactions might be. It was an exercise in keeping an open mind, even when every instinct screamed, *Close the app and run.* Somewhere deep down, I had to believe that this ridiculous process was serving a purpose. On some energetic level, I imagined I was sending out a cosmic S.O.S. to the universe. *Hey, I'm here. I'm trying. I'm ready to meet someone genuine, even if it means wading through a sea of bad puns and half-hearted winks first.* Besides, there was something endearing about the earnestness of it all. The hunt may feel like a comedy show at times, but the effort people made—even the cheesy one-liners—spoke to a shared human desire for connection. We were all just trying, in our own awkward ways, to be seen.

Noticing how late it had gotten, I switched off the TV and began my usual night routine. The dogs, as if on cue, trotted off to their beds, knowing it was time to settle down. Upstairs, I peeled back the perfectly arranged bedding, sinking into my side of the bed and cocooning myself in the soft comfort of the covers.

It seemed today was going to be another bust.

With a sigh, I closed the app on my phone, rolling onto my back and staring at the ceiling. The faint glow of the screen illuminated my face as my thoughts wandered. Biting my lip softly, I gave in to the tug of temptation, swiping to a private tab and navigating through my carefully hidden folders and bookmarks. This was my secret stash—a collection I'd never dream of sharing with anyone, not just because of its content but because of how intensely personal it felt.

I reach into the nightstand, fingers brushing against the smooth surface, and retrieve my favorite electronic boyfriend, anticipation coursing through me.

With a shuddering breath, I open my preferred go-to:

The forbidden romantic fantasy between a stepbrother and stepsister.

There's just something about the forbidden act that made me shudder *violently*.

I laid the folded towel from my bottom drawer onto the bed, a routine that had become second nature by now. Settling in, I parted my legs, sliding my panties to the side, already feeling the heat building within me. My core throbbed, slick and ready, as the stepbrother heaved his sister onto his lap on the screen in front of me. My toes curled instinctively as I propped the phone upward, angling it just right for an uninterrupted view. One hand slowly fed the thick dildo inside me, the stretch making my breath hitch, while the other roamed upward, lazily rolling my breasts. The tension building in my body matched the intensity of the scene playing out on the screen, every motion drawing me further into the blissful escape.

Fuck.

I lick my lips, flicking on as the vibration practically vibrates every nerve-ending muscle in my body. Eyes fluttering shut for a moment, I pinch my nipple, whining while I circle my clit delicately with my thumb in between fucking myself. Gradually, I start to buck up slowly against the thickness, the squelching noises growing as I watch hazily of her step brother now having her bent on their white leather sofa, breeding her senseless. I moan the same time she does, toes curling as I roll my nipple around before pinching roughly.

So good.

So damn *good*.

When I open my eyes again, I watch as she grips the edge of their sofa, drool slathering down her face as she whimpers. She looks so happy to be her brother's personal slut right in the open of their living room when their parents can come home at any time.

God, why is that so damn hot?

"*Fuck*," I mewl breaths, my eyes turning watery from the pleasure coursing through me as I focus on the moans coming out softly on my phone's speakers. His pistons are deep and powerful, almost like a rutting beast, as she now reaches to scratch at his back, begging him to hurry before their parents come home.

I picked up the speed of my toy, trying to match how deep and rapidly the man was driving into his sister, feeling my body crying out for the inevitable that was just around the corner. I can feel my inner thighs shaking, a complete mess, as I listen to the sound of those two moaning and grunting.

"Please, please, cum inside me," she whines.

"Yeah?" he grunts, but it sounds like a low growl. "You love your brother's cock that much? God, you are so fucking tight, no matter how many times I thought I had broken you in. How are you going to satisfy another man again if your pussy is already taking the shape of my cock? How about I just make you my personal fucktoy, sis?"

"*yes*," I whine at the same time she does.

I want to be bred.

I want to be fucked senseless.

I want to be taken roughly and used.

Watching as he then lays a hand on his sister's backside, the crackling noise echoing all around them as she gasps. I don't think I can last long anymore, especially when my favorite part is coming up.

Hurry, hurry, hurry.

I can feel my body starting to grow warmer, my arousal making a mess all over the bed sheets as the pool of heat in my stomach now reaches an all-time boiling point. I know that it's only a matter of when at this time when it comes to what might be the most explosive orgasm this week with how much I've been holding back.

Between crashing after working twelve-hour shifts, it's not like I even have time to breathe properly.

The man on the screen grunts.

Then I see his balls contracting up as he spills his seed into her depth.

"Fucking take it all. Take every last *fucking* drop. I watch her eyes widen before she leaps over the edge while screaming his name.

He pulls away from her gaping wet sex, pumping a few times as he paints her tits with his spill. He then groans, running his hand through his own load, massaging it like lotion into her skin as she arches her back willingly.

It's almost like he's marking her as his—And she's agreeing to every taboo with a look of complete submission in her eyes. He then takes a swipe of his mess, bringing it up to her lips as she whines and lapses it up willingly.

With a choked whine, that's all it takes.

I roll my nipple between my fingers, pinching harder as I practically buck my hips to meet every one of the dildo's fucks eagerly as I shatter entirely. My core clenches like a vise around the dildo, my finger that had been on my nipple going down to rub my clit thoughtlessly, completely a slave to my own pleasure.

"God," I mewl, bucking and writhing as I come all over my dildo, my body still shaking in pleasure.

For a few moments, I lie there, savoring the aftershocks of pleasure and trying to catch my breath.

Slowly, I remove the toy from between my legs, the warmth of its presence still lingering. I open my tired eyes to the dim light, my mind a delicious haze of desire. I turn off my phone, a thrill coursing through me as I clean and tuck the dildo away into its secure location and throw the towel into the open laundry basket.

Right as I drift off, I can't help but wonder:

Will I ever have back-blowing sex again?

| 2 |

Kisses and Confessions

When will it be my turn? They say there are plenty of fish in the sea, but I'm starting to feel like a fish stuck in a drying-up pond, flopping around while everyone else gets scooped up. The clock is ticking on my dating life—or at least that's what society loves to remind me—and the list of alluring prospects is...well, nonexistent. A year ago, I decided to focus on loving myself first, thinking that this magical act of self-care would summon my soulmate like a cosmic reward. Fast forward to now: still no sign of Prince Charming. So here I am, doubling down on this *self-love journey,* because apparently, the universe thinks I need a little more practice. Isn't it funny how people always say you need to love yourself before anyone else can? Sure, that sounds great in theory, but nobody warns you about the awkward purgatory where you're just loving your-self...alone. And let me tell you, I'm starting to feel like a professional at this point. If self-love were a competition, I'd be wearing a crown by now—not a tiara from a wedding shower but a full-on *golden sash and scepter.*

Meanwhile, my friends are pairing off like they're starring in their own rom-com montages—finding their matches, moving forward with their picture-perfect lives. And here I am, practicing self-love like it's a full-time job. Don't get me wrong; I'm great company (just ask me). I've mastered the art of solo movie marathons and splurging on fancy dinners for one. But sometimes, even I have to admit, the silence of singlehood can be deafening. It's like the universe is playing the world's longest game of, "Let's see how much patience she really has."

Despite the *radio silence* in my love life, I have to admit—I've been learning a lot about myself. New hobbies? Check. Deepened friendships? Absolutely. Independence? Oh, I've got that down to a science. Maybe the universe really is taking its sweet time, making sure the next person to walk into my life is actually worth it. I mean, at this rate, they'd better be worth the wait because I'm starting to think I deserve a medal for perseverance. So here I am, waiting for my turn—feeling like a fish out of water but still flapping along, determined to survive. Maybe I'll even grow some metaphorical legs while I'm at it. One day, I'll find my place in the sea (or pond, or wherever the hell love is hiding), and when that happens, I'll be more than ready. Until then, I'll keep fiercely loving myself and hoping the universe is cooking up something extraordinary—preferably sooner rather than later.

Over the years, I had developed a fondness for writing outdoors. There's something about the fresh air and natural light that sparks creativity. However, with the summer heat in full swing, I knew I needed something to keep me cool.

Ice cream was the perfect solution. I grabbed my favorite journal and headed to the local ice cream parlor a couple towns over. This place was known not just for its delicious treats but also for its charming outdoor seating area, filled with picnic tables and outdoor games. The drive there was a pleasant escape from my routine, giving me time to think and anticipate the delightful combination of writing and ice cream. When I arrived, I picked a spot under a large, shady tree, ordered a generous scoop of my favorite flavor, and settled in. The ambiance was perfect—a gentle breeze, the laughter of kids playing nearby, and the comforting hum of summer all around me. It was the ideal setting to let my thoughts flow onto the pages of my journal.

There's something comforting about living near small towns. It's predictable in the best possible way. The places look the same, smell the same, and are run by the same people for decades. There's a sense of reassurance in seeing familiar faces and building relationships with the staff and fellow locals. It feels like home. Every corner of the town holds a memory, from the old diner where I have my breakfast to the bookstore where I spend my afternoons browsing. The shopkeepers know me by name, and there's a warmth in their greetings that you can't find in larger cities. The local park, with its familiar walking trails and benches, offers a peaceful retreat where I can gather my thoughts.

Even the seasonal changes are a comfort—the same festivals, the same decorations, the same traditions year after year. There's a rhythm to life here that's both calming and grounding. It's a place where everyone looks out for each other, and community spirit is alive and well. Balancing this with working in the city provides the perfect blend of both lifestyles. The hustle and bustle of the city energizes me during the day, with its fast pace and endless opportunities. Then, coming back to the calm and cool of a small town in the evenings offers a much-needed respite. It's the best of both worlds—thriving in the dynamic city environment while savoring the tranquility and familiarity of small-town life.

Interrupting my thoughts of admiration for small towns, the phone chimes with a text message.

"What are you doing in my town?"

Where is he? Slightly excited and slightly creeped out, I curiously turned around to find my long-time friend Anthony standing behind me, smiling. Anthony and I go way back—we used to work together at an assisted living facility for individuals with traumatic brain injuries. He was my overnight partner, and we quickly became friends. Working overnight with someone in a home setting is like fast-tracking a friendship on steroids. You see all sides of them—there's no hiding. It's easy to develop a "work husband/wife" mentality. This person sees you at your most energized when you walk through the door and at your grouchiest when you're tired. They learn all your quirks and pet peeves, and you learn theirs. In a home setting, you split home responsibilities while caring for the individuals. It's an unfiltered, no-holds-barred kind of bonding experience. There's no way to keep up any façade when you're making late-night coffee runs and sharing stories in the wee hours.

Anthony and I would trade off duties, laugh at ridiculous jokes, and commiserate over the endless paperwork. We had an unspoken understanding that only comes from shared late-night shifts. We became each other's sounding boards, confidants, and partners in crime. Seeing him now, out of the blue, brought back a flood of memories. Nights spent navigating the chaos of our job, supporting each other through the lows and celebrating the highs. Our friendship had evolved naturally, shaped by the countless hours we spent together in the trenches of caregiving.

I eventually moved on to different work, but Anthony and I always managed to stay in touch or randomly run into each other over the years. Anthony was very attractive—he had a perfectly groomed beard and dressed in a sharp, clean-cut style. He was one of those guys with impeccable hygiene, the type you just knew would always smell good. Known as the nice guy that everyone loved, Anthony had zero enemies. We had a very playful friendship, filled with playful banter and random adventures. Our bond was a true "ride or die" type of loyalty. Whether it was play fighting or embarking on some spontaneous escapade, we always found a way to make each other laugh. It never mattered how much time had passed between our encounters; our friendship always picked up right where it left off, as if no time had passed at all. Anthony's charm was undeniable, but it was his genuine kindness and continuous support that made our friendship so special. He was the person you could always count on, no matter what. We shared countless memories of late-night conversations, road trips to nowhere, and inside jokes that only we understood.

Every time we reconnected, it felt like a warm reminder of the enduring nature of true friendship. But having a close friend of the opposite sex could be tricky at times. Romantic partners would sometimes get jealous or worried about our friendship, internally questioning if they had something to be concerned about. Out of respect for our significant others, Anthony and I usually opted to distance ourselves whenever either of us were dating someone seriously. We had a mutual understanding that we would always reconnect when the time was right. It wasn't always easy, but we both simply wanted to see each other grow and be happy. We respected the boundaries that our romantic relationships required and trusted that our bond was strong enough to withstand the occasional hiatus. Our friendship was built on a solid foundation of trust and loyalty, so we never felt the need to explain or justify our actions. We always knew we'd cross paths again.

In those moments apart, we pursued our individual dreams and navigated the complexities of life. Yet, the anticipation of our next meeting always lingered in the back of our minds. Each reunion was like picking up a cherished book, finding the exact page where we left off, and diving back into the story with renewed enthusiasm. Our bond transcended the usual constraints of time and distance. It was the kind of friendship where we could go months without speaking, yet instantly fall back into our old rhythm with a single text or chance encounter. We shared a deep understanding and genuine affection that went beyond mere companionship. It was a rare and precious connection, one that enriched our lives in countless ways. We celebrated each other's successes and supported one another through the inevitable challenges. Anthony's encouragement helped me through some of my toughest moments, and I like to think my advice did the same for him. Our friendship was a constant source of strength and joy, a reminder that true friends are always there, even when they're not physically present.

When I was with James, I shut everyone out of my life, including Anthony. Looking back, I can't help but feel deep remorse for my actions. It had been four long years since we last talked. Throughout those years, Anthony would occasionally send me messages to check in, but I ignored them, paralyzed by the fear that even the smallest connection with him might jeopardize my already fragile relationship with James. I was wrong. It's people like Anthony that I should have kept close. Perhaps he could have told me to run for the hills while I was ahead. Perhaps he could have been the much-needed shoulder to lean on while I stubbornly chose to stay and fight a losing battle. As I stood there, facing him again after all this time, a whirlwind of emotions hit me—nostalgia for the times we shared, regret for pushing him away, and relief that he was still here.

So many thoughts crossed my mind in a matter of seconds. What if I had stayed in touch with Anthony? Maybe he could have offered the clarity and perspective I desperately needed. His friendship could have been a lifeline, guiding me away from the mistakes I made. I felt a pang of guilt, realizing how my fear and insecurity had cost me such a valuable relationship. In those moments, the weight of my decisions settled heavily on my shoulders. I regretted how I had allowed James to isolate me from the people who truly cared about me. Anthony had always been there, a constant presence in every phase of my life, and I had turned my back on him. The regret was almost too much to bear, knowing that I had missed out on four years of his friendship, support, and laughter.

Now, seeing Anthony again, I felt an overwhelming urge to make things right. I wanted to apologize, to explain, and to somehow make up for the lost time. But most of all, I wanted to ensure that I never made the same mistake again. Four years had passed, and it was clear that I had changed. But something was different about Anthony too. His beard now sported a few gray hairs, but otherwise, he looked the same. It was the way he carried himself that had transformed. He exuded a more mature energy, a quiet confidence that hadn't been there before

"Hi! Long time no see!" I said, my excitement barely contained.

"Yeah, I know, jerk," he replied with a smirk, half-joking but with a hint of genuine reproach. "What are you doing here?"

"I love this place. I just wanted to come and enjoy the weather," I explained, trying to sound casual despite the rush of emotions. Seeing Anthony again after so long was stirring up a mix of nostalgia and curiosity.

Anthony was with his daughter Mia. "Hi, Mia!" I greeted her warmly, marveling at how much she had grown. It was hard to believe she was already twelve, considering I remembered her as a little five-year-old.

"Hi," she replied politely, her shyness evident.

"Well, we have to go, but it was nice seeing you," Anthony said, preparing to leave.

"Thanks, you too!" I replied, trying to mask my disappointment. I had hoped we could talk more, catch up on the years that had passed. As they headed to their car, I sat back down, feeling a pang of regret.

I picked up my journal again, trying to focus on my writing, but my thoughts kept drifting back to our brief encounter. Just then, my phone chimed with another text message. I glanced at the screen, my heart skipping a beat.

"Do you want to meet up for dinner?" I read the words, surprised but thrilled at the opportunity to reconnect.

"Okay, when?" I replied quickly, my fingers almost trembling with excitement.

"Tonight." He wasn't wasting any time, and I was here for it.

"It's a date," I texted back, a smile spreading across my face.

The anticipation of dinner brought a rush of emotions—hope, excitement, and a touch of nervousness.

It will be great to catch up and see where life has taken him, to find out what's changed and what stayed the same. We agreed to meet at Applebee's, a popular chain restaurant in the area with a happy hour menu to die for at half-off prices. It was happy hour, and I was excited to head over to the restaurant to meet up with Anthony. The place was buzzing with energy—upbeat music and lively chatter filled the air. The bar was lined with TVs broadcasting sports, adding to the vibrant atmosphere. We chose a booth, wanting to have a space where we could actually hear each other talk. True to form, it felt like no time had passed at all. Within moments, we were back to our old routine—cracking jokes, playfully speculating about the other tables, and just enjoying ourselves. We chatted about our most recent failed relationships, keeping things light-hearted and avoiding too much detail.

From that night on, our texting frequency skyrocketed. It was refreshing to have such an easy, uncomplicated conversation with someone who truly understood me. Our reconnect was a breath of fresh air, and it felt good to dive back into that effortless camaraderie. We saw each other a few more times, and I couldn't quite put my finger on it, but something was definitely different. It was like I was living in a scene straight out of a Disney movie, with that iconic "There's something there that wasn't there before" song playing on repeat in my head. Every time we met up, there was a subtle shift in the air, an unspoken energy that made me question what was happening. Was I going crazy, or was there something real going on? The connection we had always been easy and comfortable, but now it felt charged with an underlying tension I hadn't noticed before. I couldn't shake the feeling that something had changed between us—maybe it was just me projecting my own emotions, or perhaps he was experiencing the same stirrings. There were glances that lingered a bit too long, moments of silence that seemed to say more than words ever could. Was he feeling what I was feeling? Or was this all just a figment of my imagination, a trick my mind was playing on me? It was both exciting and unsettling, and I found myself caught in a whirlwind of emotions.

Movie nights and game nights quickly became our routine. With each film we watched and every game we played, we found ourselves growing closer. Quite literally closer, as we often ended up cuddling into pretzel-like shapes, melting into each other's embrace. It was clear that physical touch was a love language we both shared. With Anthony, I felt safe. He knew exactly who I was, and I never had to pretend or put on a facade. Messy hair, pajamas, mismatched socks—none of it mattered to him. He accepted me as I was, flaws and all.

One night, as we settled into our usual spot on the couch, I found myself lost in thought, appreciating the comfort and ease of our connection. Just then, Anthony grabbed my hand and kissed it, a sweet and unexpected gesture that made me smile. But Anthony, always the joker, wasn't done. He grabbed my hand again, kissed it once more, then playfully smacked it and burst into laughter.

"What was that for?" I asked, pretending to be offended.

"I just want to fight you," he said with a mischievous grin.

"Oh please, don't start. I don't want to hear you crying when I hit you too hard," I shot back, raising an eyebrow.

"Shut up," he retorted, and in an instant, he lunged at me, trying to pin me down. I used the strength of my legs to push him off, but this time, he had the upper hand.

"Yeah, not so strong now, huh?" he said, his face radiating confidence.

I started laughing, deciding to let him think he had won. "Ha!" he shouted, feeling triumphant.

Just as he was basking in his victory, I slipped out of his grip and maneuvered myself on top, pinning him down. "Ha!" I shouted back, mocking him.

He burst into laughter. "Okay, I see what you did there."

"Now you have to fight these kisses!" I declared, leaning down and attacking him with playful kisses all over his face. He tried to squirm away, but I was relentless.

I stopped for a moment and looked at him. Our eyes locked, and the playful atmosphere shifted. He grabbed my face and kissed me on the lips. My heart skipped a beat. His lips were so soft, his kiss slow and sensual, filled with a passion that made it clear he had been waiting to do this for a long time. We paused for a second and looked at each other, searching for confirmation in each other's eyes. No words were needed; our gazes spoke volumes. Both of us silently pleaded for more, and one kiss turned into what felt like an hour-long make-out session. We were both conscious of not wanting to cross any further lines, aware of the boundaries we were navigating.

As much as I wanted to take things further, I decided that this was already a significant leap. I ended our make out session with some playful baby kisses, which he respected and mimicked. He grabbed my face one last time and gave me a lingering, tender kiss before he yelled, "Okay, come on, we have a movie to watch!" He laughed, breaking the tension. We rewound the movie, though neither of us cared about it anymore, and settled back into our pretzel position. My thoughts wouldn't let me focus on the screen. What just happened? It was clear that I wasn't imagining things. My mind wasn't playing tricks on me. His kisses had felt just right, like Goldilocks finding the perfect porridge. At that moment, nothing else in the world mattered.

I couldn't stop my thoughts from diving deeper. Could it be? Was it possible that what I had been searching for all along had been right in front of me? It was certainly too soon to tell, but the thought lingered, refusing to be dismissed. Every glance, every touch held a different meaning now. The boundaries of our relationship had shifted, and neither of us seemed eager to define it just yet. We were content to let things unfold naturally, savoring the thrill of it all and the comfort of familiar companionship. As the credits rolled, we stayed entwined, the world outside fading into insignificance. In that cozy cocoon of our making, I felt a profound sense of contentment and a budding hope that maybe, just maybe, this was the start of something wonderful.

| 3 |

Doubt and Desire

The next morning, I woke up to a call from Anthony. "HELLOOOO!! GOOD MORNINGG!!" he
sounded groggy, like he had just woken up. "Good morning!" I replied, hearing a little voice in the background.

"Who's that?" I asked, curious about why it sounded like
he had a toddler with him so early.

"That's my son," he said casually.

He has a son? How did I miss that? Was he hiding it
from me? My old triggers immediately started creeping back
in, reminding me of when I found out James had a baby
on the way with Elaine. Was I naive enough to fall for the
same situation twice? I was determined not to let that happen again, to be more aware of my surroundings. But apparently, I hadn't been careful enough. Was this a trigger from
my past, or did I just have a knack for picking men who lie
through their teeth? Despite the panic brewing inside, I decided to play it cool and see where the conversation led.

"I didn't know you had a son," I said, fishing for more information.

"What do you mean?" he asked, sounding genuinely con- fused. "He's all over my social media."

Really? I had to admit, I added him as a follower but never actually clicked into his profile. And now he knew that too.

"Oh, is he?" I said, pulling up his account to check out his profile for myself.

"Wow," he said, realizing I never bothered to look at his profile.

Sure enough, there were multiple photos of his son and his daughter displayed throughout his profile. Pictures of his son's first and second birthdays, right there in plain sight for me to see. It was at this moment that I questioned how aware I really was of my surroundings. I chuckled to myself, relieved that I wasn't reliving a horrific story twice, but also feeling caught off guard. Nevertheless, I continued to play it cool.

"Aww, he's cute! How old is he?" I didn't see any birthday photos past three years old.

"He's two. He turns three in May."

"Oh, nice!" I said, unsure of what the proper response was.

"Mhm," Anthony responded, his tone carrying an under- current of understanding. He knew I was trying to play it cool, but he could sense my internal turmoil. Still, he was willing to go along with the charade. I continued reading the captions on his social media. "HBD Christian. I love you, buddy." Christian was a nice name, I thought to myself.

On the bright side, at least he wasn't hiding the fact that he had another child. What a relief. He had no idea what

I went through in my last relationship. It wasn't the existence of his second child that concerned me—I loved children and would gladly take any child in as my own. My worry was about his relationship with Christian's mother, especially given how young their child was. It dawned on me just how much had changed in the four years we hadn't talked. I needed to rip off the bandage and get to the bottom of this.

"So, what's the situation with you and his mom?" I asked, cutting right to the chase.

"We're not together," he replied. Thank goodness, I thought, considering the intense make-out session we had the night before.

He continued, "I met her at a party. We went on a couple of dates. We had sex twice, and on the third time, she got pregnant." Anthony wasn't the type to sleep with just anyone, so he must have been genuinely interested in her. "I made her my girlfriend when I found out she was pregnant, but that's when everything changed. She just became so mean."

"What do you mean?" I asked, my curiosity piqued. As a woman, I automatically assumed it must have been the hormones. As if reading my mind, he interrupted my thoughts.

"I thought maybe it was just hormones, but then Christian was born, and it didn't get any better," he explained. "Before getting pregnant, she told me she couldn't have children. She said how much she wished she could but that it wasn't in the plan for her. Clearly, it was."

Did she trap him? Miracles do happen, but what are the odds that she claimed she couldn't get pregnant and then conceived within a month? As if reading my thoughts, Anthony continued speaking while I listened patiently.

"The change was so drastic. I sometimes wonder if it was planned. But at the same time, I always say that everything happens for a reason, and I got my boy out of all this." His voice filled with joy as he spoke about his son, Christian.

"Okay, so where do you two stand now?" I needed to know.

"We tried to make it work, broke up, tried again, but it's done. She might be even crazier than the last." He was referring to Mia's mom, who had put him through hell when Mia was younger, constantly dragging him to court with false accusations. Anthony now had full custody of Mia, and her mom lived on the other side of the country.

"Well, you know how to pick 'em. You love the crazies," I joked. It was a long-standing joke between us, but now that I was no longer just a friend, I felt a twinge of doubt. I would never be one of those girls... again. What if I wasn't crazy enough for him? What if my simple and predictable life bored him? I quickly shook those thoughts out of my head. He knows who I am. But what if he turned them crazy? What if they all started out like me? No. I knew him too well. Not on a romantic level, but on every other level, and I couldn't see that being the root problem here.

"Okay." One word. That was all I needed to say at the moment. I wanted to let things play out and let his actions speak for themselves.

"I'm going to take a shower, but I'll call you when I'm done," he said. I'm sure he didn't know where to take the conversation next, just as much as I didn't.

"Okay, sounds good," I replied.

He did call after his shower. And from that day on, he called me every morning and every chance he could throughout the day until it was time to go to bed. First, he would call just to say goodnight then he started calling so we could fall asleep together on the phone. Over time, those calls became a comforting routine. We'd share the little details of our day, laugh about silly things, and sometimes, we'd just fall asleep listening to each other breathe. The consistency of his calls reassured me, slowly chipping away at my doubts.

At first, I would always make sure he fell asleep first, worried I might make any embarrassing noises or snore without knowing it. Being the jokester that he is, I knew if I made any weird noises, I would definitely hear about it in the morning. Anthony saw me every chance he could, and I wasn't used to this amount of attention. He just wanted to talk to me, tell me about his day, and be in my presence. It felt refreshingly genuine. It started with simple requests—asking me to run errands with him. We'd buy groceries, get oil changes for our cars, go to the gym, and find any excuse to utilize the limited time we had together. Physical touch was definitely our shared love language. We'd hold hands during car rides, playfully grab each other at the grocery store, and rest our heads on each other while waiting in waiting rooms. We needed to touch in some way, a constant reminder of our connection.

Christian lived with his mom three days a week and with Anthony the remaining four days. We spent time together when Christian was with his mom and while Mia was in school. This arrangement worked perfectly with my schedule since I primarily worked evenings, and he worked overnight. We wanted to take our time and get to know each other on a romantic level before involving the kids. Our days quickly became full of sushi lunch dates and exploring trending local spots we'd heard about on social media.

We'd laugh together over the smallest things, like trying to pronounce exotic sushi names or debating which local café had the best coffee. His presence became a comforting routine, something I looked forward to amidst the chaos of our schedules. I began to notice how he'd go out of his way to do little things for me, like remembering my favorite snacks or suggesting places I'd mentioned wanting to visit. Was he courting me? I struggled to decipher if this was what healthy courting looked like or if this was a potential red flag, reminiscent of when James was obsessed with spending time with me. I couldn't help but draw parallels to my past, questioning if Anthony's attentiveness was genuine or a sign of something more sinister.

With James, the constant need for togetherness had felt suffocating, like an ever-tightening grip around my freedom. His obsession with our time together quickly became a means of control, isolating me from friends and family. The red flags had been there, waving furiously, but I had been too blinded by his initial charm to see them for what they truly were. Anthony's behavior, however, felt different. His attention didn't come with the same heaviness or underlying tension. When we were together, there was a lightness, an ease that I had never experienced with James. It felt like

Anthony genuinely enjoyed my company without trying to control it. His efforts to include me in his daily life seemed rooted in a desire to share, not to possess.

Yet, doubt still lingered. Was I being naïve again? Could I be missing subtle warning signs because I was so desperate for this to be real? These questions haunted me, a constant whisper in the back of my mind. I knew I had to tread carefully, to differentiate between genuine affection and potential manipulation. Despite my reservations, it felt... good. Anthony's presence was warm and reassuring. He wasn't just filling a void; he was adding something valuable to my life. Our interactions were infused with a sincerity that was hard to ignore. The way he made me laugh, the gentle touches, the thoughtful gestures—each moment spent with him felt like a step towards something meaningful, not a calculated move on a chessboard of manipulation.

I remembered the countless times James had insisted on being the center of my world, demanding my attention and time until I felt like I had nothing left to give. Anthony, in contrast, seemed to thrive on the balance we found together. He encouraged me to pursue my interests, to spend time with friends, to maintain my independence. This wasn't a relationship built on dependency but on mutual respect and support. I realized that I needed to trust myself and my instincts more. The old me, conditioned by past traumas, might have seen shadows where there were none. The new me, stronger and wiser, could recognize the genuine care and affection Anthony was offering. It was time to let go of the past and embrace the possibility of a healthy, loving relationship. For the first time in a long time, I felt like

I could let my guard down and allow myself to truly experience the joy of being loved and cared for.

Is there such a thing as a healthy obsession? It's a curious concept, isn't it? Obsession typically carries a negative connotation, conjuring images of unbalanced fixations and unhealthy dependencies. Yet, when framed within the context of genuine affection and mutual respect, can it transform into something positive? Think about the way a gardener tends to their plants—dedicated, attentive, and nurturing. The gardener doesn't merely water the plants; they understand their needs, ensuring they get just the right amount of sunlight, the right kind of soil, and the occasional trimming to keep them healthy. This level of dedication and care could be seen as a form of healthy obsession. The gardener's love for the plants drives them to go above and beyond, creating an environment where both the gardener and the plants thrive.

Similarly, in relationships, a healthy obsession might manifest as an intense interest and investment in each other's well-being and happiness. It's about wanting to know everything about the person—not to control or possess them, but to support them fully and celebrate their uniqueness. This kind of obsession is rooted in love, not possessiveness; in care, not control. But, of course, the line between healthy and unhealthy can be thin. It's all about balance. A healthy obsession respects boundaries, promotes growth, and enhances both individuals. It's like the gardener who knows when to let the plants grow wild and when to prune them back. So, is there such a thing as a healthy obsession?

The sexual tension was building as the days went by, an unspoken energy simmering beneath the surface of our every interaction. It was in the way our eyes would linger just a little too long, each glance a silent conversation filled with unvoiced desires. The tension crackled between us, like static electricity waiting for the right moment to ignite. During our movie nights, the innocent brush of his hand against mine felt like a spark, sending shivers down my spine. Sitting close, our bodies gravitated towards each other, as if drawn by an invisible force. The air was thick with anticipation, every casual touch charged with meaning. It was as if the very act of being near each other was a delicious torture, a sweet ache that neither of us wanted to end. We found excuses to touch more frequently—his hand resting on the small of my back as we navigated crowded spaces, or our fingers intertwining during conversations. Each touch was a promise, a hint of what could be, and it left me craving more.

Our conversations, too, were laced with double meanings and playful innuendos. We danced around the topic, flirting with words and stolen glances, each exchange adding to the mounting tension. The nights we spent together grew longer, our conversations deeper, as if we were both waiting for the moment when words would no longer suffice. It was as if we were two magnets, irresistibly drawn to one another yet held apart by the thin barrier of our mutual restraint. The anticipation was intoxicating, making every moment feel heightened, every touch more electric. The tension built with each passing day, a delicious undercurrent that made our time together both exhilarating and excruciating.

Everything was perfect, yet I still found myself having to talk myself out of paranoia. "He's not doing anything wrong," I would mutter to myself. "He told you exactly what he would be doing and exactly when he'd be calling back... without being asked." It was a rational voice trying to soothe the irrational fears that kept creeping into my mind. Part of me was grateful that he was resisting his sexual urges. It prevented me from adding more unnecessary doubt of his motives. I knew I had to shake these feelings, to silence the whispers of doubt that gnawed at the edges of my happiness. "Patricia, stop it," I'd sternly tell myself, as if commanding my heart to trust what my mind already knew.

But it was hard. The scars of past betrayals ran deep, and they had a nasty habit of reopening at the slightest provocation. I couldn't always tell if my fears were old ghosts haunting me or legitimate concerns about introducing someone new into my life. Yet, it wasn't just anyone new. It was Anthony. I knew Anthony—knew his kindness, his sincerity, his unwavering honesty. He wasn't a stranger trying to win my trust; he was a lifelong friend who already had it. And that made the paranoia even more frustrating.

"Why am I like this?" I'd wonder, caught in a loop of self-doubt. Memories of James and the deceit that unraveled our relationship would surface unbidden, casting shadows over my present happiness. I remembered the lies, the secrets, the heartbreak. It was like a nightmare I couldn't wake up from, and now, those same fears were threatening to taint something beautiful. But then I'd think of Anthony. Anthony, who had been a constant in my life through thick and thin. Anthony, who had never given me a reason to doubt him. Anthony, who was now here, choosing me. I had to remind myself of that.

"Anthony loves me and respects me," I'd repeat, almost like a mantra. "He knows me." Unlike the hollow promises and empty words of the past, his actions spoke volumes. He showed up, he communicated, he cared. These were things I could hold onto, tangible proof of his commitment. It was a battle between my past and my present, between the hurt that once was and the healing that now beckoned. I had to learn to differentiate between the echoes of old trauma and the genuine foundation we were building. I had to let go of the paranoia, to let myself believe in the good that was right in front of me. Trust didn't come easy, but with Anthony, it was worth the effort.

| 4 |

Painting Memories

School was out, and Mia was set to spend a couple of weeks at her mom's house in California, a yearly tradition since her mother lived on the other side of the country. It was a chance for them to reconnect, and for Anthony, it was an opportunity to plan a special surprise for Mia.

"Can you help me decorate Mia's room? I want to surprise her when she comes back." His words hung in the air, and I froze for a moment, fully grasping the significance of his request. I had never been to his house before; he was notoriously private about his living space. Not only that, but I would also be meeting his mother. Anthony had moved back to his mother's house a year ago after his last failed relationship with Christian's mother. They had joined forces to support each other, understanding that in today's economy, two incomes were better than one. As an independent homeowner, I could attest to how rough it was out there, and I was honestly shocked I had made it this far.

I could hear the hesitation in his voice, a mixture of nerves and hope. "I'm going to talk to my mom about it tonight. She's going to know. She knows I never bring any-one over here." It was clear that he was even more anxious about discussing me with his mother. From the stories I'd heard, she was one tough cookie who sugarcoated nothing. Shit, I was nervous too.

The gravity of the situation hit me. Meeting his mother and stepping into his personal space was a huge step for-ward in our relationship. This wasn't just a casual request; it was an invitation into his life on a much deeper level. I could tell this was important to him, and it made my heart swell with affection and anxiety in equal measure.

"I'd love to help," I replied, trying to keep my voice steady despite the butterflies in my stomach. "Just let me know when and what you need."

As we ended the call, my mind raced. What would his mother think of me? Would she approve of me? I knew Anthony's mother was a strong, no-nonsense woman who had been through her share of hardships. She had raised Anthony to be the man he was, and her opinion mattered greatly to him—and now, to me. That evening, as I sat on my couch, I couldn't help but reflect on how much had changed in such a short time.

Later that night, Anthony called. "I talked to my mom," he said, his voice betraying a mix of relief and lingering nerves. "She's okay with it. She wants to meet you."

"Great!" I replied, trying to sound more confident than I felt. "When should I come over?"

"How about tomorrow afternoon? I'll send you the ad-dress."

"Perfect," I said, my heart racing.

I had never met anyone's mom before, not even James's. That should have been a glaring red flag. He always told me I couldn't meet her because his sister was combative. Looking back now, I wonder if any part of that was ever true. Shaking off those thoughts, I redirected my focus back to what mattered: What was I going to wear? I couldn't wear a dress since I was going to paint a room. I needed to look presentable but also ready to work without seeming like I was trying too hard. After much deliberation, I decided to simply be myself. Gone are the days when I masked myself for the validation of others. I would just have to pray to the gods that my shining personality would win her over because I was not a fashionable dresser by any means. My daily attire consisted of ripped jeans and T-shirts or sweaters.

It was too hot for long jeans, so jean shorts would have to do. I made sure to pick a non-revealing top, aware that I am a curvy Latina woman. There were some things I simply couldn't hide like my big butt and thick thighs. I couldn't really hide my D cup breasts either, but at least I could cover them up a bit with a crew neck tank top. I didn't mind doing this as I was naturally a pretty conservative dresser anyway.

The next day arrived, and I must have looked at myself in the mirror a million times contemplating if I should change. I checked myself in the mirror one last time. My outfit might not win any fashion awards, but it was practical and comfortable. I tied my hair up in a ponytail to keep it out of my face while we worked. I opted for minimal makeup, just enough to enhance my features without looking like I was trying too hard. After all, I wanted to make a good impression on Anthony's mom, not look like I was heading to a photo shoot. Feeling as ready as I could be, I grabbed my bag of decorating supplies and headed out the door. The drive to Anthony's house felt longer than usual, my mind racing with thoughts and what-ifs. What if his mom didn't like me? What if I made a terrible first impression? I took a deep breath and reminded myself that Anthony wanted me there, and that had to count for something.

As I pulled up to his house, my nerves kicked into high gear. It was a charming beige house with bold red shutters, standing out in a neighborhood where every lawn was meticulously kept and the landscaping was pristine. Anthony walked outside with Christian, catching me off guard. I hadn't expected Christian to be here too. Meeting Anthony's mother and son in one day felt like a significant milestone. I was excited to finally meet Christian. We had talked on the phone several times, but now he could put a face to my name. Christian had caramel-colored skin, short brown curly hair, and a big, infectious smile on his face.

"It's showtime," I whispered to myself, taking a deep breath to steady my nerves. I stepped out of the car and walked toward them, my heart pounding in anticipation.

"Hi, come on!" Christian grabbed my hand and eagerly led me toward the front door.

"Christian! Stranger Danger!" Anthony yelled out, clearly not in on the plan.

Christian looked back at his dad, who was standing there in disbelief, then gave him a look that practically screamed, "Chill out, Dad. I know what I'm doing." Clearly, this kid had inherited his father's sass. I chuckled to myself, wondering if Anthony had given him the heads-up that I'd be coming.

Anthony sighed dramatically and trailed behind us. "Mama, look!" Christian shouted as we entered the house, drawing the attention of Anthony's mom, who was seated at the kitchen table. She was beautiful, with a youthful energy and curvy figure, complemented by her wavy blonde hair. It was a relief to see her; from one curvy woman to another, I knew she'd understand.

"Hi, sweetie, it's nice to meet you," she greeted warmly, and I could tell instantly that we'd get along.

"Hi, nice to meet you! Thank you so much for having me," I replied, giving her a hug.

Anthony rolled his eyes. "Not the customer service voice," he groaned under his breath. Apparently, I'd slipped into my professional tone without realizing it.

"Okay, come on, Christian. We're going upstairs to start working on the room," Anthony announced, clearly eager to escape his own internal misery. Anthony's mother and I both glanced over at Anthony with a smile knowing exactly what he was doing.

"It was nice meeting you!" I said as Anthony was pushing me away. His mother just laughed.

"You too sweetie." As we headed up the stairs, he whispered that it was Christian's naptime and asked me to start unpacking the supplies while he put him to bed.

"Byeeee!" Christian waved enthusiastically as he was led into his bedroom by Anthony.

With a deep breath, I turned back to Mia's room, ready to dive back into our project. The day was just beginning, and despite the nerves and the bickering, I felt hopeful and excited for what lay ahead.

Once inside Mia's room, I started removing the plastic from all the painting supplies, my eyes wandering to the photos on the walls. There was a vibrant collage of her with friends, plus family photos featuring Anthony, Christian, and his mother. It felt like an exclusive glimpse into a side of Anthony I'd never seen before. The room was filled with stuffed animals, colorful toys, and posters of her favorite characters, clearly marking her as the princess of the house. Anthony soon came in, ready to get to work. You know those adorable scenes in rom-coms where a couple is painting and having a great time, maybe even engaging in a playful paint fight? Well, that wasn't us. We were both overwhelmed by the task at hand and found ourselves bickering about every little thing.

"Start taping here," Anthony instructed, pointing to the corner of the room. "No, I'm going to start here," I replied, moving to the opposite side. "Don't walk up the ladder, I'll do it," he said, his voice firm. "It's fine, I got it," I insisted, stepping onto the first rung of the ladder.

Our arguments were almost comical in their frequency and intensity. At one point, I dropped a roll of painter's tape, and we both bent down to pick it up at the same time, bumping heads and laughing despite ourselves.

"Seriously, can you just let me do this part?" Anthony said, clearly exasperated. "Only if you promise not to micromanage my half," I shot back, smirking.

His mother opened the bedroom door, interrupting our playful spat. "Oh my goodness! You two sound like an old married couple!" she exclaimed with a chuckle. We both laughed, momentarily breaking the tension.

"Christian is up from his nap. I'm going to pick up dinner and I'm taking him with me," she announced.

"Okay," Anthony replied, a hint of relief in his voice knowing that food was probably going to be the best medicine.

Anthony watched the car pull away, his eyes following it until it disappeared around the corner. He then turned his gaze to me, a smile playing at the corners of his lips as he watched me concentrate on painting. I felt his presence behind me before I saw him, a warm, familiar feeling that made my heart race. He moved closer, the heat of his body radiating towards me. I continued to paint, pretending not to notice, but I couldn't ignore the electric tension between us. Anthony's hands found my hips, and he gently pulled me back against him. The firmness of his touch and the press of his arousal against my lower back sent a shiver down my spine.

I paused, brush still in hand, as he leaned in and kissed my neck. His lips were soft and warm, trailing a path of gentle kisses down to my shoulder. I closed my eyes, savoring the sensation, and leaned back into him, letting the paintbrush fall to the floor. His kisses were sweet and tender, each one igniting a fire within me. As he continued, his hands roamed over my body, his touch firm yet gentle. I turned in his embrace, our bodies pressing together as I faced him. His eyes locked onto mine, and for a moment, we just stood there, breathing each other in. The intensity in his gaze sent a thrill through me, and I knew exactly what was about to happen. We moved in sync, as if drawn together by an invisible force. Our lips met in a slow, passionate kiss, the kind that made everything else fade away. His hands slid up my back, pulling me closer, while my fingers tangled in his hair, holding him to me.

Anthony deepened the kiss, his lips exploring mine with a hunger that matched my own. We were both lost in the moment, the room around us forgotten. The only thing that mattered was the connection between us, the overwhelming desire that had been building for so long. His hands moved down to my waist, lifting me effortlessly onto the nearby dresser. The cool surface contrasted with the heat of our bodies, making me gasp. He stepped between my legs, pressing closer, his kisses becoming more urgent. I wrapped my legs around him, pulling him even closer, not wanting any space between us.

His fingers slipped between my thighs, finding the aching heat that was already desperate for him. My breath hitched as he teased me, his touch slow at first—deliberate, tantalizing. Then his movements quickened, circling my clit with just the right amount of pressure, sending sparks of pleasure coursing through me. I clung to him, a moan spilling from my lips as he pushed me closer to the edge, every stroke making me wetter, hungrier. My body begged for more, silently pleading for him to fill the space inside me. Unable to resist the pull of his need, I leaned forward, my lips brushing his neck, tasting the salt of his skin as my hand slid lower. I wrapped my fingers around his cock, stroking him in time with his motions on me. His groan was low and guttural, vibrating against my lips.

"Take off your pants," he commanded, his voice rough with desire, the restraint in his tone barely holding on.

"Here?" I asked, glancing around the familiar space. We had already crossed boundaries, but something about going all the way in her room felt daring—maybe even forbidden.

"Mhm," he murmured, his dark gaze locking with mine, his need overpowering any hesitation. His lips brushed mine in a kiss that left no room for second-guessing, his hands already tugging at the waistband of my shorts, impatient and relentless.

With a nervousness, I got up and unbuttoned my shorts and he lowered them along with my underwear to the floor followed by his own. He turned me around and bent me over leaning over the edge of his daughter's bed. Within seconds he slipped inside me.

"Oh my God," he murmured, his voice a low, gravelly hum that sent a shiver down my spine. He slid into me with deliberate slowness, giving my body time to adjust to the stretch. Each movement was calculated, teasing, before his rhythm shifted. The slow, sensual strokes morphed into something deeper, harder—his grip tightening on my hips as he claimed me.

The raw intensity ignited something feral in me. "You feel so good," he groaned, his voice thick with desire. His words melted into my skin, and I couldn't stop the breathy moans escaping my lips. My fingers clenched the sheets, the comforter muffling my cries as he drove me closer to madness.

"You're making me so wet," I gasped, the confession spilling out as I felt his resolve waver, his pace faltering ever so slightly. Sensing his impending release, he tangled his fingers in my hair, tugging gently to lift my head. His lips captured mine in a searing kiss, deep and possessive, as he pushed himself even deeper, his cock hitting all the right places.

He paused, teasing me, holding still just long enough to make me squirm. His wicked grin told me he enjoyed the way my body writhed beneath him, pleading for more. "You're such a tease," I whispered, circling my hips to coax him back into action.

"You're too good at this," he growled, his voice filled with delicious frustration. He shoved me back down, gripping my waist with unrelenting dominance, and began to thrust again, faster this time. I pushed back against him, meeting his movements, feeling the heat build between us. The sound of skin on skin and our shared moans filled the room, an erotic symphony of pleasure.

"God, you're going to make me cum," he rasped, his voice breaking with desperation. The moment he edged closer, I twisted out from under him, spinning around and sinking to my knees. His eyes widened as I took him into my mouth, my lips wrapping around him with precision and hunger. My tongue teased his sensitive head before sliding him deeper, taking all of him in a way that made his legs tremble. I continued to deep throat showing him that I did not have a gag reflex. He braced himself against the dresser, a guttural cry tearing from his throat as I worked him with my mouth, my tongue, my throat.

"Fuck," he gasped, his body shuddering as he spilled himself into me. I didn't stop, savoring every drop, drawing him out until he was completely spent.

"Okay, okay," he laughed breathlessly, pulling back as his knees threatened to buckle. "I can't take anymore."

We both dissolved into laughter, our bodies still humming with the aftershocks of pleasure. As we gathered our clothes, the air between us was electric, alive with a connection that words couldn't capture. The timing couldn't have been more perfect. Just as we finished straightening up, we spotted his mother's car pulling into the driveway. Quickly, we grabbed our brushes and pretended to focus on the half-finished wall, masking the lingering flush in our cheeks. It was hard to believe we had just shared the best quickie of our lives. Moments later, his mom came up the steps, balancing a bag of takeout as she opened the door.

"Oh wow, you two are almost done!" she exclaimed, beaming with excitement.

Thank God that's what she noticed and not, *What have they been doing this whole time?* My heart thudded, but he played it off smoothly, chuckling. "Yeah, we've been working hard!" he said, his tone steady, though the corner of his mouth quirked with a secret grin. I bit my lip to keep from laughing as I turned back to the wall, carefully adding a final touch to the paint, pretending the heat of his gaze wasn't still on me. Less than an hour later, our work was done. Beautiful lilac walls with white trim. Wanting to show off our work that we were proud of, I posted pictures of the room on my social media along with some still shots of Anthony in action and a selfie we took holding up our brushes as if it was hard to tell who had done the work. The comments started flowing in within seconds.

"Omg so cute!"

" I love it!"

"Great job!"

Reading all the positive comments brought a smile to my face. I put the phone down for a second and the sound of another Ping caught my attention. The smile on my face was quickly wiped away by the element of surprise as I read the notification on my screen. " You have a friend request from James Sterling." Impeccable timing James. This could NOT have been a coincidence. I felt myself breathing heavier. My body was frozen in shock and the only thing I could think of was " Oh Shit."

| 5 |

Ghosts in the Feed

I swiped right to remove the notification from my phone. This was definitely a matter I had to deal with later.

" Hey I'm going to head home to feed the dogs."

" Okay, are you okay?" He could sense the shift in my energy.

" Yup, all good. I just feel bad that I haven't been home all day." I felt terrible lying to Anthony. It was my first time ever lying to him and of course it was because of this piece of shit.

" Okay, I can go over there after I put Christian to bed." I absolutely loved that he wanted to spend more time with me despite already spending the majority of the day with me but today was not the day. I could already feel my mind spiraling. How could such a perfect day be ruined within seconds. I knew that he wanted to stop by because he didn't believe me. He knew something was wrong.

" Yeah, that sounds nice." I responded with a gentle smile to reassure him that nothing was wrong. I walked down the stairs to find his mother and son. They were cuddled up on the couch watching a dinosaur cartoon show. Gosh his mom is amazing.

" I'm going to head out. It was nice meeting you!" I walked up to her to give her a kiss on the cheek. This was a standard practice for the Hispanic culture. It was considered rude if you did not do this upon entering or leaving a home. Christian stood up to give me a big hug.

" You come back right?" he said in broken English.

" Yeah baby, I'll come back." My heart filled with joy.

" Okay!" he yelled with excitement as he plopped back down on the couch. I laughed to myself as I turned around to walk to the front entrance. Anthony was patiently waiting at the door and listening in on the conversation. He always needed to know what was going on at all times. He gave me a big hug and gentle kiss. " Thank you for helping me today. Text me when you get home." I thought it was sweet that he was so attentive.

"I will."

As soon as I got in the car, the joyous ride my mind had been on came to an abrupt halt. Reality snapped back as I pulled up the app on my phone and stared at the pending friend request. *Delete. Delete. Delete.* Without hesitation, I cleared it away, knowing I needed to reset my head before heading home.

I decided to stop by the local coffee shop to journal, hoping to find clarity in the soothing chaos of its familiar surroundings. There's something strangely calming about watching the busyness of other people's lives. Seeing them rush in with their work uniforms, juggling online meetings on their laptops, or quietly seeking their own escape in a book while nestled on one of the worn, comfy couches in the far corner—it was a reminder that everyone had their own story. It made my own life feel less overwhelming. This coffee shop had become my sanctuary, a routine that steadied me when my thoughts ran wild. But today, something—or rather, *someone*—caught my attention. Actually, *two* someones.

They were clearly on what looked like a first coffee date. The girl, an African American woman with long, gorgeous curls parted to one side, exuded nervous energy as she sat down at their table. Her outfit was flawless—a perfect blend of effort and ease. It showed she cared but didn't try so hard as to make it seem forced. *Simple yet chic,* I thought, appreciating her attention to detail. I watched as she fidgeted slightly, adjusting her clothes and running a hand through her hair, her nerves barely hidden beneath her composed exterior. *Girl, you look perfect,* I thought, silently rooting for her. *Please let at least one of us win at this game called love.*

A few moments later, an African American man walked through the door, and I saw her perk up instantly. She straightened in her seat, a hopeful smile spreading across her face as he approached. He was definitely a man with style—clean-cut, with a perfectly groomed beard. He wore a jean jacket and a hat to cover his bald head. *Oh no, please don't let him be a hat-fisher,* I thought, stifling a laugh. For the uninitiated, a hat-fisher is someone who hides their baldness behind the clever use of hats in every single photo, leaving you to wonder if there's a full head of hair under there or just a secret they don't want you to discover. Was I seriously this invested in their date already? Apparently so.

First impressions are everything, I reminded myself, watching intently as they started with a handshake. Okay, safe and respectful. Points for that.

"Shall we order?" he suggested, gesturing toward the counter and letting her take the lead as they walked. *Chivalry isn't dead, after all.* Though, to be fair, he might've just wanted a good look at her backside. Either way, well played, sir.

As time passed, I watched their awkward first-date energy start to fade. The initial vibes screamed "formal interview"—good posture, polite smiles, and responses that felt overly rehearsed. But within thirty minutes, something shifted. Their smiles became easier, their hand gestures more animated. Laughter floated over the quiet hum of the coffee shop. They had officially crossed into the "I'm interested and not bolting for the door" phase. By the time they left, walking out together like they'd known each other longer than the hour they spent inside, I found myself smiling. *Not bad,* I thought, silently rooting for them as the door swung shut behind them.

As I continued writing in my journal, I couldn't help but glance up occasionally, watching people come and go through the door. At one point, it was just me and the employees left inside. The thought nagged at me—*What does that say about me?*

Am I now *that* person? The one who spends hours in a coffee shop, nose buried in a journal or a book, because nothing else exciting is happening in her life? Or... is this what peace actually feels like? To have the freedom to sit here as long as I want, in a place where the employees know my name, where I can decompress whenever I need to. Maybe it's all in the perspective, a matter of how you choose to see it. I thought back to a different version of myself. The days when I couldn't even afford to keep my cell phone service on. I used to sit in the parking lot of this very coffee shop, stealing Wi-Fi so I could respond to people on apps that only required an internet connection. I spent days, even months, parked out there. Never stepping inside. Never imagining I could.

"Ridiculous," I muttered aloud, laughing softly to myself.

And yet, here I am now, sitting comfortably inside, ready to take on the world, casually paying eight dollars for a cup of coffee that's mostly caramel, whipped cream, and creamer. I poured my thoughts and feelings into my notebook, feeling like just another person in the crowd. My mind wouldn't stop its interruptions, though. *Patricia: the quintessential coffee shop girl who secretly doesn't even like coffee but drinks it because it's required for her sweet concoctions.* I laughed again, probably looking a little unhinged if anyone was observing me as closely as I was observing others.

Life has changed so much. *I* have changed so much. But one thing that hasn't changed is James. He lingers like a ghost I can't shake. No matter what, there's nothing he could say or do to undo the pain, to mend the wounds that tore us apart. The baby that was never born. The future that shattered into pieces. There are some things that can't be fixed, no matter how hard you wish for them to be different. So why does the mere sight of his name make me feel like I'm reliving the torture all over again? Is this what PTSD feels like? Or am I simply overreacting? I could feel paranoia creeping into my thoughts. What are the odds that he'd send me a friend request on the exact day I posted a picture with Anthony in it? It wasn't a coincidence. He was watching me—*but how?*

I turned the page of my notebook, my pen hovering over the blank space as I took a deep breath. Instead of spiraling, I started writing. A letter to the powers that be. Not to James, not to myself, but to something bigger.

Dear Universe,

What the actual fuck? Things are finally starting to go right for once, so please, I beg you, do not sprinkle your "charming" sense of humor into my life right now. Seriously, your last joke—the whole fiasco with the magician—was a real showstopper. I mean, kudos to you, it was a class act. But let's be honest, trying to pull something like that again would be like remaking a classic movie with a cast of B-list actors. It would flop. Big time. So, let's not, okay?

Also, while I have you here, thank you. Thank you for bringing Anthony back into my life. That was a solid move on your part, and I truly appreciate it. Thank you for showing me not to give up. I got the message loud and clear the first time, though, so no need for a sequel on that lesson. We're good.

And a massive shout out for making his mom and son like me. You have no idea how much anxiety that little detail caused me. Lord knows I was sweating bullets about it, so thanks for coming through on that one.

But yeah, just to reiterate—keep the cosmic fuckery over there. No curve balls, no twists, no "plot development." Let me ride this good thing for a while, okay? Please and thank you.

Over and out,
Patricia

| 6 |

Family Matters

Anthony coming back into my life is a good thing. A *really* good thing. I can't let James ruin this for me. *Fuck him.*

Maybe if I just ignore it, it'll go away. Like when a kid says a bad word and adults are supposed to pretend they didn't hear it, hoping the lack of reaction will make the kid stop. What's the psychological term for that? Extinction, maybe? Whatever it's called, that was my plan for James. No reaction. No satisfaction. He'd give up eventually, right? Deep down, though, I knew better. As much as I wanted to believe that my amateur psychology tactic would work, the odds weren't in my favor. And by "odds," I mean there was a solid 99% chance it wouldn't.

I knew James too well—or at least, the persistent side of him. The manic side. He *had* to be manic to reach out to me after all these years, especially after how disastrously things ended. It's the only explanation that made sense. This is the same man, after all, who spent thirty minutes every day picking me up from work and "courting" me—while leading a full-blown double life. *Manic.* That's the only word that fits.

"I'm on my way," Anthony's text popped up on my phone. *Okay, Patricia, time to put on your best smile and act like you've got everything under control.*

Anthony lived thirty minutes away, so I had just enough time to prep. I darted around the house, tidying up like my life depended on it, making sure there wasn't a single stray bra or other evidence of my single-woman chaos lying around. *God forbid he thinks I'm anything less than effortlessly put together.*

The dogs, meanwhile, just lay there, their heads swiveling from left to right like they were part of some cartoon. They could tell something was happening but had no clue what. The frantic energy probably tipped them off. A short while later, I saw the glow of headlights cutting through the night, shining onto the side of my house. *It's showtime,* I thought, taking a deep breath. I unlocked the door so he could walk in without setting off the dogs. The doorbell was like their secret alarm system—a clear signal that whoever dared to enter wasn't fully welcome. But tonight? Tonight, I needed everything to go smoothly. Even the dogs had to stay on script.

"Heyyy! Long time no see!" I said, putting on my brightest, happiest voice.

Anthony rolled his eyes as he walked past me. *Okay, maybe it was a little over the top, but at least I tried.*

"So, are you going to tell me what's wrong?" he asked, tone sharp and direct. *Wow, he's not wasting any time.* Having someone who knows you inside and out really is a blessing and a curse. Moments like this make you wish you could get away with a white lie or two.

"There's nothing wrong," I replied softly, trying to sound convincing.

Another eye roll.

"There's a lot of eye rolling happening here," I said, raising a brow.

"There's a lot of lying happening here," he shot back without missing a beat. His quick wit made me laugh despite myself.

"I don't know what you're talking about." The words were barely out of my mouth before I saw another exaggerated eye roll as he kicked off his shoes and sprawled out on the chaise of my sectional sofa.

"Okay, *Patricia*, whatever you say." His tone was dripping with skepticism, but at least he didn't press further. Small victories, right?

Hearing him say my name gave me pause. We didn't really use nicknames for each other, but when either of us used the other's name, it was never a good sign. Still, he seemed to let it go for now, and I'd take that win. I turned on the TV and sat down next to him. Without a word, he shifted, opening his arm in an unspoken invitation for me to curl up against him.

With Anthony, everything felt so natural. Like second nature. I didn't need to signal or ask; he just knew. We loved watching movies together—though, to be fair, he almost always fell asleep halfway through. Today, I was strategic. I picked a rom-com, knowing it would knock him out in no time. Sure enough, within minutes, I could hear his soft snores.

This was his usual nap time before his overnight shift, and I couldn't help but feel a little relieved. Was it terrible of me to be thankful he was already asleep? As long as he was out, he couldn't ask questions I wasn't ready to answer. It gave me some breathing room, a temporary reprieve from the hot seat. Nestled in his embrace, the warmth and comfort made it easy for me to drift off too.

Before we knew it, the sound of birds chirping woke us both up. His alarm. It was 10 p.m., time for him to head to work.

I'm in the clear... or so I thought.

He gave me a hug and a kiss before leaving. "Whenever you're ready to talk, I'll be here," he said with a gentle smirk.

Persistent.

"Have a good night at work," I replied, subtly nudging him toward the door, making it clear this was his queue to leave. He laughed, catching the hint but not entirely giving in.

"Okay, okay. I'll text you when I get there," he said with a grin as he stepped out.

Persistence and consistency.

Deep down, I had to admit—I kind of loved it.

The weeks that followed felt like stepping into a dream—the kind that lingers when you wake, leaving a warm, fuzzy imprint you carry throughout the day. Anthony and I were in sync, moving effortlessly from one moment to the next. Our connection deepened with every text, every lingering glance, every conversation that stretched late into the night. If I had to describe it, I'd call it a *healthy obsession.* If that's even a thing. We weren't just interested in each other—we were captivated, pulled into each other's orbit in a way that felt both exciting and safe. There was a weight-lessness to being with him, as if the heaviness of the world had momentarily lifted.

He was always present, whether it was a random text that made me laugh in the middle of a hectic workday or showing up at my door with my favorite breakfast sandwich after his overnight shift. And I couldn't deny it: I was just as invested. I'd find myself scrolling through my phone at night, reading back our conversations with a stupid grin on my face. It was ridiculous, but I didn't care. For the first time in a long time, I felt truly seen, valued—and dare I say it—loved. Anthony wasn't just letting me into his world. He was including me in parts of it I didn't expect, parts that mattered deeply to him. One of those parts was his kids—Mia and Christian.

Mia lived with Anthony full-time but spent a couple of weeks during the summer with her mother, Christina, on the other side of the country. Christian, on the other hand, was home all year round since his mother lived close by, and throughout the weeks, I found myself bonding with him just as much as I was with Anthony. Christian was sharp and full of energy, constantly surprising me with his quick wit and boundless curiosity. We spent hours together doing every-thing from baking cookies (which somehow always ended with more flour on the floor than in the mixing bowl) to sit-ting in the backyard, talking about anything and everything. Anthony often joined us, but sometimes, it was just me and

Christian, laughing about silly things or debating on which dinosaur was more cool. Those moments, as small as they seemed, felt monumental to me.

There was a time when I had the choice to bring a child into this world with a man I deeply loved. But the reality of what that would mean weighed heavily on me. It would have meant raising a baby in chaos—a world where I couldn't guarantee stability, where I wasn't even sure if I could provide a roof over their head or food on the table. A world where they might grow up witnessing their father struggle with mental health, just as I had seen before. I couldn't bear the thought of willingly subjecting someone else—someone so innocent—to the pain and uncertainty I had lived through. So, I made the hardest decision of my life. I chose to let go of that dream, and instead, I chose my career. I chose survival, focus, and building a life that felt secure, even if it came at a personal cost. But now, standing on the other side of those years, I find myself longing for something more. The fear hasn't vanished, but neither has the hope. This time, I want to choose differently. I want to give life a second chance—to create something new from the pieces of the life I've built. Something beautiful. Something whole.

Including me in his children's lives wasn't just a gesture from Anthony—it was a statement. It showed me how much he trusted me, and I felt honored to be part of their world. Still, there was Christina, the ever-present storm cloud over Anthony's otherwise sunny life. Despite only having Mia for a few weeks, she called constantly, creating drama from across the country. It started with a phone call one evening while Anthony and I were curled up on the couch, half-watching a show and half-talking about nothing. His phone buzzed on the coffee table, the name *Christina* flashing on the screen.

"Again?" he grumbled, running a hand down his face.

"She calls often huh?" I asked casually, though I could already guess the answer from his exasperated tone.

"Constantly. She's got this habit of calling just to stir the pot. Every little thing turns into a crisis—whether it's about Mia or something that has nothing to do with me. I think she just enjoys yelling at me sometimes."

He answered reluctantly, and sure enough, within seconds, I could hear Christina's voice on the other end of the line. Loud. Angry. Accusing him of being an unfit parent because Mia hadn't done a chore up to her standards. Anthony handled it calmly, his voice measured and steady despite her tirade. But as the calls became more frequent over the next couple of weeks, I could see the toll they were taking on him. One night, after he'd hung up from another exhausting call, he turned to me with a sigh. "I don't know what to do about her, Patricia. She's impossible to reason with, but I don't want Mia to feel like she's caught in the middle. What do you think?"

It was a simple question, but it hit me deeply. Anthony wasn't just venting—he was asking for my opinion. He valued my perspective enough to include me in one of the most important areas of his life: parenting.

"Well," I began, trying to organize my thoughts. "First of all, you're doing an amazing job with Mia. She's happy, stable, and thriving because of you. Don't let Christina make you question that. As for her constant calls, maybe it's time to set some boundaries. If it's not an emergency or directly about Mia, maybe those conversations don't always need to happen."

He nodded, his expression thoughtful. "That's... a good point. This is just too much. Enough is enough."

From that point on, things shifted. Anthony started implementing boundaries with Christina, and while she didn't take it well at first (predictably calling to yell about it), he stood firm. And through it all, he continued to lean on me—not just for advice but for emotional support. It wasn't lost on me how significant this was. Anthony didn't just care about me; he trusted me with something deeply personal, something vulnerable. And I cared just as deeply—not only for him but for the life he'd built with Mia and Christian. As we grew closer, I found myself looking forward to the moments we shared, no matter how small. Whether it was helping him brainstorm solutions to Christina's drama, laughing over Christian's latest antics, or watching Anthony and Christian tease each other during dinner, it all felt right. Natural. Like we were becoming something solid, something real. And tomorrow, Mia will be coming home. Anthony and I had spent the last couple of days decorating her room, transforming it into something magical just for her. Christian even helped pick out some of the final details, adding his own little touches to the space. I couldn't wait to see her face when she walked in and saw it all. I found myself feeling hopeful. Hope for love, for connection, for a future that felt whole. With Anthony and the life we were building together, it all seemed possible.

The next day arrived, and it was time for Mia to come home. Anthony had gone to pick her up from the airport, and I stayed back, anticipating the moment she'd see her surprise. "I'll call you when we get to the house," he had said before leaving. Not long after, my phone vibrated. I didn't even get a chance to say hello before Anthony's excited voice came through.

"Shh. Just listen," he said, his tone brimming with anticipation.

From the faint background noise, I could hear him guiding Mia. "Go to your room to put your bags down," he said.

There was a brief pause, followed by the creak of a door opening. Then came the sound of a delighted scream.

"AHHHHHHHH! This is so cool! I love it!" Mia's voice was filled with pure joy.

"Patricia and I did it. We hope you like it," Anthony said, making sure to include me in the credit. He could've easily claimed the glory for himself, but he didn't.

"I love it! Thank you, Patricia!" Mia yelled into the phone, her excitement making me smile.

"You're welcome! Your dad wanted to surprise you, and he worked very hard on it," I replied, trying to shift the spotlight back to Anthony.

Later that day, I went over to Anthony's house to spend some time. He and I were sitting on the floor in his bedroom, folding laundry and talking about random things. The easy rhythm of our conversation was interrupted when Mia opened the door and walked in, carrying her usual vibrant energy.

"Wanna hear about my trip?" she asked, her big eyes locked on mine.

"I'd love to," I said with a laugh, amused by her eagerness.

"Well... I didn't do much," she said, completely anticlimactic.

Anthony and I couldn't help but burst into laughter at the unexpected turn.

"Okay, but what *did* you do?" I asked, trying to steer the conversation back to her experience with her mother.

"Well, I went to the movies one day, and we went to a birthday party another day, but Mom had to work, so we stayed home most of the time."

Anthony and I exchanged a look, the same thought running through both of our minds. *You only see your daughter for a few weeks, and you still put work first?* It was disheartening. Mia needed her mother—a strong, guiding presence in her life—but it seemed like Christina wasn't ready to be that person.

"Okay, well, did you enjoy seeing your mom?" I asked gently.

"Yeah, it was nice," Mia said, shrugging.

"Well, that's good," I said, trying to keep the mood light.

"Okay, I'm going to go watch TV in my room. See you later!" Mia chirped before hopping up and leaving the room.

Not long after, I decided it was time for me to head out, too.

"Thanks for stopping by," Anthony said, walking me to the door.

On my way home, my phone rang. It was Anthony.

"So... we have a problem," he said. His tone was serious, and my heart sank.

"Oh great. What now?" *Did James contact him too?* I asked, trying to mask my growing worry.

"It's Mia. She called her mom and told her that you and I were in my bedroom together, and Christina blew it out of proportion."

I couldn't help but laugh, even though I knew it wasn't a laughing matter. I could only imagine how that must've sounded coming out of a child's mouth.

"Well, what did you tell her?" I asked, trying to keep calm.

"I told her it wasn't like that, that we were just folding laundry. But, of course, she told me I shouldn't be bringing women into my bedroom with a young girl in the house. Then she threatened to come here."

"Oh, so she'll come here to start a fight but not to spend time with her daughter? That's cool," I said sarcastically, unable to hold back the sting in my words.

Anthony didn't respond to my jab. I realized it wasn't the time for snark.

"We're going to have to chill and not be together while Mia is around," he said, his voice laced with guilt. "Christina's right. I know we weren't doing anything wrong, but it just sounds bad. And I don't want to give her more ammunition."

I understood his point, but the thought of having to tiptoe around Christina's insecurities and dramatics left a bitter taste in my mouth. How could a relationship grow when it was forced to hide behind a veil? Still, his children came first, and I knew I'd have to adapt. But the shift didn't last long. A few days later, it was as if Anthony woke up with a new determination to show Christina that I wasn't going anywhere. I had been visiting him while the kids were in school, keeping a low profile, when one day, Anthony casually said, "Come on. We have to pick up Mia from school."

I paused, confused. "*We?*"

He ignored my look, brushing it off as if it were no big deal. "Hurry up and put on your shoes!"

Still unsure, I slipped on my shoes and followed him out the door. From that day on, it became part of our routine: picking up Mia *together*. It wasn't just a statement—it was a turning point. Anthony wasn't going to let anyone dictate our relationship, not even Christina. And in that moment, I realized just how deeply he valued me—not just as someone in his life, but as someone in his family's life.

| 7 |

Steps Toward Forever

Stepping into the role of a stepmom isn't something you can prepare for, no matter how many books you read or stories you hear. It's a delicate dance, one that requires patience, understanding, and a whole lot of trial and error. Some days, it felt natural, like I'd always been a part of Anthony's family. Other days, it felt like I was stumbling in the dark, trying to find my footing in a space that wasn't entirely mine but one I wanted to nurture with my whole heart.

Mia was the biggest challenge, but not in a bad way. She was smart, observant, and fiercely protective of her dad. I could tell early on that she was still trying to figure out where I fit in her life—and honestly, so was I. The bond we were building was rewarding, but it wasn't without its hurdles. Some days, I felt like we were making progress, sharing laughs and connecting over little things. Other days, I'd feel like an outsider, unsure if I was doing too much or not enough. Christian, on the other hand, was much easier. He was younger and more open to letting me into his world. He loved having someone new to dote on him, whether it was baking cookies together or letting me help him with his school projects. His innocence made it easier to bridge the gap, and his mom didn't seem to stir up much trouble—at least, not yet.

For Anthony, this was a learning curve too. He had spent so much of his life doing everything on his own, and now, he had to learn how to let go of some of that control. That wasn't always easy for him. He wanted to protect me from the harder parts of parenting, as if shielding me from the challenges would somehow make things easier. But I didn't want to be protected—I wanted to be involved. One of the places this tension showed up most was when it came to buying things for the kids. I loved picking up little gifts for Mia and Christian, whether it was a book that reminded me of Mia or a new art set for Christian. Gifting was my love language; it was my way of saying, *I see you, I care about you.* But for Anthony, it felt like a line he wasn't ready for me to cross. He didn't want me spending my money on them, maybe because he saw it as his responsibility.

This became one of our biggest points of contention—not because either of us was wrong, but because we were coming from different places. He wanted to maintain control, ensuring I wasn't overstepping or taking on too much. I, on the other hand, wanted to express my love in the way I knew best. Compromise wasn't just a suggestion; it was a necessity if we wanted to make this work. That said, even at our worst, we were still better than most people's best. There are definite perks to dating someone you've already built an established friendship with. You skip the awkward "impressing each other" phase, the overcompensating, and the guesswork. There's an authenticity that feels grounding, a balance that comes from knowing you can call each other out when needed.

But that's also where the flipside comes in. They know you *too* well. Sometimes, you just want to fake a smile and coast through a tough moment, but nope—they'll see right through it, every single time. It's equal parts comforting and maddening, but it's also what keeps you honest, both with yourself and with each other. Through these challenges, though, I began to see the beauty in what we were building. This wasn't about being perfect; it was about showing up, trying, and learning together. For every struggle, there was a moment of connection—a shared laugh, a quiet conversation, or a simple smile from one of the kids that reminded me why this was all worth it.

The kids were home, but the quiet of the afternoon was golden. Christian was napping in his room after a full morning of cartoons and running around the backyard, and Mia was absorbed in her latest art project. Anthony and I exchanged a glance in the kitchen, the kind of look that carried an unspoken question—and an even clearer answer.

"We've got, what? An hour?" he murmured, his lips curving into that irresistible grin.

"If we're lucky," I whispered back, my voice barely audible over the soft hum of the dishwasher.

Without another word, he took my hand, leading me quietly to the master bathroom. The door clicked shut, and I leaned against it, my heart already racing as his hands found my waist.

"We've got to be quick," I breathed, trying to sound practical but failing miserably as his mouth grazed my neck, sending a shiver through me.

"We'll be quick," he promised, though the way his hands were sliding under my shirt said otherwise.

The shower knob squeaked as he turned it on, steam filling the small space almost instantly. Before I knew it, we were shedding clothes in a flurry, his lips never straying far from mine. The heat of the water wasn't half as intense as the fire building between us. I stepped into the stream first, the water cascading over my shoulders as Anthony pressed in behind me, his hands roaming possessively over my slick skin. His lips trailed along my neck, down my shoulders, as his hands settled on my hips, pulling me back against him. Pressed up against him, I felt his lips trail along my neck, warm and tantalizing, as his hand slipped between my thighs, his fingers finding me with deliberate, electrifying precision.

"God, you feel so good," he whispered against my ear, his voice low and heavy with desire.

I turned to face him, my hands sliding up his chest, the water dripping between us. His eyes locked on mine, dark and filled with hunger, before he crushed his lips to mine in a kiss that made my knees weak. One hand pressed against the cool tile behind me for support as the other tangled in his wet hair. His hands slid lower, lifting me effortlessly as I wrapped my legs around his waist. The pressure of him against me was enough to make me moan softly, the sound swallowed by the rush of the water.

"Quiet," he whispered, his grin teasing as his mouth claimed mine again.

The way he entered me was deliberate yet urgent, his movements fueled by the stolen nature of our time together. I bit my lip to keep quiet, my body arching into his as the rhythm of his thrusts grew faster, deeper. My back pressed harder against the tile as he held me steady, his lips finding every sensitive spot along my neck and shoulder. The sensation of the water cascading over us mixed with the heat building inside me, and I struggled to suppress the soft cries threatening to escape. His hand moved between us, his fingers finding the spot that sent me spiraling. My hands gripped his shoulders as I buried my face against his neck, my body trembling as the waves of pleasure hit me hard and fast.

"God, Patricia," he groaned.

"Quiet," I whispered, mocking him.

"Shut up" His voice was rough and strained. I could feel the pressure of his climax building up as I increased my speed to give him the best sense of release. His breathing got heavier as he gripped me tighter.

"Oh my god I'm cumming" he said as I felt his cock pulsating inside me making me orgasm simultaneously. We stayed like that for a moment, his forehead resting against mine, both of us catching our breath as the water continued to fall around us. By the time we cleaned up and stepped out of the shower, Christian was still peacefully napping, and Mia was tucked away in her room, music blasting as she worked on an art project. This was our life—stealing moments of intimacy whenever and wherever we could, making the most of the little pockets of time we had.

| 8 |

Sweet Pea, Sour Memories

Morning light seeped through the blinds as I stirred awake, still cocooned in the comfort of warm blankets. My phone buzzed on the nightstand. Half-asleep, I reached for it, expecting nothing more than the usual notifications. But the moment I saw three consecutive messages, my drowsiness evaporated. The number wasn't saved, but I didn't need to see a name to know who it was.

"Good morning, sweet pea."

"You didn't add me."

"That wasn't very nice."

My heart skipped a beat. Then another. Sleep was a distant memory as I stared at the screen, my breath shallow, panic flooding my chest. *What the fuck is wrong with this guy? Why the hell is he contacting me?!*

I could feel Anthony's steady breaths beside me, still lost in sleep, completely unaware that my entire body felt like it was vibrating with tension. *DELETE.* Out of sight, out of mind—that was the mantra. If I didn't give it attention, maybe the problem would go away. That's what worked the last time. My thumb hovered over the delete button, and I forced myself to press it. But the words lingered in my mind, like a scratch on a record I couldn't smooth out.

James. He always knew how to stir something inside me, whether it was rage, fear, or the kind of anxiety that left you doubting your own strength. I could feel my pulse pounding in my ears, my mind spiraling. Why was he doing this now? What did he want? I sat up, clutching the phone like it might somehow bite me again. My heart raced as I took a shaky breath, trying to steady myself. I would not let him win. Whatever game he was trying to play, I refused to give him the satisfaction of knowing he'd gotten under my skin. Sliding out of bed as quietly as I could, I padded down to the kitchen, needing the soothing ritual of making tea to distract me. The soft hum of the kettle filled the silence, grounding me just enough to keep from completely unraveling. I was lost in my thoughts, staring into the steam rising from my mug, when I heard Anthony's footsteps. His warm presence filled the room as he wrapped his arms around me from behind, planting a gentle kiss on my cheek.

"Good morning," he said softly, his voice still groggy from sleep.

I forced a smile and turned to him. "Good morning."

But I should have known better. Anthony had a knack for reading me like a book.

"What's wrong?" he asked, his brows furrowing slightly as he studied my face.

"Nothing, I'm okay," I said quickly, waving it off. "I just had a weird dream, that's all."

"You and your weird dreams," he teased, brushing a hand through his hair. His tone was light, but his eyes lingered on me, searching for something beneath the surface.

"Yeah," I replied, trying to sound casual. I turned back to my tea, willing myself to focus on the rhythmic stirring of the spoon instead of the storm brewing in my chest. He stood there for a moment longer, and I could feel the weight of his gaze. I knew he wasn't fully convinced, but thankfully, he let it go.

"Alright," he said finally, leaning down to give me another kiss. "Let me know if you want to talk about it."

I nodded, offering him a small smile, grateful that he didn't push further. As he walked out of the kitchen, I leaned against the counter, gripping the edge until my knuckles turned white. The truth of James's text burned in the back of my mind, but I couldn't bring myself to tell Anthony—not yet. Anthony had enough to deal with, and dragging him into this mess felt like giving James even more power. But as I stared into the swirling tea in my mug, I couldn't shake the feeling that ignoring James wouldn't be enough. The next morning, my phone buzzed again. I hesitated before picking it up, already dreading what I might see. Sure enough, there it was—another text.

"Good morning, sweet pea."

My jaw clenched as I stared at the words, a mix of frustration and unease bubbling in my chest. He was trying to get to me, and I hated to admit it, but it was working. *Oh, this is going to be a problem.* It had been three years. Three long years. Why now? Why would he decide to reach out after all this time? Someone must have told him about Anthony. That was the only explanation that made any sense. But even if that were true, why would he care? The last I'd heard of James, he had moved on. *Shockingly,* things hadn't worked out with the other woman he left me for. I even heard from friends at the station that he had remarried someone new. That news had hit me like a punch to the gut—not because I wished it had been me, but because of the sheer injustice of it. How could someone who caused so much pain be able to start fresh like that? To create a new life, as if the wreckage of the old one didn't exist?

It wasn't jealousy. God, no. It was the deep, unsettling feeling of watching someone who had left a trail of destruction seemingly move on without consequence. Meanwhile, I had spent years picking up the pieces of my life, learning from my mistakes, and trying to do better. I shook the thought away, unwilling to let James consume any more of my energy. I glanced over at Anthony, who was still peacefully asleep beside me. I didn't want to freak him out with this. He already had enough to handle. Something I kept telling myself in efforts to convince myself that I was doing the right thing.

I'll block the number, I told myself. *There. Problem solved.*

For a while, it seemed like it worked. The rest of the day passed without any interruptions, and I started to feel the tension in my chest ease. But then came Day 3.

There was no text this time. Instead, I woke up to a message request on yet another app. My stomach dropped as I opened the notification.

"Hi, sweet pea. Miss me yet?"

My breath caught in my throat. Clearly, James had no intention of stopping anytime soon. Blocking him wasn't enough, and I knew now that ignoring the problem wasn't going to make it go away.

I had to tell Anthony.

This wasn't just about me anymore. James wasn't going to back off, and the last thing I wanted was for this to escalate further without Anthony knowing. I could feel my heart pounding as I reached for my phone again, preparing myself for the conversation I knew I couldn't avoid any longer. When Anthony woke up that morning, he immediately noticed something was off. The moment his eyes met mine, his brows furrowed with concern.

"What?" he asked, his tone sharp with worry.

I hesitated, feeling the weight of the confession I was about to make. "There's something I need to tell you," I said, my voice trembling slightly.

"What?" he repeated, this time louder, his tone edged with impatience.

"A while back, my ex, James, sent me a friend request," I began cautiously, trying to gauge his reaction.

"Okay, Patricia..." His tone was calm, but the slight edge in his voice wasn't lost on me.

"I deleted it right away and left it alone. I didn't think it was even worth bringing up at the time."

He nodded slowly, his expression unreadable. "Okay... so why are you bringing it up now?"

I swallowed hard. "Well, this week... he's been texting me."

"This week?" His tone shot up, his face twisting with a mix of confusion and frustration.

"Yeah, for the past couple of days."

"And what does he want?"

"I don't know," I admitted quickly, shaking my head. "I haven't been responding."

"Okay," he said, his voice firm now. "Then block him everywhere. There's no reason he should be reaching out to you, and there's definitely no reason why you shouldn't have told me about this from the start."

"I know," I said softly, guilt pressing down on me. "I'm sorry."

He stared at me for a moment, his jaw tight, before letting out a long breath. "Just block him," he said finally, turning away to get out of bed.

I didn't tell him the full story—not about how I'd already blocked James in two places and how he'd managed to find another way to contact me. I didn't want to add fuel to the fire. Instead, I resolved to block James from every form of communication I could think of and pray that it would be enough.

Although Anthony handled the situation well on the surface, I could tell it bothered him that I hadn't been upfront with him. He didn't say anything else about it, but his mood for the rest of the day was noticeably different. He was present—doing everything he needed to do—but he wasn't going out of his way to show affection like he usually did.

I didn't blame him. Trust was a fragile thing, and I knew I'd shaken it.

Anthony was working overnight, and I was home alone. Normally, he'd call me on his way to work—a routine we both cherished—but tonight, my phone stayed silent. The absence of that call felt heavier than it should have, a quiet reminder that things between us weren't quite right. I tossed and turned, unable to sleep, my mind spiraling with guilt and anxiety. Had I ruined our almost-perfect relationship? I replayed the conversation over and over in my head, dissecting every word, every pause. Anthony hadn't yelled or stormed off, but his disappointment was palpable, and it ate away at me. There were so many thoughts swirling in my mind, yet no one I could really share them with. Sighing, I opened the drawer of my nightstand and pulled out my notebook—the one place I could pour out my heart without fear of judgment. I clicked my pen and began to write.

Dear Universe,

I think I really fucked up this time.

I don't know how to handle this situation, and I feel like I'm drowning in it. James has been nothing but a bad memory for years, and now he's popping up out of nowhere, turning my life upside down. What does he even want from me? Closure? Attention? To stir up trouble? It's like he's haunting me, even though I've done everything to leave him in the past.

And Anthony... he didn't deserve this. I should've told him from the start. Maybe then, he wouldn't feel blindsided. I hate that I made him feel like I was keeping secrets from him, like I couldn't trust him. That's not how I see it, but I can't blame him if he does.

This relationship with Anthony is so good, so solid—something I never thought I'd have again. I don't want to lose it, but I don't know how to fix this. Is honesty enough? Is time enough?

I'm trying, Universe. I'm trying to do the right thing, but I feel like I'm failing. I don't even know what James is looking for, but I can't let him ruin what I've built with Anthony. Please give me a sign, some kind of guidance to help me navigate this mess.

I don't want to let my past destroy my future.

Over and out,
Patricia

| 9 |

Silent Sirens

In the midst of the changes I was making in my personal life, I decided it was time to make a shift in my career as well. If I truly wanted a life where I could settle down, I needed a job that would allow me to do so. My days of traveling across the country four to five times a week at all hours of the night weren't going to cut it anymore—not if I wanted stability, not if I wanted to build something real with Anthony.

So, I took a leap. I got a job at a hospital in the city.

Although I excelled in the transplant specialty, transitioning to a new hospital wasn't as seamless as I'd hoped. Not every place offers transplant, and that meant I had to start from scratch—learning new systems, new protocols, and new dynamics. The pressure felt heavier this time around. Straight out of school, you have the excuse of being green, still learning the ropes. But walking into a new job with experience in a prestigious specialty? People expect you to know *everything*.

I didn't.

During my probation period, they put me through a rotation of all the surgical specialties to see where I'd be the best fit. And while most new hires are given several weeks to get acclimated, my experience meant they cut my rotation time in half. I really had to hit the ground running. Every day was a whirlwind of information. I was thrown into cases with little time to breathe, my brain constantly trying to absorb everything—equipment, techniques, protocols. I went home most nights exhausted, mentally replaying my day and figuring out how I could do better the next. The stakes felt higher than ever, but so did my determination.

Then, I found it. My specialty.

Neurology.

Brain and spine surgery turned out to be exactly what I was looking for. Brain surgeries were slow and meticulous, requiring an almost meditative level of focus. Spine surgeries, on the other hand, were fast-paced and often unconventional—a stark contrast that felt familiar and exciting for someone coming from the radical world of transplant. It was the perfect balance for me, a blend of precision and unpredictability that kept me on my toes.

Once I settled into neurology, my confidence started to grow. The steep learning curve began to level out, and I finally felt like I was finding my rhythm again. Working four days a week and having three days off gave me the space to breathe, recharge, and, most importantly, focus on my relationship with Anthony and the children.

Every day off became an opportunity to connect, to nurture the bond we were building. Whether it was lazy mornings in bed, cooking dinner together, or taking spontaneous day trips out of the city, those three days became sacred. After years of chasing career milestones and prioritizing work above all else, it felt like I was finally learning how to balance ambition with love, stability with excitement. But the changes weren't without their challenges. Some nights I'd come home so drained that all I could do was collapse on the couch, too tired to hold a conversation, let alone be emotionally present. Anthony, patient as ever, would simply sit beside me, holding my hand or rubbing my back, reminding me with his quiet presence that I wasn't alone.

"I'm proud of you, you know," he said one night as we sat on the couch, the glow of the TV flickering across the room.

"For what?" I asked, leaning my head against his shoulder.

"For everything. For putting yourself out there, for building a new life, for figuring out what you want and going after it."

His words stayed with me long after the moment had passed. In all the chaos of starting over, I hadn't stopped to give myself credit for how far I'd come. But Anthony saw it. He saw me. And in those moments, I realized that the leap I'd taken wasn't just about a new career or a new specialty. It was about creating the kind of life I wanted—a life filled with purpose, love, and a sense of belonging. Neurology gave me the spark I needed to reignite my passion for my work. And Anthony gave me the grounding I needed to keep going, to believe that I could have it all. He worked overnight, so we found ways to make it work. Sometimes, I'd visit him at the hospital after my shift, and other times, he'd stop by to see me at home in the few hours before he went in for his. We had to get creative, but we made it work.

For now, our arrangement was manageable because we didn't live together, and his mom played a big role in helping with the kids. Working nights, Anthony made the most of the time while the kids were in school, catching a nap before switching into full-on daddy mode when they got home. He wasn't perfect—no one is—but Anthony was as close to perfect as you could get in a realistic, no-rose-colored-glasses kind of way. He balanced his responsibilities with such grace, juggling work, fatherhood, and our relationship without ever losing his humor or his heart. With Anthony, I felt secure in a way I hadn't in years, like I could finally let my guard down. But even Anthony's steady presence couldn't erase the shadows creeping into my mind.

The unease began as a whisper, a fleeting thought I could dismiss if I tried hard enough. But whispers can grow louder, and shadows have a way of creeping into the corners of your safe places. At first, I thought I was imagining it. The faint sound of a siren in the distance, an ambulance passing by my house. Nothing out of the ordinary, right? But it wasn't random, and it wasn't just once. James wasn't content to stay behind the screen anymore. He was making his presence known in a way that sent my sense of safety crumbling.

Anthony made me feel secure in our relationship—he always had—but James was unraveling my sense of security in my own home.

He was driving by my house.

It wasn't random, either. It was calculated.

He wasn't stupid; he used the ambulance vehicle. A convenient cover—after all, who would question an EMT driving through a residential area? But I knew better. Every time he passed, he'd sound the siren, just for a split second. Not long enough to cause alarm for anyone else, but just enough to catch my attention. To let me know he was there. Watching. I was starting to feel unsafe in my own home. The place that was supposed to be my sanctuary now felt like it had invisible eyes on every corner. I'd hear the faint sound of a siren and my chest would tighten, my body bracing before my mind could even process it. I'd catch myself glancing out the window, scanning the street for any sign of him, even when I knew he wasn't there.

Am I going crazy?

The more I thought about it, the more paranoid I became. The scenario played on repeat in my head: *"I think this man who's an EMT is stalking me because he's driving by my house on a main road in an ambulance, briefly sounding the sirens to get my attention."* It sounded ridiculous, even to me.

Who would believe that?

More importantly, how could I explain this to Anthony? The last thing I wanted was for him to think I wasn't over James. The idea of bringing it up felt like opening a Pandora's box, one filled with doubt and unnecessary drama. I couldn't risk that—not now, not when things between us were so good.

So, I decided to stay quiet..at least for now..

I convinced myself I needed solid proof before I could say anything. But in the meantime, the silence was suffocating. I was constantly on edge, my mind running wild with what-ifs. What if he escalated? What if he was trying to intimidate me into responding? What if this didn't stop?

At night, I double-checked the locks on my doors and windows, feeling foolish but unable to stop myself. The shadows outside seemed darker, the usual noises of the street suddenly more sinister. My phone became a source of dread; every notification made my stomach drop, even if it wasn't him. I didn't know how much longer I could keep this to myself. Anthony noticed the change in me—how distracted I was, how I seemed to jump at little things. But every time he asked if something was wrong, I brushed it off. "Just tired," I'd say, or, "Work's been stressful." The truth was, I didn't know how to handle this. James was unraveling the fragile sense of security I'd worked so hard to rebuild, and I felt powerless to stop it. For now, I could only wait. Wait for proof. Wait for something concrete to show Anthony so I wouldn't seem delusional. Wait for a sign that I wasn't losing my grip on reality.

| 10 |

A Diner Full of Lies

James had escalated.

It wasn't just the drive-bys anymore. Now, he was leaving things on my car—small, innocuous objects that felt anything but innocent. A single flower, and even a note that simply said, *"Thinking of you."*

He wanted my attention? Fine. He was going to get it. Unblocking his number, I sent the simplest, most direct message I could muster:

"Please leave me alone."

The reply came almost instantly, as if he had been waiting for me to crack.

"Hi sweet pea, I'm happy to hear from you. I'd like to meet for coffee to talk. There are some things I'd like to tell you."

I stared at the screen, my blood boiling at his audacity. It was as though he'd crafted the message with just the right amount of urgency, knowing I'd consider it even if I didn't want to. Perhaps he thought if he got it all out in one text, I wouldn't block him again.

What could he possibly need to talk about?

My mind spiraled with possibilities, each one more absurd than the last. Maybe he wanted to apologize for being a piece of shit. Maybe he wanted to tell me I was the one that got away. Or, maybe he just wanted to gloat about how happy he was in his new marriage. Was it egotistical to think any of this was about me? Or was I right to assume that his sudden reappearance had nothing to do with closure and everything to do with control? I didn't see a single scenario in which this conversation would end with me feeling better. But as much as I hated to admit it, my curiosity was gnawing at me. Maybe if I went, he'd say his piece and finally leave me alone. Maybe this would close the door for good.

Against my better judgment, I responded.

"Fine. Tell me when and where."

The address came back almost immediately: the diner where we had first met.

Of course, he chose *that* location.

I rolled my eyes, already annoyed. He clearly wanted to evoke some kind of nostalgic connection, as if meeting there would somehow soften me. It wouldn't.

"Okay," I replied. One word. That was all he was getting from me.

It was the following morning, and luckily for me, Anthony had a doctor's appointment. Normally, he liked me to go with him, but he opted to go alone this time, predicting it would be a quick in-and-out visit. *One hour,* I thought. That's all James gets—if that.

I pulled up to the diner, and there he was, already waiting. Time hadn't been kind to him, or maybe my feelings had just changed so drastically that I no longer saw him through rose-colored glasses. His once clean-cut appearance had given way to a slightly shaggy look, and a potbelly now pushed against the fabric of his shirt. *Where did that come from?* Yet, there he was, chin held high, a cocky smile plastered on his face as he rushed to hold the door open for me, his eyes locking onto mine with deliberate intensity. *Cocky son of a bitch.* The sight of him already irritated me to the core, and he hadn't even said a word. The waitress, kind and unsuspecting, led us to our table. Of course, it had to be *that* table—the exact one from our first date. The universe really has a twisted sense of humor.

"Sweet pea," he said, standing as I approached.

"Don't call me that," I snapped, sliding into the seat across from him without bothering to look up.

He raised his hands in mock surrender, his grin unwavering. "Fair enough."

The waitress returned, and I ordered a black coffee, silently hoping she'd sense the tension and minimize the interruptions.

"So," I said, folding my arms and cutting straight to the point. "What do you want, James?"

He leaned back in the booth, still radiating that infuriating smugness. "I wanted to see you. It's been a long time."

"Just how I like it," I shot back, my voice cold enough to cut glass.

He chuckled, shaking his head. "You haven't changed much, I see. Still sharp as ever."

"And you're still wasting my time, I see" I replied, my patience already wearing thin. "What do you want to say?"

For a moment, his cocky facade faltered, and I thought I caught a glimpse of something real—regret, maybe. Then he spoke, his words tumbling out quickly, almost desperately.

"I haven't been sleeping much," he admitted. "I've been thinking about us, about everything that happened. I talked to..." He paused, then continued. "I talked to my ex wife recently about the anniversary of our baby's death. We went to the beach to lay out the ashes, and all I could think about was you. I called you, but it went straight to voicemail."

I froze, my stomach turning at his words. That must have been the universe protecting me because I never got a phone call—and I was grateful for that small mercy. What was his plan? *"Hey, I'm at the beach with the woman I married behind your back, grieving the loss of our wedlock child, and I thought it'd be a great time to reminisce about our baby that never was."* Hard pass.

I stayed silent, letting him keep talking. He was speaking too fast, his words rushing together. I recognized the signs: impulsive actions, sleepless nights, rambling. This wasn't just guilt or regret—this was James in the midst of a manic episode.

"When your phone went to voicemail, I went on Facebook to send you a message. That's when I saw your profile picture with your new man. And... as much as I want to see you happy with someone else, it kills me. That's all I can think about now."

I took a slow sip of my coffee, unsure of how to respond. Then, as if on cue, the waterworks began.

"I'm sorry," he said, his voice cracking. "I'm sorry for everything I did. For everything I put you through. I'm sorry we didn't get a chance to see our baby grow up. I'm sorry for all of it."

I stared at him, stunned. This 6'4" stocky man was sitting across from me in a diner, crying, while I remained stoic, a blank expression plastered on my face. He leaned forward, his voice softer now, more measured. "I've been doing a lot of thinking," he continued. "My marriage now... it's not what I thought it would be. It's made me realize a lot about myself, about my mistakes. And you... you were one of the biggest."

His words hung in the air between us. I couldn't tell if he was being genuine or if this was just another one of his manipulations.

"So, what?" I said finally, my voice even. "You want me to forgive you? Is that it?"

"I don't expect anything," he replied, shaking his head. "I just needed to tell you. To say it out loud. You don't have to forgive me."

I took another sip of my coffee, letting the silence stretch out as I tried to process what I was hearing.

"Are you done?" I asked after a long pause.

He nodded slowly. "Yeah, I'm done."

"Good. I'm glad you got it out of your system." I stood, reaching into my purse and tossing a few bills onto the table to cover my drink. "Don't contact me again, James."

I turned and began to walk away, relief starting to wash over me, when I felt his hand grab my arm.

"Patricia, wait," he said, his grip firm enough to stop me in my tracks. I knew that was a little too easy.

I froze, staring down at his hand gripping me. My skin crawled at the contact.

"Let go," I said evenly, my voice steady but icy.

His hand dropped immediately. "I'm sorry," he said, his voice small and defeated.

"Please sit just a bit longer." He said with a tone of desperation. Reluctantly, I sat back down to see what else he had up his sleeve. I had spent years imagining this moment. The day James would come crawling back, apologizing for everything he'd done, begging for forgiveness. In my mind, I'd tell him I was in a happy relationship, flash him a smug smile, and walk away feeling victorious, vindicated.

But when the moment finally came, I felt... nothing.

No anger, no sadness, no satisfaction. Just a hollow void where I thought there might be some grand sense of closure. There he was, a grown man crying in the middle of a diner, confessing his regrets, and I couldn't even muster a flicker of emotion. He was unraveling in front of me, but I wasn't responsible for stitching him back together.

"Thank you for your apology," I said flatly, the words feeling as empty as I did. It was all I could think to say.

His red-rimmed eyes locked onto mine, and then he said it: "I'm going to make it right."

Make it right? What the hell did that mean?

I raised an eyebrow, confusion plain on my face. "There's no need. That's what you're doing right now—by apologizing."

"No. You'll see," he said, a strange intensity in his voice that made my stomach twist.

Oh, great. This wasn't going to end here. It was clear that he had no intention of letting this be our last interaction.

"Well, listen," I said, trying to keep my voice firm but calm. "I appreciate your apology. Let's move forward and leave this in the past so we can both live our lives in peace—*separately.*"

His face hardened, and his tone shifted. "Oh no, sweet pea," he said, leaning forward, his voice low and deliberate. "I don't think you understand. I'm going to leave my wife, and I'm going to fight for you. You are mine, and I was a fool to let you go before. I will never let that happen again."

My blood ran cold.

This was so much worse than I could have ever imagined.

"No, you're not," I said firmly, shaking my head. "You are happy with your new life. I am happy with my new life. This will be the last time we see each other or speak to each other. Thank you for your apology—it's accepted." (It wasn't.) "But I have to go now."

I stood up, ready to bolt. He didn't stop me this time. He sat back in his seat, watching me leave. I didn't waste another second. The minute I got into my car, I blocked his number, his Facebook account, and every other platform I could think of. I wasn't leaving any doors open.

"Never let that happen again, my ass," I blurted to myself, gripping the steering wheel as I sped out of the parking lot. I didn't look back.

| 11 |

The Weight of We

"We have to talk."

It was the kind of text no man ever wanted to receive. Four words heavy with implications, words that felt like they were holding a grenade, just waiting for the pin to be pulled.

Anthony called almost immediately.

"What's wrong?" he asked, his tone a mix of concern and irritation.

"This isn't something I want to discuss over the phone," I said, trying to keep my voice calm, even though my hands were already trembling. "I'm on my way to your house."

"You can tell me now. What's going on?" His voice sharpened, pushing against the vague wall I'd just built.

"I said I'm on my way," I repeated, firm but shaky. I needed time to gather my thoughts, and I wasn't ready to have this conversation through a phone line.

"Fine," he muttered before hanging up.

The thirty minutes it took to get to his house felt like a lifetime, and judging by his expression when I pulled into the driveway, it had felt even longer for him. Anthony was outside, leaning against his car, a Black & Mild between his fingers. His posture was tense, his jaw set in a way that immediately put me on edge. I parked, turned off the car, and sat there for a moment, watching him. He wasn't going to let me off easy—not this time. Not when I'd left him hanging with a cryptic text and thirty minutes to spiral into worst-case scenarios. Stepping out of the car, I walked toward him, each step feeling heavier than the last. Anthony's eyes followed me, sharp and questioning. I leaned against his car, deciding not to waste any more time.

"Remember when I told you about my ex sending me a friend request and texting me?" I began cautiously, my voice soft but deliberate.

"Mhm," Anthony replied, his expression hardening just slightly, the calm exterior beginning to crack.

"Well… he didn't stop there."

"Yeah, you told me he reached out again, and you blocked him," he said, his tone calm but now threaded with suspicion.

"I did," I admitted. "But it really didn't stop there either."

"What do you mean?" His voice sharpened, his eyebrows knitting together as his body tensed.

I hesitated, the words catching in my throat. My heart pounded, and for a moment, I considered not telling him the full truth. But I knew better than to keep this from him any longer. "After that, he started driving by the house… and leaving things on my car."

Anthony's expression darkened instantly, his jaw tightening as his posture shifted. His shoulders squared, and his grip on the Black & Mild he was holding tightened. "What kind of things?" he asked, his voice low and controlled, but I could hear the storm brewing beneath.

"A pink rose," I said, my voice barely above a whisper. "And then... a note."

"A note?" he repeated, his eyes narrowing. "What did it say?"

I reached into my bag, pulling out the folded piece of paper that had been haunting me since I found it on my windshield. I handed it to him without a word, my hands trembling slightly as I placed it in his.

Anthony unfolded the note carefully, his eyes scanning the words: *"Thinking of you."*

The paper crinkled slightly under his tightening grip. "This... this guy is out of his mind," he muttered, his voice low and seething. He looked back at me, his expression a mixture of anger and disbelief. "How long has this been going on?"

"It's been going on for a while," I admitted quietly, my gaze dropping to the ground.

"And you didn't think to tell me?!" he snapped, his tone louder than I'd expected, forcing my attention to be directed back at him.

He was pissed, and I couldn't blame him.

"I wasn't completely sure... at first," I stammered, even as the excuse felt hollow and unconvincing. Anthony's arched brow and the hard line of his jaw told me he wasn't buying it.

"That doesn't answer why you didn't tell me," he pressed, his voice sharp and pointed.

"I didn't want you to think there was a reason to worry," I said, though the words sounded weak even as I said them.

"Patricia," he said sharply, his frustration spilling over. "We've been through this before. Why are we having the same damn conversation again?"

"You're right," I admitted, my voice trembling. "You're absolutely right. But I was scared, Anthony. Because now... now I think there is a reason to worry."

"And why is it that you only hide things when it comes to him?" His voice dropped, quieter now but no less cutting.

"I don't know," I said honestly, looking down at the ground.

The truth was, this terrified me more than I wanted to admit. No matter how much I tried to fight it, James was like a hot stove—a lesson learned the hard way. Once you've been burned, you never want to go near it again. James *was* the stove, and I had no intention of ever touching, seeing, or even thinking about it again. But now, here I was, being forced to confront it. And the worst part? I didn't even know how to deal with it. Anthony's silence was heavy. I could see his mind racing, his thoughts spiraling as he pieced everything together. I knew he was imagining the worst—that everything we'd built together was about to crumble because of this ghost from my past. His family, his children, his friends—they all knew me now. To him, it must have felt like James was threatening to destroy all of that.

"I met him for coffee today," I finally said, the words slipping out in a rush.

Anthony's jaw clenched, his eyes narrowing as he processed what I'd just said.

"And what happened?" he asked, his voice carefully measured, his tone controlled but edged with frustration.

"I met him because I thought... maybe if I let him say whatever he needed to say, that would be the end of it," I said quickly, trying to get it all out. "But after talking to him, I'm scared. He's... he's not well, Anthony."

Anthony's eyes hardened as he stubbed out the Black & Mild on the concrete floor next to his car. He took a moment, inhaling deeply before looking at me.

"I dont give a fuck if this man is well or not Patricia. You knew this man was driving past *your house*, where my kids often are, and you didn't tell me?" His voice was sharp, each word landing like a blow.

He was right. I had fucked up—again.

He continued, his frustration spilling over. "You're so damn stubborn. You always think you have to figure everything out on your own, and now look. You've got this clinically diagnosed crazy man *telling* you he's going to create a problem. Now we're both going to be stuck looking over our shoulders. And this—" he gestured to me—"this is why you've been on edge for weeks."

He said *we*.

Despite everything, despite the intensity of his words, that single word reassured me. He wasn't planning to leave me. He wasn't giving up. He was pissed, but he was still here and by his words, he didn't seem like he had any intentions of leaving any time soon. *Is this what a healthy reaction looks like?* I thought, absurdly, even as I tried to process everything. It wasn't the time, but I couldn't help the heat that rose in me at how protective he was.

"I know I messed up," I said, my voice trembling. "I should have told you sooner. I didn't think it would get this bad, and I didn't want to drag you into it."

"We're already in it, Patricia," he said firmly, his tone leaving no room for argument. "You should've come to me the moment this started."

"We're"—there it was again.

He softened slightly, stepping closer and placing his hands on my shoulders. "I just need to know that you're safe. That *we're* safe."

"You better stop turning me on with all this 'we' talk," I said, attempting to lighten the mood with a playful smile.

He took my hand, kissed it gently, then looked up at me with a smirk. "Shut up. It's not the time," he said, trying—and failing—to hold back his laughter.

"I'll do whatever it takes to make sure we are safe," I said, meeting his eyes. "I promise."

"Good," he said, his voice softer now, but still firm. "Because we're handling this together. No more secrets. No more trying to deal with this alone. Understand?"

I nodded, relief washing over me in waves. Before I could say anything more, he pulled me into a tight hug, his arm strong and reassuring around my shoulders. He leaned down, pressing a kiss to my forehead.

"You're so hardheaded, you know that?" he said, his tone somewhere between exasperation and affection.

"I'm sorry," I whispered, the words heavy with sincerity. It was all I could think to say.

"Mhm," he responded, his lips twitching into the faintest hint of a smirk. His arms tightened around me briefly, a silent acknowledgment that while he was frustrated, we were still a team.

| 12 |

The Periwinkle Warning

The unease in my life had taken root, spreading its toxic vines into every corner of my day. What had started as unnerving texts and drive-bys had now grown into something far more invasive. James's behavior was escalating, and I couldn't pretend anymore that it wasn't affecting me—or everyone around me.

The first sign was the flowers.

At first glance, they seemed innocuous enough—a simple bouquet left on my doorstep. No card, no message. But the color of the roses—*periwinkle blue*—sent chills down my spine. It was the exact shade I had once told James I wanted for our would-have-been wedding day. I knew instantly who they were from. That wasn't a color you could just pick up at the grocery store. These roses had to be specially ordered. The man had an irritating attention to detail. I'll give him that. But it was too late. If only he had put this much effort in years ago, when it actually mattered. This much work to be better, to honor my trust, to just not be a complete douchebag. Maybe then, these flowers could have meant something. Instead, they felt hollow, like a mockery of what could have been. I picked them up and purposely walked them to the outdoor trash can, making sure to toss them in with deliberate care—in case he was watching. The next day, there was a ring at my door. I opened it to find a delivery man from Flora's Florals standing on the porch, holding a massive bouquet that made the previous day's flowers look like an afterthought.

"Special delivery for a lucky lady!" he said with a cheerful grin.

"Oh no," I said immediately, shaking my head. "I'm sorry, I have to decline this delivery."

His smile faltered. "Ma'am, it's a really big bouquet and fully paid for. I have to make sure it gets to the proper location."

"Are you married?" I asked flatly. "Give it to your wife."

He looked startled. "Uh, no ma'am, we're not allowed to do that. You can always just toss them if you don't want to keep them."

I sighed, knowing there was no way out of this without making the situation worse. Reluctantly, I signed for the package.

I'm not going to lie—when I saw the arrangement up close, it was stunning. Easily the most beautiful flower arrangement I'd ever seen. A large bouquet of at least fifty roses in a pristine white vase. Periwinkle, white, and yellow roses, perfectly arranged and dusted with a delicate coat of silver glitter spray.

The same colors I once told him I wanted for our wedding.

My heart sank, a mixture of anger and sadness swelling inside me. It hurt to know I was going to have to throw away something so beautiful.

"Would you like me to carry them inside for you?" the delivery man offered, noticing the weight of the arrangement.

"No, thank you," I replied quickly. "You can just leave them out here."

Later that day, Anthony came over to the house. His eyes landed on the massive bouquet still sitting on the porch. To my dismay, he brought it inside and set it on the counter.

"This has to stop," Anthony said firmly, crossing his arms as he stared at the flowers.

"I know," I replied, my voice small and hesitant. "But why did you bring them inside?"

"They're nice," he said with a shrug.

I stared at him in disbelief. "What?"

"What? They *are*," he said matter-of-factly, gesturing toward the bouquet. "But this is too much. This is harassment, Patricia. He's testing boundaries. He's escalating."

"Yeah," I replied, still incredulous, "and you just brought the flowers into the house."

Anthony looked at me, his expression calm and unbothered, which somehow only added to my disbelief.

But then it hit me. This man was so confident in his place in my life, so secure in what we had, that he could bring another man's flowers into my house without a flicker of insecurity. He wasn't threatened. Not even a little. It was... kind of hot. I couldn't help the faint smile that tugged at my lips, even in the middle of all this chaos.

"You're unbelievable," I said, shaking my head. Anthony simply laughed it off.

"But what can I do if he just keeps sending flowers?" I said looking for some type of insight.

"Yeah but he's not *just* sending flowers," Anthony snapped, his frustration bubbling over. " This has been a problem for a while now. It's the fact that he knows where you live. It's the fact that he's deliberately trying to get a reaction out of you. What's next, Patricia? What happens when he crosses the next line?"

His words stayed with me long after the conversation ended, replaying in my head like a broken record. *What happens when he crosses the next line?*

And then, inevitably, the next line was crossed.

It was a quiet Saturday morning, and Anthony was at work. I'd stepped out to grab coffee, grateful for a few minutes of normalcy outside the suffocating tension that had become my life. But when I returned, I noticed something off as I walked up the driveway.

The mailbox was open. Frowning, I approached cautiously, peering inside. My stomach dropped.

There, tucked neatly inside, was a photograph.

My hands trembled as I pulled it out. The image was grainy, zoomed in from a distance, but there was no mistaking it was me. I was sitting on the porch swing in Anthony's backyard, a book in my lap, completely unaware that I was being watched. Bile rose in my throat as I clutched the photo, my pulse pounding in my ears. This wasn't just flowers anymore. This was something far more sinister. When

Anthony saw the picture, his reaction was immediate and visceral.

"That's it," he said, pacing back and forth in my living room, his fists clenching at his sides. "We're calling the cops. Tonight."

"No," I said quickly, panic rising in my chest.

"What do you mean, no?" He turned to face me, his expression incredulous.

"I mean, I'm not ready to go to the police," I said, my voice trembling.

"Patricia, this man is stalking you. He's leaving things at your house, taking pictures of you. Do you understand how dangerous this is?"

"I know!" I said, my voice cracking. "But you don't understand what he's like. If we involve the police, it could make him spiral. It could make things worse."

Anthony stared at me, his jaw tight, his eyes searching mine for some semblance of reason. "And what happens if you don't involve the police? Do you think he's just going to stop on his own?"

I didn't have an answer.

Anthony sighed, running a hand through his hair. "I get that you're scared. I get that you don't want things to get worse but you can't keep pretending that ignoring it will make it go away."

I nodded slowly, tears welling in my eyes. "I just... I need time to figure out what to do."

"Time might not be something we have," he said softly, his frustration giving way to concern.

That night, after Anthony left, I found myself sitting at the kitchen table, staring at a blank sheet of paper in my notebook. Writing had always been my way of processing things, and tonight was no exception.

Dear Universe,

I don't know what to do.

James's presence in my life has taken over my thoughts, my actions, my sense of safety. Every time I hear a car drive by, my stomach tightens. Every time the doorbell rings, I feel a wave of dread. Anthony wants me to call the police, to take legal action, and part of me knows he's right. I can't keep living like this—always looking over my shoulder, always wondering what James will do next.

But another part of me is terrified of what will happen if I do.

James isn't stable. I've seen him spiral before, and I know how unpredictable he can be. If I get the police involved, what's to stop him from retaliating? What's to stop him from doing something worse? I want to protect myself. I want to protect Anthony and his family. But I'm scared, Universe. I'm scared of making the wrong choice.

Please, give me a sign. Show me what to do. I can't keep living in this state of paranoia, but I don't know how to move forward.

Over and out,
Patricia

That night, sleep didn't come easily. My mind raced, replaying every interaction with James, every moment of unease I'd felt since he forced his way back into my life. When I finally drifted off, it wasn't long before I woke again—drenched in sweat, my heart pounding violently against my rib cage.

The nightmare had been so vivid, so real.

James was standing over me, his face shadowed but unmistakable. His hand gripped a knife, the blade gleaming in the faint light filtering through the window. I tried to scream, but no sound came out. I tried to move, but my body was frozen. He leaned in closer, his breath hot against my ear as he whispered, "You're mine. You'll always be mine."

Then, without hesitation, he plunged the knife down—

I bolted upright, gasping for air, my hands clutching at my chest. The darkness of my bedroom closed in around me, and for a moment, I wasn't sure if I was still dreaming. It took several minutes for me to calm down, to remind myself that I was safe. But was I? I glanced at the locked bedroom door—a habit I'd recently developed—my mind racing with a thousand what-ifs. I couldn't keep living like this. Something had to change.

Whether I was ready or not, the time for action was drawing near.

| 13 |

When Roses Turn to Thorns

The words **FRANKVILLE POLICE** stood out in large yellow letters on a black sign, flanked by a gleaming police badge. They were emblazoned on the white municipal building, commanding my full attention, leaving me unable to focus on anything else. Anthony and I sat in the car outside the police station, the engine still running. Neither of us made a move to get out. The weight of the situation pressed down on us, making the air in the car feel heavier than it had ever been.

"You ready for this?" Anthony asked, his voice low but steady.

"No," I admitted, staring straight ahead. "But we need to do it anyway."

He nodded, reaching over to give my hand a reassuring squeeze. "Let's go."

The fluorescent lights inside the station were harsh and sterile, a stark contrast to the turmoil churning inside me.

Anthony led the way to the front desk, where a tired-looking officer glanced up from his paperwork.

"Can I help you?" the officer asked, his tone more business than warmth.

"Yes," Anthony began, his voice calm but firm. "My girlfriend is being stalked, and we need to know what steps we can take."

The officer's expression shifted slightly, a flicker of seriousness crossing his face. "Alright, let's start with the details."

We were led into a small room with mismatched chairs and an old desk. The officer asked me to recount everything—every text, every drive-by, the flowers, the photograph in the mailbox. Saying it all out loud felt surreal, like I was describing someone else's life. Anthony sat beside me, his presence grounding, though I could feel his tension radiating. Every time I hesitated, he gently urged me to continue. When I finished, the officer leaned back in his chair, his notepad filled with scribbled notes. "This is serious," he said plainly. "It's good that you're here. Stalking cases like this can escalate quickly, especially when the behavior becomes invasive, like leaving items or taking photos."

"What are our options?" Anthony asked immediately.

"Well, first and foremost, you can file a police report. That establishes a record of the incidents, which is crucial if this continues or escalates. From there, you could consider a restraining order."

"A restraining order?" I repeated, my stomach tightening at the thought.

"Yes," the officer said. "It's a legal document that prohibits him from contacting you or coming near you. Violating it would result in immediate legal consequences."

"But wouldn't that... provoke him?" I asked hesitantly.

The officer's gaze softened. "It's possible. In some cases, restraining orders can escalate the behavior initially, but they also give you legal recourse. It's about weighing the risks and deciding what makes you feel the most secure."

Anthony's jaw tightened. "So basically, we're damned if we do and damned if we don't."

The officer didn't deny it. "It's not a perfect system, but it's a starting point. My advice? Document *everything*. Every text, every visit, every item left at your house. The more evidence you have, the stronger your case will be if you decide to move forward."

After leaving the station, we didn't say much. The weight of the conversation lingered between us as we drove to meet with a lawyer Anthony had found online. The lawyer, a sharp-dressed woman with a no-nonsense demeanor, wasted no time diving into the legal aspects of the situation.

"You have two priorities here," she said, flipping through her notepad. "First, protect yourself. Second, build a strong case. That means gathering as much evidence as possible—texts, photos, video footage if you can get it. Anything that establishes a pattern of harassment."

"What about the restraining order?" Anthony asked, his voice tight with tension.

"It's a useful tool," she said, nodding. "But it's not foolproof. It's a piece of paper. It's meant to deter, but it can't physically stop someone from doing something reckless."

"That's what I'm afraid of," I admitted.

She looked at me, her expression softening slightly. "I understand. These situations are incredibly difficult, especially when you're dealing with someone unpredictable. The goal is to create barriers—legal, emotional, and physical—that make it harder for him to access you."

"And if he doesn't stop?" Anthony asked, his protective instincts clearly kicking in.

"Then you escalate. More documentation, more evidence, more legal action. But the sooner you start, the better positioned you'll be if this goes to court."

By the time we left the lawyer's office, the sun was setting, casting a dim orange glow over the city. The day had been long and emotionally draining, but it had also been productive. We had a plan—or at least the beginnings of one.

"Do you feel better?" Anthony asked as we walked back to the car.

"Not really," I admitted, leaning against the door. "But I feel… clearer. At least we have a plan now"

He nodded, wrapping an arm around me. "We're going to get through this. One step at a time."

I leaned into him, grateful for his steady presence even as my mind raced with the reality of what lay ahead.

As we pulled out of the parking lot, Anthony glanced at me. "We have one more stop," he said.

"Where?" I asked, my voice weary but curious.

"We need cameras," he replied, his tone leaving no room for argument.

I didn't protest. If anything, I was relieved. Anthony had been steps ahead of me this whole time, his protective instincts kicking into overdrive in ways I hadn't even considered. While I had been paralyzed by fear and uncertainty, he had been quietly putting together solutions to make sure we were safe. We drove to the nearest electronics store, the atmosphere in the car heavy but slightly lighter than it had been earlier. Anthony parked and got out with purpose, holding the door for me as I followed him inside. The store was brightly lit and bustling, the normalcy of it a stark contrast to the tension that had been hanging over us all day. Anthony headed straight for the security section, scanning the shelves with a focused intensity that made me feel oddly comforted.

"This one," he said, pointing to a system with multiple cameras and motion detection. "It's got a wide range and alerts straight to your phone."

"You've done this before," I teased lightly, trying to break the tension.

He smirked but didn't look away from the box as he read the specs. "Let's just say I like being prepared."

We loaded up the cart with two sets—one for my house and one for his—and a few extras: motion sensor lights, smart locks, and even a couple of dummy cameras to deter anyone from getting too close. By the time we got back to my house, the sun had set, casting the street in shadows. Anthony didn't waste any time. He set to work immediately, unboxing the cameras and mapping out the best spots to install them.

"Here," he said, pointing to the front porch. "One for the driveway, one for the walkway, and one angled toward the mailbox."

He moved to the backyard next, placing a camera near the fence line and another overlooking the porch swing—the very spot where James had taken that photo of me. As I watched Anthony work, meticulously ensuring every angle was covered, a wave of gratitude washed over me. While James was trying to make me feel unsafe, Anthony was doing everything in his power to make me feel protected. He wasn't just listening to my fears—he was acting on them, turning them into a tangible sense of security I hadn't felt in weeks.

"You're amazing," I said, leaning against the door frame as he adjusted the last camera.

He glanced back at me, a faint smile tugging at his lips. "Just doing what I need to do."

Later that night, after everything was set up and the app was installed on both of our phones, Anthony walked me through the features.

"See? Anytime there's movement, it'll send an alert," he explained, demonstrating on his phone.

I nodded, overwhelmed but grateful. "You didn't have to go this far, you know."

"Yes, I did," he said simply. "I need to know you're safe. That *we're* safe."

There it was again—that *we*. Every time he said it, it hit me in a way I couldn't quite describe. James might have been trying to tear me down, but Anthony was building me up, piece by piece, with every gesture, every word, every action. Once the house was quiet and the tension of the day had started to fade, I found Anthony in the kitchen, leaning against the counter with a glass of water in hand.

"I just want you to know," I began, stepping closer to him, "how much I appreciate everything you've done today. You didn't have to take this all on, but you did. You always do."

He set the glass down, his eyes softening as he looked at me. "You don't have to thank me for that. I'm just doing what anyone would do."

"No," I said, shaking my head. "You're doing what *you* would do. And I'm grateful for that. For you."

I closed the distance between us, wrapping my arms around his neck and pulling him into a kiss. It started slow, but the weight of the day melted away in the heat of the moment.

"I'm going to show you just how much I appreciate you," I murmured against his lips, feeling his hands slide to my waist.

His smirk returned, playful and teasing. "Oh yeah? Is this part of the security plan?"

"Let's just say, I like being prepared," I teased, my voice dripping with seduction as I unbuckled his belt. Slowly, I lowered myself to my knees, making sure to keep my eyes locked on his. The intensity in his gaze sent a shiver through me, and I could see the anticipation darkening his expression.

Without breaking eye contact, I leaned in and carefully wrapped my lips around the swollen tip of his cock, swallowing just the head.

"Oh my fucking god," he groaned, gripping the edge of the kitchen counter for support.

The salty taste of pre-cum teased my tongue as I let it pool in my mouth. Slowly, I licked a deliberate path from the tip of his cock down the thick, veined shaft to the root, savoring the way his body responded to every touch. I didn't stop there. I licked lower, my tongue exploring further, drawing a sharp gasp from him. When I sucked one of his balls into my mouth, rolling it gently with my tongue, his hips jerked involuntarily, and a deep, guttural moan escaped his lips.

"Fuck, just like that," he murmured, his fingers tangling in my hair.

I didn't rush—I wanted to savor every moment, every reaction. Shifting to the other, I gave it the same slow, tantalizing attention, rolling it gently between my lips while tracing it with my tongue. His body trembled ever so slightly, his breathing ragged, as though he was trying to hold himself together. Licking my way back up his shaft, I let my tongue trace the pulsing ridges, the heat of him throbbing against me. By the time I reached the glistening tip, a fresh bead of pre-cum had formed. I eagerly swirled my tongue over the slit, collecting every drop before it had the chance to drip down.

But it was time to change the pace.

With a sudden surge of hunger, I took him fully into my mouth, sliding down until he filled me completely. His hand tightened in my hair, his groan echoing through the kitchen. I set a steady rhythm, hollowing my cheeks and letting him guide me as I moved up and down, taking him deeper with every stroke. As his cock began to swell, I felt his body tense, his grip on my hair becoming firmer. My eyes widened as he held my head in place, thrusting into my mouth with a primal urgency. His hips moved faster, his groans growing louder, and I could feel the heat building, the moment drawing near.

Then it hit.

Load after load of cum shot into my mouth, the warmth spilling down my throat as I pulled him closer, swallowing every drop. His body shuddered as he gasped for air, the pressure on the back of my head easing. I lifted my head slightly, giving him the illusion I was done, his heavy breaths filling the room. But I wasn't finished—not yet. With a mischievous smile, I leaned back down, my lips teasing the sensitive head. His cock twitched as I circled my tongue in fast, deliberate motions, alternating between shallow licks and deep, slow throating.

"Jesus Christ," he groaned, his hand gripping the counter again, his knees nearly buckling.

I didn't stop until his body jerked back instinctively, his hands pushing me away.

"Oh my god, I can't," he gasped, pulling back with a laugh of disbelief.

With a satisfied smile, I stood back up, my chest heaving as I caught my breath. Before I could say anything, he pulled me into a deep, passionate kiss, his tongue teasing mine. To my surprise, he wasn't done. His hand slipped down the front of my pants, sliding into my underwear, and his fingers found the wet heat between my legs.

"Mmm," he moaned, pulling back just enough to look into my eyes before capturing my lips again. His fingers began circling my clit with expert precision, sending jolts of pleasure through me. I clung to him, moaning into his mouth as my hips instinctively moved against his hand. With a low grunt, he suddenly yanked my pants down, the fabric pooling around my ankles in an instant. Spinning me around, he pushed me down onto the kitchen counter. He didn't waste any time. With one smooth motion, he slid inside me, stretching and filling me completely. A gasp escaped my lips as he set a relentless pace, his thrusts deep and powerful.

"You gonna be a good girl and cum for me?" he growled, his voice thick with desire as he leaned over me. His hand slipped beneath me, his fingers expertly teasing my clit while he continued driving into me.

"Yes," I gasped, my words breathless. "You feel so good inside me."

His pace quickened, his movements precise and unrelenting. I gripped the edge of the counter, my knuckles turning white as waves of pleasure built inside me, coiling tighter and tighter until I couldn't hold back any longer. My muscles clenched around him as my legs trembled uncontrollably. A scream tore from my throat as I came, squirting over the both of us.

"Mmm," he groaned in approval, his thrusts never faltering.

He didn't stop. If anything, the intensity of his movements increased.

"Oh my god," I cried out, my voice cracking. "You're going to make me cum again!"

He angled his hips slightly, hitting just the right spot, and within seconds, another wave of pleasure crashed over me. My body convulsed as another gush of fluid spilled out, my legs shaking so violently I thought they might give out beneath me.

"Good girl," he said, his voice low and commanding.

My entire body trembled as he continued to move inside me, prolonging the sensations that left me breathless and utterly at his mercy. I clung to the counter, my mind blank except for the overwhelming ecstasy that consumed me, and the sound of his voice pushing me over the edge again and again.

This man was going to kill me.

Pushing up inside me to get even deeper, he sent a whimper spilling from my lips. My body was already too sensitive, trembling with the aftershocks of everything he'd done to me. I didn't know how much more I could take, but I couldn't bring myself to stop him. Sensing my struggle, he gripped me closer, holding me steady and giving me the support I needed as my legs shook uncontrollably. His hand found my clit again, and just when I thought he couldn't push me any further, he sped up his motions.

I gasped, bracing myself against the counter, my breath hitching with every deliberate circle of his fingers.

"Oh my god," I cried out, the pleasure building so quickly it felt almost unbearable. And then it hit.

A scream louder than any before tore from my throat as I shattered completely, my release soaking both of us.

I couldn't control the way my body trembled, my muscles spasming as wave after wave of ecstasy rolled over me. Before I could even catch my breath, he propped me up on the counter and dropped to his knees. His tongue pressed against my inner thigh, then moved to my center, licking and sucking up my release like it was his favorite meal.

"Anthony," My voice was weak as I watched him with my chest still heaving and my legs wrapped around his head. He didn't stop until he was satisfied, his tongue exploring every inch, teasing me with gentle flicks that made my already sensitive body tremble even more. When he finally pulled back, he rose to his feet and began kissing a trail up my stomach, each press of his lips a soft contrast to the intensity of everything before. When he reached my lips, he kissed me gently, his hands cradling my face as I leaned into him.

As I sat up, still catching my breath, I laughed softly. "That was not how that was supposed to go."

He grinned, his confidence radiating as he locked eyes with me. "That was exactly how that was supposed to go," he said, his tone low and satisfied. And with the way he looked at me, like I was the only thing that mattered in the world, I couldn't even argue.

| 14 |

Shadows in the Light

For the first time in what felt like forever, I woke up feeling at ease. The soft light of the morning sun filtered through the curtains, warming the room with its gentle glow. The air felt lighter, almost as though the suffocating weight I'd been carrying had lifted, even if just for a moment. I stretched lazily, my muscles pleasantly sore from the night before. As my hand brushed against the edge of the bed, I realized something that stopped me in my tracks—I hadn't locked my bedroom door.

That realization hit me like a wave, but instead of panic, I felt... calm. Safe, even.

It had been weeks since I'd gone to bed without checking the locks three, sometimes four times. Weeks since I hadn't felt the need to create a barrier between myself and the world outside. The knowledge that I had fallen asleep so easily, without my usual ritual of double-checking, was almost startling. I glanced at the empty side of the bed where Anthony had been the night before. His scent still lingered faintly, a mix of his cologne and the natural warmth of his skin. It made me smile. He had a way of doing that—making me feel like everything was okay, even when it wasn't. Like no matter what came next, I wouldn't have to face it alone.

I swung my legs over the edge of the bed, my bare feet meeting the cool floor. The house was quiet, the kind of peaceful silence I hadn't realized I missed. No paranoia, no racing thoughts, just calm. Walking to the kitchen, I made myself a cup of tea, savoring the stillness as I watched the steam curl into the air. I couldn't remember the last time I'd felt this settled. Maybe it was Anthony. No, it wasn't *maybe*. It *was* Anthony. He had brought something into my life that I hadn't realized I'd been missing—a sense of security.

Anthony had gone home to get the kids ready for school, his usual calm efficiency bringing a sense of routine to the day. He was going to drop them off and meet me at the grocery store to pick up some necessities before my evening shift. I'd arrived a little early, deciding to get a head start on the shopping. The aisles were quiet, and I let myself enjoy the mundane task of filling my cart. It felt normal. Simple. Something I hadn't had in a while. As I wheeled the cart to the corral in the parking lot, I heard a car door slam behind me. The sound sent a jolt of unease through me, and when I turned, my stomach dropped.

James.

He was standing just a few feet away, leaning casually against his car like he had every right to be there.

"Patricia," he called out, his tone almost friendly. But there was something in his eyes—something unsettling.

I gripped the handle of the cart tightly, my heart racing. "What are you doing here?" I demanded, trying to keep my voice steady.

"I needed to see you," he said, stepping closer.

My pulse quickened. This wasn't a coincidence. He'd followed me.

"You have no reason to be here," I said firmly, taking a step back. "You need to leave."

James didn't budge. Instead, he took another step forward, his eyes narrowing. "It's a public place. Plus you didn't answer my messages. You didn't give me a chance to explain. I'm not leaving until you hear me out."

"I have nothing to say to you," I replied, trying to keep my voice calm but forceful.

"Don't do that," he said, his tone dropping, now laced with frustration. "Don't act like I'm the bad guy here."

As I gripped the handle of the cart, preparing to push it toward the corral, James took a step closer, his smirk deepening.

"Did you like the flowers I sent?" he asked casually, as if we were old friends catching up.

My stomach churned, but I kept my face as neutral as possible. "What flowers?" I replied flatly, though the bile rising in my throat told me he already knew the answer.

"The periwinkle roses," he said, his tone smug. "I noticed you didn't like the first ones, so I made sure to go bigger the second time. You didn't throw *those* out, did you? I knew you'd love them. They're our colors."

The nonchalance in his voice made my skin crawl. How did he know I hadn't tossed them immediately? Was he watching the house more closely than I thought?

I stiffened, forcing myself to hold his gaze. "You need to stop," I said firmly, my voice trembling just slightly.

James tilted his head, his smirk never faltering. "Stop what? Showing you how much I care? You can lie to yourself, Patricia, but you can't lie to me. I know you felt something when you saw them."

I swallowed hard, my chest tightening as a wave of unease washed over me. He wasn't just trying to get under my skin—he was enjoying it. Before I could respond, I heard Anthony's voice calling out my name. Relief washed over me, but it was quickly replaced by dread. Anthony parked and stepped out, his eyes immediately locking onto James. His expression darkened as he strode over, his movements deliberate.

"What the hell is going on here?" Anthony demanded, his voice low but firm.

James turned to face him, his stance shifting. "This doesn't concern you," he said dismissively.

"The hell it doesn't," Anthony shot back, stepping between us. "You need to leave. Now."

James smirked, his eyes flicking between the two of us. "Oh, I see how it is. Playing the knight in shining armor, huh? You don't know a damn thing about us."

"I know enough." Anthony growled, his voice rising slightly.

The tension was suffocating. The two of them stood face-to-face, the air thick with hostility.

Anthony was a nice guy, but even the nicest people have their breaking point. There were two things to know about Anthony:

1. He would do anything to protect the people he loved.
2. When he got close to his breaking point, his words became few and far between.

I could see the signs—his sentences were getting shorter, his tone sharper, and the tension in his body was palpable. With every clipped response, my anxiety grew stronger, a knot tightening in my stomach as I braced for what might come next.

"Anthony," I said softly, placing a hand on his arm. He didn't look at me, his focus locked on James.

"You need to go," Anthony repeated, his voice cold.

"Or what?" James challenged, his smirk fading into something darker.

I felt panic rising. This was escalating too quickly. I couldn't let it get worse.

"Anthony," I said again, louder this time. "Please. Let it go."

Still not breaking eye contact from James, Anthony didn't say a word.

"I don't want this to escalate. Please." I begged.

Anthony hesitated, his anger warring with his instinct to protect me. Finally, he stepped back, his gaze still fixed on James.

James smirked again, his confidence returning. "You should listen to her," he said smugly. "She knows me better than you ever will."

Anthony stiffened, but I stepped in quickly, putting myself between them.

"Go," I said to James, my voice shaking with anger. "Get in your car and leave. Now."

For a moment, he didn't move, his eyes searching mine. Then, with a shrug, he turned and walked back to his car. "I'll see you later Sweet Pea."

"The fuck you will." Anthony yelled back. Anthony stepped forward once more as I put my hand on his chest to stop him.

Anthony watched him go, his hands clenched into fists at his sides.

"Are you okay?" he asked once James was gone, his voice softer now.

I nodded, though my hands were still trembling. "I'm fine. Let's just finish what we came here to do. I already started looking around but I came back out to meet you."

Anthony hesitated, clearly torn, but he nodded. "Alright," he said, his voice tense. "But this isn't over. Not by a long shot."

As we walked back to the store, I couldn't shake the feeling that James's actions were building toward something bigger. And I couldn't ignore the growing fear that Anthony might be right—this wasn't over. Not even close.

| 15 |

Signed, Sealed, Guarded

How did we get here? Filing for a restraining order wasn't something I ever thought I'd have to do. It felt surreal, like I was living someone else's life—a life filled with court dates, legal jargon, and the constant dread of waiting for the next escalation. Anthony and I sat in the small, fluorescent-lit office of a local attorney. The lawyer, a no-nonsense woman with sharp eyes and a commanding presence, outlined the process for us.

"We'll need to document everything," she said, her pen tapping against her notepad. "Every text, every encounter, everything and anything. The more evidence we have, the stronger your case will be."

I nodded, the weight of her words settling on my shoulders. My stomach churned at the thought of recounting every interaction, every invasive moment James had forced into my life.

"This isn't just about protecting yourself," Anthony chimed in, his voice steady but tense. "It's about setting boundaries and making sure he knows he can't keep doing this."

I glanced at him, grateful for his presence but also painfully aware of how much this was taking out of him too. Anthony had been my rock through all of this, but I could see the stress etched into his face—the tightness in his jaw, the faint dark circles under his eyes. The process began with paperwork—endless forms that felt cold and clinical compared to the reality of what I was dealing with. I sat at the dining table late into the night, filling out each detail as Anthony sat across from me, quietly reading over everything I wrote.

"What about the time he left the flowers?" I asked, my voice shaky.

"Include it," Anthony said without hesitation.

"And the picture in the mailbox?"

"Definitely include that," he replied, his tone clipped.

I could tell this was weighing on him too. Anthony was a man of action, someone who fixed problems head-on. Watching me struggle through this process without being able to immediately make it all go away was wearing on him. The court hearing was even more emotionally draining. Sitting in a sterile courtroom, surrounded by strangers, as I recounted the details of James's behavior felt invasive and humiliating. James wasn't present—restraining order hearings didn't require the other party to be there—but it felt like he was. Each stare from a stranger was like his eyes beaming at me, trying to intimidate me not to follow through with it. Anthony sat beside me. He held my hand tightly as I spoke, his silent support grounding me when I thought I might falter.

When the judge finally granted the restraining order, it felt like a small victory—a shield, albeit a fragile one, against the storm James had brought into my life. But the emotional toll didn't stop once the papers were signed. The stress lingered, like a shadow hanging over everything. At home, Anthony and I found ourselves snapping at each other over small things. The tension that had built up over weeks was finally bubbling to the surface.

"I know you're trying to protect me," I said one night as we sat on the couch, the air between us heavy. "But this is hard for both of us. I don't want to lose us in all of this."

He sighed, rubbing a hand over his face. "You're not going to lose me, Patricia. But seeing you go through this, knowing I can't just fix it—it's killing me."

His honesty hit me hard, and I realized that while I was consumed with my own fears and anxieties, I hadn't fully considered how much this was affecting him too.

"You're not supposed to fix it," I said softly, reaching for his hand. "Just being here, being you—it's enough. I couldn't do this without you."

He looked at me then, his eyes tired but filled with a determination that reminded me why I loved him. "You're stronger than you think," he said. "We're going to get through this. Together."

I rested my head against his chest, the weight of everything finally breaking through my fragile composure. Silent tears slid down my cheeks, soaking into his shirt as we sat on the couch. Without a word, he wrapped his arms around me tighter, holding me like he was the only thing keeping me together. He didn't speak—he didn't need to. His steady presence, the warmth of his embrace, was all the support I needed in that moment. It was enough to let me cry, to let me feel without judgment or expectation. I had fallen asleep in his arms without even realizing it. The soft press of kisses on my forehead stirred me awake.

"I have to leave for work," he said quietly, his voice low and gentle. "Do you want to come with me?"

I shook my head, too exhausted to speak.

"Okay," he said, brushing a strand of hair from my face. "Well, call me if anything happens. I've got the alerts on my phone for the cameras, and I'll be up all night. You don't need to worry."

"Okay," I whispered, my voice barely audible. "Thank you."

I didn't have many words left. The weight of every-thing—the day, the stress, the emotions—had drained me completely. But his presence, his calm reassurance, was enough to ease the edges of my fatigue as I sank back into the comfort of the couch. When Anthony left, the silence of the house settled over me like a heavy blanket. My eyes drifted to a nearby notebook on the coffee table. I reached for it instinctively, knowing that writing was the healthiest way I could release the flood of emotions threatening to overwhelm me. I flipped to a blank page, picked up a pen, and let my thoughts spill out.

Dear Universe,

Today, I filed a restraining order against James.

I never thought my life would come to this. A legal document to keep someone I once trusted so deeply at arm's length. It feels surreal—like I'm stuck in a nightmare I can't wake up from. How did it get this far? How did he get this far? I used to love James. Truly. He wasn't always the man he is now. Or maybe he was, and I just didn't want to see it. Either way, the person I thought I knew is gone, replaced by someone I can't recognize—someone who scares me. Today should have been a relief—a step toward protection and peace—but instead, it feels like I've dragged Anthony deeper into this mess.

Anthony.

God, I'm so grateful for him. He's been my anchor through this chaos, never once making me feel like I'm in it alone. But it hurts to see how much this is taking out of him. He's sleeping less—I can see it in the way his shoulders slump just a little more when he thinks I'm not looking. He already carries so much on his plate: his kids, his work, his life. And now I've added this to his list of responsibilities. He doesn't deserve it. He does everything in his power to keep me safe, and yet I can't help but feel like I'm failing him by putting him in this position.

Universe, I'm begging you—please help me with this situation. Protect me. Protect us.

I'm reaching a breaking point. I'm tired of looking over my shoulder, of feeling unsafe in my own home, of worrying about what James will do next. The fear, the paranoia, the guilt—it's eating me alive. Please, give me peace of mind. Help me find the strength to keep going, because right now, it feels like I'm crumbling under the weight of it all. I need guidance. I need protection. I need this to end.

Over and out,
Patricia

| 16 |

A Mostly Yes Day

In the midst of all the chaos James had brought into my life, there was at least one silver lining: the overwhelming support I received from the people who mattered most. Friends, family, and even colleagues rallied around me, offering everything from words of encouragement to practical help.

"I can't believe you're dealing with this," my best friend Layla said during one of our late-night phone calls. "You should've told me sooner. I would have been there in a heartbeat."

"I didn't want to bother you," I replied honestly, though I was kicking myself for not reaching out sooner.

"Patricia, please," she said firmly, her tone leaving no room for argument. "You're not a burden. And if this James guy shows up again, he's going to regret it. Trust me on that."

Her fierce loyalty brought a smile to my face—something I hadn't experienced much of lately. I was struck by how much I'd missed leaning on her, the way she always had my back no matter what. Years ago, she was the first person to notice the subtle signs of my pregnancy with James. She'd been my rock then, so why hadn't I turned to her sooner this time? Maybe it was shame. Maybe embarrassment. Or maybe it was just my stubborn habit of trying to handle things on my own. Whatever the reason, I knew now that I should have trusted her from the beginning, and should have let her in when I needed her most.

Even my colleagues at the hospital pitched in. My supervisor had adjusted my schedule to make room for court dates and lawyer meetings, while coworkers stepped up to cover shifts when I needed time off. Their quiet gestures of support reminded me that I wasn't as alone in this fight as I sometimes felt. But just as the pieces of my support system started to strengthen, another crack appeared in the form of Christina.

It started with a message on my phone late one evening. I was sitting on the couch, exhausted from the day, when the notification buzzed. At first, I thought it might be Anthony, but when I opened it, my stomach dropped.

It was Christina, Mia's mother, and the tone of the message was exactly what I'd expected: accusatory and sharp.

Christina: *I've heard about what's going on. This is completely unacceptable. I don't feel comfortable with Mia and Christian in that house. I'm seriously considering taking legal action to get full custody.*

My jaw clenched as I read the words. *Legal action?* Christina, who barely even saw Mia, was suddenly concerned about her well-being. *Okay Christina.* Although, I had to admit, she had reason with this one. I stared at the message, debating whether to respond, when Anthony walked into the room.

"What's wrong?" he asked immediately, his eyes narrowing as he saw the look on my face.

I handed him my phone without a word, watching his expression darken as he read the message.

"Unbelievable," he said in disbelief. "She barely knows Mia, and now she wants to play mother of the year?"

"Anthony, I don't want this to turn into something bigger," I said cautiously.

"It's not going to," he replied firmly, already pulling out his phone. "I'll take care of it."

It didn't take long for him to get Christina on the line. I could only hear his side of the conversation, but the intensity in his voice was enough to make me sit up straight.

"Christina, let's get one thing straight," he began, his tone sharp and unwavering. "No court in their right mind is going to take Mia out of my house and hand her over to a mother who never even sees her when you're really supposed to be seeing her every weekend."

I could hear her muffled response, though I couldn't make out the words. Whatever she said didn't faze him.

"You're worried about her safety? Give me a break," he shot back. "You don't worry about her safety while you are out living your best life. Full custody? You can't even handle taking care of her throughout the couple of weeks that she stays with you. What's her favorite color Christina? What's her favorite food? Stop pretending this is about Mia and admit what it really is—a perfect excuse to stir up drama."

He was spitting out words like a wildfire, each one more heated than the last. I had never heard him talk like that before—sharp, unrelenting, and raw. Then it hit me: the first thing to know about Anthony was that he would do anything to protect the people he loved and Christina had just crossed that line. She didn't just push a button; she pulled the lever.

Anthony wasn't just angry—he was in full-on primal mode, the kind of protective rage that left no room for negotiation.

He paused, his grip tightening on the phone. "You can threaten all you want, but we both know you can't handle the responsibility. And the next time you feel like messaging Patricia, don't. You have an issue, you come to me directly."

With that, he ended the call and tossed his phone onto the couch, letting out a deep breath.

For a moment, we sat in silence, the tension in the room thick.

"Are you okay?" I asked softly.

Anthony ran a hand through his hair, his shoulders sagging slightly. "I'm fine. It's just... frustrating. I would get it if she was actually concerned, but she's not. After this conversation she'll never ask about Mia's safety again. She just wants to feel that she has control."

His words hit me hard. I could see the toll this was taking on him—the way it wore on his patience and chipped away at his energy.

"But she won't do anything," he continued, his voice more resigned now. "She can't. She'd have to step up, and we both know that's not going to happen."

I nodded, placing a hand on his arm. "You're doing everything right, Anthony. Don't let her get to you."

He looked at me then, his eyes softening. "I'm not worried about me," he said. "I'm worried about you. You've already got enough on your plate without her adding to it."

I smiled faintly, grateful for his support, even when he was dealing with his own struggles. The tension had been palpable in our house lately, and no matter how much Anthony and I tried to shield the kids from the chaos swirling around us, they weren't oblivious. Children had an uncanny way of sensing when something wasn't right, even when words were left unsaid. I watched Anthony after the call with Christina, the way his shoulders seemed heavier, his usual easy demeanor dimmed by the weight of everything going on. I hated seeing him like that, and I hated knowing that the kids, even without understanding the full extent of it all, could feel it too. That's when the idea struck me.

"How about a fun family day?" I blurted out as we sat at the kitchen table that evening.

Anthony raised an eyebrow, his lips curving into a faint smile. "A fun family day?"

"Not just any family day," I said with a grin. "A *mostly yes day.*"

The kids perked up instantly, their eyes lighting up.

"Mostly yes day?" Mia asked, intrigued.

"Yeah," I explained. "You pick the activities, and we say yes to pretty much everything—within reason. No, we're not buying ponies, and no, you can't drive the car, Christian."

Both kids burst out laughing, their giggles bringing a warmth to the room that had felt absent for days. Anthony leaned back in his chair, his smile growing. "Alright, I'm in. What do you guys want to do?"

Mia and Christian huddled together, whispering like they were plotting the biggest event of their lives. When they finally turned back to us, their answer was unanimous: an indoor water park and ice cream after.

Anthony and I both looked at each other and back at the kids. "We can do that." we said at the same time.

" Fun day, all day tomorrow." I said with enthusiasm.

"Okay!" Both the kids yelled out bursting with excitement.

The next day, we packed up our swimsuits and headed to the water park. As soon as we walked inside, the kids' excitement was infectious. The air was filled with the sound of rushing water, the delighted squeals of children, and the occasional lifeguard whistle.

"Let's go to the slides first!" Mia shouted, already tugging Anthony's hand toward the biggest one in sight.

"Christian, do you want to go too?" I asked, but he was already running after his sister.

Anthony shot me a grin over his shoulder as he followed the kids, and for the first time in what felt like weeks, I saw a glimpse of his usual self. Watching them together was everything I needed. Anthony, completely in his element, laughing with Mia and Christian as they splashed each other in the wave pool. Mia's shrieks of joy as she zipped down the slide, followed by Christian's triumphant yell as he bravely tackled it right after her. I stayed back at times, soaking it all in. Their laughter echoed in the cavernous space, and for a moment, the world outside didn't exist.

"Mom, come on!" Christian called, waving me over to join them in the lazy river.

The word stopped me in my tracks. *Mom.*

I glanced at Anthony, half-expecting him to react, but he didn't seem fazed. In fact, his smile widened as he nudged me forward.

"Better get moving, Mom," he teased, his tone light and playful.

My heart swelled. Christian's words felt so natural, and the fact that Anthony wasn't bothered by it—if anything, he seemed content—made it all the more meaningful.

"No really, don't make me go alone with them," Anthony teased, his eyes sparkling with humor.

I waded in and let the gentle current carry us along, Christian paddling ahead while Mia tried to race us. Anthony floated beside me, and I could see the tension leaving his face little by little.

"You okay?" I asked softly.

He nodded, giving me a small smile. "This was a good idea."

I reached for his hand under the water, squeezing it gently. " We needed this."

After hours at the park, we were all ravenous, so we made good on our promise for ice cream. Christian insisted on the biggest sundae they had, while Mia opted for a double scoop of cotton candy and chocolate—an admittedly questionable combination. Anthony and I kept it simple, but watching the kids devour their treats, faces smeared with melted ice cream, was better than any dessert.

"This was the best mostly yes day ever!" Mia declared, licking her spoon.

"Yeah," Christian chimed in, his cheeks sticky with fudge. "Can we do it again next week?"

Anthony chuckled, shaking his head. "No way. You wore us out."

We all couldn't help but laugh, the sound filling the small ice cream shop and making the day feel even more complete.

That evening, as we settled back home, the kids were exhausted but happy, their energy finally spent. They fell asleep almost instantly, their soft breathing a comforting backdrop as their laughter echoed in my mind. Anthony and I stayed up a little longer, sitting on the couch in the quiet of the living room. The weight of the day, the week, the month—it all seemed lighter somehow, at least for now.

"Thank you," he said suddenly, his voice soft and sincere.

"For what?" I asked, turning to look at him.

"For this," he said, gesturing around us. "For reminding me that even when things are hard, we've got this. We've got them. And no matter what, we're still us."

"Always," I replied with a smile.

I grinned mischievously, climbing onto his lap and pinning him down. "Now, give me kisses!" I demanded playfully, leaning down to attack his face with kisses. He laughed, grabbing my face gently and pulling me in for a long, lingering kiss that sent warmth coursing through me.

"I love you," he said softly, his voice full of meaning.

"I love you too," I replied, resting my forehead against his.

"Mother fu —" I started jokingly, as he cut me off with another kiss. I resumed peppering his face with playful kisses. He laughed, trying to fend me off but making no real effort to stop me.

"Okay, okay, you win!" he said between laughs, his hands gently holding my arms.

"I *always* win," I declared triumphantly, a wide smile spreading across my face.

Both of us tired from the day's events, he shifted slightly, propping his arm open for me. I nestled into his chest, the rhythmic rise and fall of his breathing instantly soothing me.

As the quiet of the house wrapped around us, we drifted off to sleep, the weight of the world feeling just a little bit lighter.

| 17 |

The Final Rose

The chaos in our lives hadn't subsided, but somehow, amid all the noise and stress, Anthony and I found ourselves growing closer. Maybe it was the way he had stood by me through everything, or the way we both made an effort to protect each other's peace despite the chaos. Whatever it was, something about this bond felt unshakable. I hadn't expected this, not in the way it had unfolded. For years, I had been chasing a feeling, searching for that elusive fairy tale love I'd grown up believing in. I wanted the butterflies, the sweeping romantic gestures, the magic. But as I got older, I'd convinced myself it was all a lie. After all, real life wasn't a Disney movie. There were no talking animals, no fairy godmothers waving wands, no instant happily-ever-afters.

But now, sitting across from Anthony as we talked about our future, I realized I'd been wrong—at least, partially.

The fairy tales weren't entirely about the glitz and magic; they were about the core of love, about finding someone worth slaying a dragon for. The talking animals and enchanted castles were just the packaging. The real message was that love could come unexpectedly, that it could change everything, and that when it did, it was worth holding onto. Anthony had been in my life for years, a steady presence in the background while we each navigated our own journeys. It was almost ironic that neither of us had seen what was right in front of us until the timing was right. Maybe it was fate—or maybe it was simply that we had to grow into the people we needed to be before we could fully see each other. One evening, after the kids were tucked away in their rooms and the house had finally settled into a peaceful quiet, Anthony and I sat on the back porch. The cool night air wrapped around us, the faint sound of crickets filling the space between our breaths. His arm rested comfortably over my shoulders, pulling me close as we both stared at the stars.

Out of nowhere, he broke the silence. "You ever think about what life will look like in a few years?" he asked, his tone casual but thoughtful.

I blinked, caught off guard. Anthony wasn't a big talker—he was more of an *acts of service* kind of guy. The kind of man who showed his love through fixing things around the house, making sure I ate when I was stressed, or installing security cameras to keep me safe. Him initiating a deep conversation about the future? That was a *big deal*.

"Sometimes," I replied, leaning into his warmth. "It used to scare me to think about the future. Now, it feels...different. Calmer."

"Calmer?" he repeated, tilting his head slightly to look at me, his eyebrow raising in curiosity.

I smiled softly. "Because I see you in it."

The corner of his mouth twitched, and without missing a beat, he said, "Well, don't get too comfortable."

I turned to look at him with a quickness, my jaw dropping slightly. "What did you just say?"

He burst out laughing, clearly pleased with himself, but I wasn't letting him get away with it. I smacked him lightly on the arm. "Shut up, Anthony! You're ruining my moment!"

Still grinning, he pulled me closer, pressing a kiss to the top of my head. "Alright, alright," he said, trying to stifle his laughter. "You're lucky I like you."

"Lucky you like me?" I scoffed, sitting up to glare at him playfully. "Excuse me? You're the lucky one here."

"Oh, is that right?" he teased, his grin widening as he leaned back, clearly enjoying my response.

"Absolutely," I shot back, crossing my arms mock-defiantly. "Do you know how many women would kill to be in my position right now? To be in the arms of one man while having another one sending her flowers?"

He raised an eyebrow, his grin turning skeptical.

"There are men practically flocking at me for a chance that you have been so graciously given," I added, my tone dripping with playful dramatics.

Anthony snorted, shaking his head. "Flocking, huh?"

"Oh, yes," I said, leaning closer. "It's like the *Bachelorette* out here, and you, sir, got the final rose. You should feel honored. *This* sir, is a once in a lifetime opportunity."

He laughed, the kind of deep, genuine laugh that made my chest warm. "Well, if that's the case, maybe I should be worried," he said, feigning seriousness. "Sounds like I've got some stiff competition."

I rolled my eyes, settling back against him. "Don't worry," I said with a smirk. "You're holding your own... for now."

He chuckled, pulling me closer. "Good to know."

"Yeah, no problem," I quipped, grinning as I leaned into him again.

Moments like this, filled with laughter and teasing, reminded me why this relationship worked. We talked that night about everything—our hopes, our fears, and the things we wanted to build together. It wasn't the kind of grand, sweeping conversation you'd see in a movie. It was quiet, steady, and real.

"What about the kids?" I asked, glancing up at him.

"They adore you," he said without hesitation. "And Christian calling you 'Mom'? I think that says it all."

I couldn't help but smile at the memory. "That meant more to me than I can even explain," I admitted.

"I know," he said softly. "It felt...nice.."

We sat in silence for a moment, letting his words settle between us. Anthony had given me a kind of security I didn't know I needed. It wasn't just the cameras he installed or the way he defended me against James and Christina. It was the way he made me feel seen, heard, and valued. It was the fact that I loved who I was with him in it. I didn't have to dim my light in fear that it would overshadow his. I didn't have to give up my hopes, values and morals in order to fit into his life. For the first time in my life, I didn't feel like I had to fight to earn someone's love. I had spent so much of my life chasing a fairy tale, and now I understood that the magic wasn't in the grand gestures or the dramatic moments. It was in the quiet support, the shared laughter, and the presence of someone who truly cared.

"We're not perfect," I said, brushing a stray hair from my face as I looked up at him. "But I think that's what makes us work. We don't expect perfection. We just... show up for each other."

Anthony raised an eyebrow, a smirk tugging at the corner of his lips. "You're right—we're not perfect. Let me emphasize that again. *Not perfect,*" he teased, earning an eye roll from me.

"Don't start," I said, poking him lightly in the chest.

He chuckled, pulling me closer. "But you're right," he admitted, his voice softening. "We do show up for each other. We do... well, *everything* for each other."

I couldn't help but laugh. "Everything, huh?"

"Everything," he said with mock seriousness, then grinned. "I mean, I even brought flowers into the house from another man. That's dedication."

"Okay, fine," I said, laughing. "You win this one."

He leaned in, brushing his lips against my forehead. "But seriously, you're right. I wouldn't trade it for anything."

I smiled, resting my head on his chest. "Me neither," I said quietly, feeling the steady rhythm of his heartbeat beneath me.

Anthony's question about the future lingered in my mind, though. For a man who wasn't prone to romantic monologues, him bringing it up meant something. It was his way of saying, *I'm in this with you,* without actually saying the words.

And honestly, that meant more to me than any flowery speech could.

"Alright, since you asked," I said, breaking the silence. "What do *you* think the future looks like?"

He exhaled deeply, the sound almost contemplative. "I think...it looks like less chaos," he said with a small laugh. "More days like today. The kids happy. You happy."

I looked up at him, my expression softening. "What about you?"

"What about me?" he asked, feigning innocence.

"What would make *you* happy?"

He smirked, his fingers brushing gently against my arm. "This. You. Us. *Everything,*" he joked. His response was simple yet spoke a thousand words. It was quintessentially Anthony—straightforward, honest, and heartfelt. And it was all I needed to hear. The laughter and teasing eventually faded, giving way to a quiet, comforting sense of peace. Anthony shifted slightly, pulling me even closer, and I let myself melt into his warmth.

"Hey," he said softly, breaking the silence.

"Yeah?"

"We're gonna be okay."

I closed my eyes, letting the weight of his words settle over me like a blanket. "I know."

Simple, honest, and heartfelt —and exactly what I needed.

| 18 |

Poinsettias and Paranoia

The restraining order was supposed to be a barrier, a line James couldn't cross. But like every other boundary in the past, he found ways to twist and manipulate it, testing its limits in ways that felt both calculated and maddeningly subtle. At first, it was small things—things I couldn't immediately tie to him but left me uneasy nonetheless. Anonymous emails would pop up in my inbox, filled with vague phrases that could've been innocuous to anyone else but felt unnervingly familiar to me. Messages like, *"Beautiful day for a walk in the park, don't you think?"* when I had just come back from a stroll with Anthony.

Then there was the car. A white sedan had begun appearing at odd times, always parked just far enough away from my house to seem coincidental but close enough to unsettle me. I started noticing it on my drive to work, in the grocery store parking lot, and even on the route I took to pick up Mia and Christian from school. Every time, I told myself it wasn't him—that it couldn't be. The restraining order was in place. He wouldn't dare risk violating it. Would he?

Shit. Who am I kidding? I thought bitterly. I was no longer in the head space to give James the benefit of the doubt. If anything, I was now fully convinced he was capable of anything. And then my mind would spiral into other questions—the kind I wished I didn't care to ask but couldn't stop from surfacing. *How does his wife feel about any of this?* Maybe she didn't know at first, but now there was an entire restraining order. She *had* to know by now. Does she just turn a blind eye, or worse, does she support him?

Does he not care at all?

I clenched my jaw, frustration bubbling under my skin. Why do I even bother asking myself these questions? I already know the answers, and none of them make me feel any better. He doesn't care. He never has. That much has been made abundantly clear. *The rose-colored Prince strikes again,* I thought, my stomach twisting. Breaking another woman's heart, no doubt. Either she's great and hopeful, desperately clinging to the man she *wants* him to be, or... she's just as crazy as he is.

And honestly, the second possibility was even scarier.

The more I thought about it, the more my anxiety spiked. James wasn't just unpredictable—he was relentless. Whether his wife knew, didn't know, or simply didn't care didn't change the fact that I felt trapped in a situation where the rules didn't apply to him. The boundary of a restraining order was meaningless to someone who didn't believe rules were meant for them. One evening, Anthony and I sat in the living room, reviewing footage from the security cameras he'd installed around the house.

"There it is again," I said, pointing to the screen. The white sedan had appeared on the footage, slowly driving past the house at least three times that day.

Anthony's jaw tightened. "It has to be him," he said, his voice low and controlled.

I rubbed my temples, the stress pressing against my skull like a vice. "I don't understand why he's doing this. The restraining order was supposed to stop this."

"It's because he knows exactly how far he can push without getting caught," Anthony said, leaning back on the couch. "But he's not as smart as he thinks he is. We're going to figure this out."

His confidence was reassuring, but the constant vigilance was wearing me down. Every small noise, every unfamiliar car, every moment of silence felt like it could be something. I was constantly on edge, my peace chipped away bit by bit. A few days later, James crossed another line.

It was a Saturday morning, and Anthony had taken the kids out for breakfast to give me some quiet time to journal before they came to spend the day at my house. He knew writing was how I found clarity, how I sorted through the chaos in my mind. I sat at the kitchen table, a steaming cup of tea beside me and my notebook open to a blank page. Taking a deep breath, I let the pen glide across the paper, pouring out my thoughts in a familiar, comforting rhythm.

Dear Universe,

It's me again. You're not going to believe this shit. This man just can't seem to get the hint. I'm really starting to think this is my life now. Is this some kind of karmic payback I wasn't aware of? Because if it is, I think I've suffered enough.

Also... I haven't really been able to focus on work. I don't know if it's because of everything that's going on, or if I just don't have the same passion for the OR that I used to. The spark I felt for it seems... dimmed.

But what would be the next step? I can't just up and leave—

I paused, tapping the pen against the paper. The truth was, I didn't know what I wanted anymore. The constant stress was making it hard to focus on anything, let alone what my next move should be. My thoughts were interrupted by the sound of my phone vibrating on the table.

I glanced at the screen, expecting to see a text from Anthony or one of my friends. Instead, it was from an unknown number. My heart sank as I opened the message.

"Poinsettias. They really brighten up the place."

My stomach twisted, and my breath caught in my throat. At first, I thought the unknown number was a text from a telemarketer or scammer "trying to reach me about my extended warranty". But then the reality sank in, chilling me to the core. I didn't have to look outside to know what the message meant. The day before, I had hung two synthetic poinsettia arrangements on the porch, a simple decoration to add some holiday cheer.

That son of a bitch had been here. Watching.

I stood slowly, my legs feeling unsteady as I moved toward the front window. Peering outside, I saw nothing unusual—no lingering cars, no sign of movement. Just the two poinsettias swaying gently in the breeze. My hands shook as I clutched the phone, the weight of the text sinking in. He wasn't just sending cryptic messages anymore. He was confirming, in his own twisted way, that the restraining order meant nothing to him.

Anthony's words from earlier in the week echoed in my mind: *He's escalating, Patricia. This isn't going to stop unless we make it stop.* He was right. The message wasn't just unsettling; it was a calculated move to remind me that James could still reach me whenever he wanted. That he was always watching, always one step ahead. I dropped back into the chair with no motivation to continue writing, trying to steady my breathing. The poinsettias, which had seemed like a harmless, cheerful decoration the day before, now felt like a cruel joke. This wasn't just paranoia anymore. It was real. And I wasn't sure how much longer I could endure it. By the time Anthony and the kids got home, I was pacing the living room, my nerves frayed.

"What happened?" Anthony asked the moment he walked in, his expression instantly shifting to concern. I handed him my phone, unable to speak. He read the text, his face darkening as he looked out the window toward the porch.

"That's it," Anthony said firmly, his tone leaving no room for argument. "We're not waiting for this to get worse. I'm calling the lawyer and the police. He's escalating, Patricia."

I watched as he grabbed his phone and dialed the lawyer, pacing the living room with tension radiating off him.

"Unfortunately, Mr. Garcia," the lawyer's voice came through on speaker, calm but disheartening, "we cannot prove that the text was from him, so it would not hold in court. Were you able to get the plates of that white sedan?"

Anthony's jaw tightened, his frustration evident. "No," he admitted through clenched teeth. "It's never clear enough to see the plates on the cameras. They're too blurry."

There was a pause on the other end. "Then there's nothing we can do right now. Without concrete evidence tying this directly to him, any legal action is likely to get dismissed."

Anthony ended the call with a sharp press of his finger, his face a mix of anger and exasperation. "This is bullshit," he muttered, running a hand through his hair. He turned to me, his expression softening slightly but his determination unyielding. "Come on. You're coming to my house today. I'm over this shit."

Before I could protest, he called out, "Come on, kids, we're leaving!"

Mia and Christian poked their heads into the living room, confused but obedient. "Where are we going?" Mia asked.

"Home," Anthony said simply, his tone gentle with them but still tinged with the frustration he was trying to contain. As I stood to gather my things, Anthony placed a hand on my arm, his gaze locking with mine. "We're not letting him scare you out of living your life," he said firmly. "You're coming with me today, and we'll figure out a plan." I nodded, feeling both grateful and overwhelmed. That night, Anthony and I sat down to discuss what came next.

"We need to consider all options," he said, his tone gentle but resolute.

"Like what?" I asked, though I already sensed what he was going to say. Anthony looked at me without saying a word, his steady gaze telling me everything I needed to know.

"You're talking about moving," I said, though it wasn't a question.

"Yes," he admitted, exhaling deeply.

I leaned back in my chair, crossing my arms. "You just said earlier today that we're not going to let him run me out of my own life. Plus, the housing market is insane right now. I'd never be able to find another house with the same rates."

Anthony rubbed the back of his neck, his frustration evident. "I know it's a big step, but I don't see another way to put some real distance between us and him. He's clearly not stopping, and I don't want to wait until he does something worse."

I opened my mouth to argue, but before I could, he added, "This is about safety, Patricia. Yours, mine, the kids'. I don't care what the market is doing—we'll figure it out."

"Wait." I paused, narrowing my eyes at him. "Are you saying we should get a house *together*?"

The thought hadn't even occurred to me until that moment. Sure, he and the kids were already staying at my house most weekends, but this? Moving in together, especially with everything going on, felt monumental.

Anthony met my gaze, his expression unreadable. "If it makes sense," he said simply.

My mind reeled. As much as I loved the idea of us living together—building a life together—it didn't feel like the right time. There was too much happening, too much uncertainty. I let out a sigh, the thought of leaving the home I'd built weighing heavily on me. "It's just... a lot," I said, my voice barely above a whisper. Anthony reached across the table, his warm hand enveloping mine. "I know. We'll do it together," he said softly. "Wherever we go, we'll make it ours. It's just a house, Patricia."

But it wasn't *just* a house. It was so much more.

"This isn't just a house for me," I said, my voice cracking slightly. "It's where I reset my life. I was living in my car at one point, remember? Everything you see in that house, I worked hard to get. Every upgrade you see inside of that home, I did on my own. It might just be a house to you, but this house *saved* me." I had to admit that I was clearly on the defense.

Anthony's grip on my hand tightened. "I know what it means to you. I'm not trying to take that away. I'm just trying to protect you. You don't feel safe there." I nodded slowly, tears threatening to spill. "Maybe. Let's just wait a bit before we make any rash decisions."

Anthony's jaw clenched, and I could see the worry etched into his face. "I'm worried about *him* making irrational moves."

"Yeah, well, he sent that picture of me at *your* house," I shot back. "It doesn't really matter where we go. If he wants to find me, he will."

His expression darkened, and he leaned back in his chair, crossing his arms. "You're not wrong," he admitted. "But that's not a reason to do nothing."

"We're not doing nothing," I said firmly. "We're taking precautions, keeping records, and making sure the kids are safe. Moving doesn't guarantee he'll stop."

Anthony sighed, running a hand through his hair. "Alright," he said finally. "We'll wait. But if he escalates again, I don't want to wait anymore."

I nodded, knowing he was right but still feeling the weight of everything pressing down on me. As much as I hated to admit it, the idea of leaving my home—my sanctuary—was becoming more real with every passing day.

| 19 |

Permission to Pause

"10 Blade... 10 Blade... Patricia!"

The surgeon's sharp tone snapped me back to reality. My hands instinctively reached for the blade on the tray, passing it to him without hesitation.

"Sorry," I mumbled, heat creeping up my neck. "Didn't get much sleep last night."

The surgeon glanced at me, his expression softening slightly. "It's okay," he said. "Let us know if you need someone else to step in for you. This one's going to be a long one."

I nodded, silently grateful for his understanding, but I couldn't shake the knot of embarrassment in my chest. Losing focus in the operating room wasn't just a small mistake—it could be dangerous. Normally, I was sharp, anticipating the surgeon's every move, but today, my mind was elsewhere.

Get it together, Patricia, I scolded myself.

With the holidays approaching, the hospital was a flurry of activity. Everyone wanted their surgeries scheduled before Christmas so they could recover in time to enjoy the festivities, which meant our workload had doubled. Surgeons were scrambling to fit in as many procedures as possible, and the rest of us were struggling to keep up. The hospital administration, desperate to retain staff during the chaos, was offering bonuses for anyone willing to stay beyond their shifts or come in early. The old me would've jumped at the opportunity, signing up for every bonus shift without a second thought.

But now?

Now, my priorities had shifted.

Work used to be my everything—a way to prove myself, a way to distract myself, a way to keep moving forward. But life outside the hospital had become more demanding than I ever could have anticipated. And while work served as a temporary distraction from the chaos with James, adding more hours was something I mentally couldn't handle. Still, I relied on muscle memory to get me through the days. I knew the surgeries like the back of my hand, anticipating the surgeons' next moves even when hiccups occurred. Years of experience carried me when my mind couldn't. By the time the surgery was over, my body felt like it had run a marathon. I scrubbed out and headed to the locker room, where I sank onto the bench and rested my head in my hands.

Why does everything feel so heavy lately?

I used to thrive under pressure. The fast-paced environment of the operating room, the adrenaline rush of a complicated procedure, the satisfaction of a job well done—it all used to fuel me. But now, it felt like I was running on fumes, just trying to make it through the day without completely falling apart. The new neurology role was supposed to be exciting, a fresh challenge in my career. And in some ways, it was. I loved the intricacy of the procedures, the blend of precision and problem-solving required. But the mounting pressures, both at work and at home, were starting to feel insurmountable.

"Hey Patricia!" one of the nurses who had been assigned to the last case called as she entered the locker room, pulling me out of my thoughts. "You okay? You seemed a little off in there today."

I forced a small smile. "Just tired. It's been a long week."

She nodded sympathetically. "I hear you. These holiday schedules are brutal."

I wanted to tell her it wasn't just the schedule—that the exhaustion went far beyond the hospital walls. But instead, I nodded and kept the rest to myself. Later that evening, as I sat in my car in the hospital parking lot, I thought about the conversation Anthony and I had about moving. About starting fresh somewhere else. The idea was tempting, especially after a day like this. But deep down, I knew running away wouldn't solve anything. James wasn't just a physical presence—he had burrowed into my mind, into my peace, making it impossible to fully focus on anything. I took a deep breath, gripping the steering wheel tightly. I couldn't keep living like this—mentally checked out, constantly looking over my shoulder, and letting my fears overshadow the life I was trying to build. Something had to give. But I didn't know what, or how, or when. All I knew was that I couldn't do it alone. When I got to Anthony's house, Anthony was sitting on the couch, scrolling through his phone while the kids played quietly in the next room.

"How was work?" he asked, looking up as I walked in.

"Busy," I replied, sinking onto the couch beside him.

"You okay?"

I hesitated, then shook my head. "Not really."

Anthony immediately put his phone down, his full attention on me. "Talk to me."

I sighed and leaned into his shoulder, feeling the weight of the day settle even heavier now that I'd admitted it out loud. "I'm just... overwhelmed. Work, home, everything. I feel like I'm barely holding it together."

"Come here," he said gently, patting the couch next to him.

I slid closer, and he wrapped his arm around me. "It's okay. It's a lot. You're doing the best you can."

I sat in silence for a moment, letting his words soothe me. "I think..." I started, then paused, unsure if I wanted to say it out loud.

"What?" he prompted.

"I think I want to take a leave of absence."

Anthony didn't even flinch. "I think that's a good idea," he said without hesitation. "You've been carrying so much, and you deserve to take care of yourself." He didn't feel the need to follow up with further questions. Honestly, it was a relief to hear his blind support.

The next day, I made an appointment with a therapist to get the necessary documentation for the leave. To my surprise, they had an opening for the same day. Walking into the office building, I was immediately struck by how modern it was. The exterior was sleek, with glass panels and clean lines, and inside, the lobby was bright and open, with teal accents and white furnishings that made the space feel calming yet professional. The receptionist greeted me with a warm smile and directed me to the second floor. When I entered the therapist's office, I noticed how the theme continued—a minimalist setup with soft teal and white tones, accented by potted plants and abstract art. The space felt inviting, which helped settle some of my nerves.

Dr. Monroe, the therapist, was already seated when I arrived. She stood to greet me with a friendly handshake, and I took in her appearance: a woman in her late 30s or early 40s, dressed in a tailored cream blouse and navy slacks. Her auburn hair was pulled into a neat ponytail, and her glasses gave her an air of warmth and intelligence.

"Hi, Patricia," she said, gesturing for me to sit on the plush chair across from her. "It's nice to meet you."

"You too," I replied, settling in.

After some initial small talk to get me comfortable, she asked, "What brings you here today?"

I took a deep breath. "Well, it started with needing a leave of absence for work," I began. "But honestly, there's a lot more to it."

She nodded, her expression patient and encouraging. "Take your time."

I told her about the stress I'd been under, the challenges at work, and, of course, James.

"You know," I said with a hint of sarcasm, "I once pressured my ex—you know, the one stalking me—to see a therapist."

Dr. Monroe raised an eyebrow. "Do you feel that it helped him?" she asked, a slight smile tugging at her lips.

"Well, he's stalking me now, so.." I said dryly.

She chuckled softly but quickly returned to seriousness. "Do you feel that it helped him during the time you were with him?"

I nodded, surprising myself with how easily I could admit it. "Yes, I do. I don't regret doing it. At the time, it felt like the right thing to do. He needed help."

Dr. Monroe leaned forward slightly, her tone gentle but firm. "It's important to remember that mental health comes in ebbs and flows. It's a lifelong condition that requires ongoing care. It doesn't go away with a few good months or even years."

"I know," I said, my voice quieter now. "But I guess I was just hoping that after all this time, it wouldn't still be directed at me."

She nodded, letting my words linger for a moment before responding. "It's understandable to feel that way. But now, it's about refocusing on *your* mental health and what *you* need to feel safe and secure."

She was right. Amazing. Once again, I was letting this man's actions dictate my life, handing over control to someone who didn't deserve it. By the end of the session, Dr. Monroe had written me a prescription for the leave of absence. As I folded the paper into my bag, I felt a small wave of relief wash over me. Although it wasn't my initial intention, I had to admit that it was nice being able to talk openly without worrying about how it might burden someone else. I realized then why I'd been so hesitant to share everything with Anthony—I didn't want to add to the weight he was already carrying. He had been my rock, but even rocks had limits. As I left the office, I felt lighter, like I could breathe just a little easier.

| 20 |

Under the Mistletoe

The crisp morning air hit my face as I stepped outside, my bag slung over my shoulder, ready to head to my car for what would be my last day of work before starting my medical leave. But as soon as I stepped off the porch, my stomach dropped.

There it was—my mailbox, vandalized.

Bright red spray paint covered the once-pristine black surface, smeared with crude, angry streaks. My chest tightened, and a single thought shot through my mind: *James.* I scanned up and down the street, searching for any signs of similar damage. But no, the other mailboxes were untouched. Pristine. It was only mine.

It had to be him.

I rushed back inside, my heart pounding as I immediately pulled up the footage from the security cameras. Finally, I was going to get the proof I needed. This was it—the moment James's obsessive behavior would be caught on camera. I fast-forwarded through the footage, my eyes glued to the screen. And then, there they were.

Not James.

A group of teenagers.

At 2:04 am., the camera caught them running down the block, darting toward my mailbox. They sprayed it quickly, laughing and shoving each other before disappearing into the night as fast as they had come. I stared at the screen, my stomach sinking. My proof, my big moment, was a dead end. It wasn't James. Not directly, anyway. But I knew better. These kids didn't pick my mailbox by coincidence. He had sent them. This was exactly the kind of thing James would do—calculated, subtle, and just out of reach of consequences. He didn't need to lift a finger when he could manipulate others to do his bidding. I replayed the footage over and over again looking for some kind of clue that could link to him. My disappointment grew with each loop. The police wouldn't take this seriously. They'd chalk it up to random mischief, nothing more. But it wasn't random.

It was him.

I sighed heavily, glancing at the clock. I was running late for work, but the frustration lingered, twisting in my gut. How much longer could this go on? When I got to work, the nurse manager approached me with a curious look on her face.

"Your uncle called," she said.

"My uncle?" I asked, confused.

"Yeah," she replied. "I told him you weren't in yet, so he left a message. He said he heard about the vandalism on your street and wanted to make sure you were okay. He also mentioned he tried calling you, but it went straight to voicemail."

My stomach twisted. *That son of a bitch.* Keeping my face neutral, I forced a calm response. "Oh, yes, that's actually why I was late. Some kids vandalized my mailbox."

The nurse manager nodded sympathetically. "I'm sorry to hear that. Let me know if you need anything."

"Thank you," I replied, my voice steady despite the anger simmering beneath the surface.

Inside, I was fuming. James had reached a new level of manipulation, disguising himself as a concerned "uncle" to worm his way into my work life. He was not only invading my personal space but he was creeping into my professional life, too. I clenched my fists, willing myself to stay composed. There was no way I was letting him derail me here, not today. Luckily, this was my last day here, so there wasn't too much damage he could do even if he tried. That thought offered a small shred of relief, but it didn't entirely calm the simmering rage and unease bubbling inside me. James was pushing boundaries, again, and it was getting harder to stay one step ahead.

I had just gotten to work, and I already couldn't wait for the day to be over. The schedule was packed with laminectomies, a procedure where the surgeon removes part of the vertebra, called the lamina, to relieve pressure on the spinal cord or nerves. While fascinating in theory, the repetitive nature of these surgeries and the level of precision required made for an exhausting day. By the time the clock struck 7 pm., I was practically hovering near the time clock, badge in hand, ready to swipe out. *So long,* I thought to myself as I left the OR behind, eager to trade the sterile air of the hospital for the warmth of Anthony's company.

Once I was in my car, I called Anthony.

"Hey," I said when he picked up.

"Hello Miss Unemployed!. Done with your last day of work?"

"Yes finally" I said while slightly laughing at his comment.

" I'm on my way over, but there's something I need to talk to you about when I get there."

The slight pause on his end didn't go unnoticed. "Something I'm not going to like, huh?"

I sighed. "Probably not."

"Can't wait," he said, a touch of sarcasm in his voice, though I could hear the underlying concern.

"See you soon," I replied before hanging up, my thoughts already spinning over how the conversation would go. When I arrived, we sat down at the dining table. I wasted no time diving into the latest absurdity.

"Can you believe he had the nerve to call my job and pretend to be my uncle? TO CONFIRM HE DID IT?!"

Anthony, ever the steady one, simply said, "Yes."

Disappointed by his level of calm, I threw my hands up. "Come on! Get hype with me here!"

Without missing a beat, Anthony straightened in his chair, throwing his arms in the air dramatically. "HE DID WHAT? THAT SON OF A BITCH!" he shouted, feigning outrage.

"I know, right?! That's exactly what I said!" I replied, unable to keep a straight face.

We both burst into laughter, the absurdity of the situation momentarily lifting the weight of it off my shoulders. It felt good to laugh, even if only for a moment.

"Okay Listen," I said, breaking the laughter, my tone resolute. "For now, I need you and the kids to stay at your house. We'll meet in public places."

Anthony immediately shook his head, his jaw tightening. "What? No, Patricia."

"Yes, Anthony," I said firmly, though my heart ached at the thought.

"You're right. I don't like this. You're giving him what he wants," he argued, his voice rising slightly.

"I don't care," I shot back, my own frustration bubbling to the surface. "This is about keeping everyone safe. That's all I care about."

He leaned back in his chair, rubbing a hand over his face. "So what's the plan, then? Just avoid the house forever? Let him keep scaring us into a corner?"

I exhaled, trying to keep my emotions in check. "Friday is Christmas," I said, softening my tone. "I'll be at your house in the morning, and we'll spend it together, like we planned. But after that, I don't want the kids around my house right now. I can't handle another text from Christina, another close call. This is what has to be done for all of us."

Anthony stared at me for a long moment, his expression a mix of frustration and understanding. As much as he didn't want to admit it, he knew I was right.

"Okay," he said reluctantly, his voice quieter now. "But we're going to at least start looking at houses."

I nodded, relieved he was willing to compromise. "Okay," I said softly.

Friday morning, I arrived at Anthony's house bright and early, eager to soak in the holiday spirit. The warmth of the home enveloped me the moment I stepped through the door, carrying the comforting scent of hot chocolate and freshly buttered bread. Anthony's mom was in the kitchen, stirring a pot of hot chocolate on the stove with care, just as my mother used to. It was rich and creamy, with the unmistakable aroma of cinnamon wafting through the air. On the counter sat slices of bread, the "good bread" as we used to call it in my house, each piece perfectly coated with a generous layer of butter. The scene immediately took me back to my childhood. Sunday mornings with my family came rushing back—my mom humming softly as she stirred the hot chocolate, my dad returning from the bakery with fresh bread still warm from the oven. We'd sit around the table, dipping the buttery bread into the steaming cups of chocolate, sharing laughs and stories.

"Patricia!" Anthony's mom called out, her smile lighting up her face as she wiped her hands on a towel. "Merry Christmas! Come on in."

"Merry Christmas!" I replied, shrugging off my coat and setting it on the back of a chair.

The kids came bounding into the room, their excitement palpable. Mia twirled in her reindeer-patterned pajamas, while Christian showed off his elf outfit, complete with a tiny green hat.

"Look, Patricia!" Mia exclaimed, grinning from ear to ear.

"You two look amazing," I said, kneeling to hug them both. "I think Santa definitely stopped here last night."

"Yeah, and he brought me *everything* I wanted!" Christian chimed in, his face lighting up.

We all gathered around the table, mugs of steaming hot chocolate in front of us. Anthony's mom handed out plates of buttered bread, and the kids wasted no time dunking their slices into the hot chocolate, giggling at the mess they made.

"This," I said, holding up my mug, "is a delicacy in my house. We used to have this on Sundays, just like this. My mom would make the hot chocolate, and my dad would get the freshest bread from the bakery."

"It's a tradition for us, too," Anthony said, his smile warm. "Mom swears it's the best way to start Christmas morning."

"She's absolutely right," I said, taking a bite and savoring the taste. It was simple, yet it brought so much comfort and joy.

The kids chattered away about their presents, their laughter filling the room. Anthony's mom watched them with a contented smile, clearly enjoying the happiness her family brought her.

Across the table, Anthony caught my eye. The look he gave me was full of gratitude and love, and for a moment, it felt like the world outside didn't exist. As the kids tore through their presents later, the house was filled with the sounds of excitement and joy. Anthony sat on the floor, helping Christian assemble a toy while Mia showed me how her new art supplies worked.

"Look, Patricia, I made this for you!" Mia said, holding up a painting of a house with a big, colorful tree in front.

"It's beautiful," I said, touched. "Is this your house?"

"No," she said with a giggle. "It's *our* house. All of us together."

I glanced at Anthony, who was watching with a soft smile. The moment felt so full, so complete, it almost brought tears to my eyes. Later, as the kids played with their toys, Anthony and I sat quietly on the couch, his arm draped around my shoulders.

"This," he said softly, gesturing to the lively scene in front of us, "this is what it's all about."

"It really is," I replied, leaning into him.

"Are you ready for your gift?" Anthony asked, his eyes sparkling with excitement.

"Yes, I have yours too," I said, unable to hide my grin.

I had put together a box filled with his favorite things—a gift card for gambling, something he loved to do in his rare free time, and something much more personal. Inside was a Christmas card with a scannable code that linked to a video I'd made. The video was a heartfelt thank-you for all he'd done, not just this year, but over the years we'd known each other. It included photos and video clips from the memories we'd shared over the last decade.

"You have to open mine first," I said, my voice filled with anticipation.

"It better not be anything crazy. I know how extra you are," he teased.

"It's not, just open it."

He carefully opened the box, pulling out each item one by one. "Okay, this isn't too much! Good job!" he said, clearly surprised.

I stayed silent, knowing the video would change that.

"Aw, you even put a card in here!" he said, smiling at me.

"There's a code inside. You have to scan it."

"A code? Here you go being extra," he joked, rolling his eyes.

"Just do it," I urged, barely able to contain my excitement.

He scanned the code on his phone, and the video started playing. His face softened as the images and clips began to unfold.

"What is this?! Nooo, this is too much! I hate you!" he said, his voice cracking as his eyes filled with tears.

I laughed. "You're very conflicting right now. I don't know if you're happy, mad or sad." I joked.

"Shut up. Come here," he said, pulling me into a hug. "Thank you, you asshole," he added, wiping his face. "This makes my gift look like shit."

"That's not true! I'll love it no matter what," I said enthusiastically.

"Close your eyes," he said suddenly, his tone shifting.

I looked at him suspiciously. "Why?"

"Just do it," he said with a smirk.

Reluctantly, I closed my eyes. I felt him take my hand, kiss it softly, then slap it playfully.

I burst into laughter. "What was that for?"

"Shh! Keep them closed," he said, trying not to laugh at himself.

"Okay, okay," I said, shaking my head.

I heard the kids giggling in the next room, which only made me more curious. Then I felt him take my hand again, kiss it tenderly, and slip something cold and metal onto my finger.

"Open your eyes," he said.

I opened them and froze, my eyes immediately falling on the ring now sitting on my finger. It was stunning—a pear-shaped diamond with a delicate accent stone on each side, set on a sleek white gold band.

I looked at Anthony, who was now down on one knee, grinning up at me.

"Surprise! Will you marry me?"

My jaw dropped. I looked back at the ring and then at Anthony, my heart racing.

"Okay, hurry up already! My knee hurts!" he joked, pretending to wince.

"Let me have my moment!" I shot back, still in shock.

Anthony rolled his eyes dramatically.

His mom, who had been quietly watching from the kitchen, burst into laughter. "You two are ridiculous!" she said, shaking her head with amusement.

"Okay, yeah, I guess I'll marry you," I said teasingly, a wide smile spreading across my face.

"Finally!" he exclaimed, standing up and pulling me into a deep, heartfelt kiss.

Mrs. Patricia Garcia. That was going to be my name.

"Your gift was way better, by the way," I said, looking at him with a playful smirk.

"I know," he replied, leaning in for another kiss, his grin as big as mine.

| 21 |

The Master Plan

For the moment, everything else faded away—James, the stress, the constant state of vigilance. None of it mattered as I sat on the couch, absentmindedly twirling the ring on my finger. I was *engaged.* To Anthony.

Anthony Garcia.

The man who once told me he couldn't tell the difference between parsley and cilantro and blamed the vegetables for "looking too much alike." The same man who, just last week, accidentally put dish soap in the dishwasher and flooded his kitchen with suds. He was also the same man who's been there for me since day one. That Anthony. Every time I wanted to pinch myself to see if it was real, I saw the proof sparkling on my finger.

I couldn't help but laugh at the thought. "You sure you want me?" I'd asked him earlier, half-joking but with just a tinge of seriousness. "Maybe you lost your mind for a second. Blink twice if you need help."

His response? "Yes. Stop being ridiculous." He'd said it with so much certainty, like he hadn't just committed to a lifetime of *this*.

The thing is, deep down, I always wondered if I was someone people could commit to—truly, fully commit to. I mean, come on, I'm a walking contradiction half the time. I want things perfectly planned, but I thrive in chaos. I'll fight you for the last piece of bread but share my dessert without hesitation. Anthony knew all of that, and still, here we were. The realization hit me like a freight train: everything I'd been looking for really *was* right in front of me all along. Anthony had been my friend for years before he was anything else, and maybe that's why this worked. He didn't just love me; he *knew* me. He saw the good, the bad, and the *are-you-seriously-eating-ice-cream-for-breakfast-again* moments and still thought, *Yep, that's the one.*

I sat back, staring at the ring again, and let my mind wander. How long had he been planning this? Was it spur-of-the-moment? Did he buy the ring last week while picking up milk at the grocery store? Or was this something he'd been thinking about for months, quietly waiting for the perfect moment? I smiled, imagining him pacing the aisles of a jewelry store, overwhelmed by the options. *Does she like gold or silver? Wait, is white gold considered silver? What the hell is a pear cut?* The thought was so vivid, I almost wanted him to ask. Then again, it didn't really matter. The man could've tied a twist tie around my finger, and I probably still would've said yes. Not because of the gesture, but because of him. My curiosity got the best of me. I decided to ask anyway, the question practically bubbling out of me.

"So... how long were you planning this?" I asked, trying to sound casual, though the excitement in my voice betrayed me.

Anthony smirked, leaning back on the couch. "I've known for a while," he said, his tone nonchalant.

"Really?" I replied, my eyebrows shooting up. I was genuinely shocked, though I wasn't entirely sure why.

"Yeah," he said with a small laugh. "Why do you think I was asking all those questions about our future plans and a house? I was planting seeds."

"Oh, *that's* what that was about," I said, narrowing my eyes playfully.

"Yep. Honestly, I for sure thought you were going to say we needed to be married first, and I was ready to pounce on that. That was supposed to be my gateway."

I stared at him, blinking in disbelief before bursting into laughter. "So you were trying to trap me!"

"Trap you? Please," he said, feigning offense. "If anything, I was setting the scene for *you*. I thought you'd say something like, 'Well, we can't move in together until we're married,' and then, *bam*, I'd hit you with the ring. Perfect timing."

"Wow," I said, shaking my head in amusement. "So calculated. I almost feel bad for ruining your master plan by not saying it."

"Almost?" he teased, leaning toward me with a grin.

"Almost, because that was not the right timing" I confirmed, leaning back into the cushions and smirking.

He laughed, pulling me closer. "Well, you said yes anyway."

"Oh, don't get too comfortable," I joked, poking his chest. "You've still got a lifetime of convincing me this was a good idea."

He raised an eyebrow, his expression dripping with confidence. "Okay ,that's fine. I've been putting up with your ass for years already."

"How romantic," I said, narrowing my eyes at him.

"But seriously... you've known for a while?" I couldn't help but ask one more time.

Anthony's face softened, the teasing slipping away as he took my hand. "Yeah," he said quietly. "I've known for a while. I just wanted to make sure it was the right time for both of us."

I looked at him, my heart swelling in a way I hadn't expected. Leaning in, I kissed him gently on the cheek, catching the faintest hint of a smile as he squeezed me tighter.

"I just might have to show you later how grateful I am for you," I whispered, letting my lips linger near his ear.

"Grateful, huh?" he asked, his voice low and teasing as he turned to meet my gaze.

"Mhm," I replied, my eyes sparkling with mischief.

We held each other's gaze for a moment, flirtatious and playful, before turning our attention back to the kids. They were immersed in their new toys, their laughter mingling with the soft hum of a Christmas movie playing on the TV in the background. Later that evening, Anthony and I were curled up on the couch after the kids had gone to bed. The Christmas lights still twinkled softly in the corner, casting a warm glow over the room. I turned to him, an idea I'd been mulling over for days suddenly bubbling to the surface.

"What if I did some freelance writing work?" I asked, breaking the comfortable silence.

Anthony raised an eyebrow, his lips twitching with amusement. "You don't know how to stay still, do you?"

I laughed. "What do you mean?"

"You took off from one job to give yourself another job," he teased, his grin widening.

"Yeah, but this would be different," I insisted, sitting up straighter. "Writing is fun for me. It's calming. It doesn't feel like work."

He nodded, clearly still amused. "Well, do it then. If it's something you love, go for it."

"I'll rest," I promised, though we both knew I'd already started mentally drafting an article in my head.

Anthony shook his head, clearly catching on to my thoughts. "You're impossible, you know that?"

"Impossible but lovable," I shot back, grinning.

He laughed, pressing a kiss to the top of my head. "Yeah, yeah, you've got that going for you too."

"Enough talk about this, though. Want to see something else I love?" I said, my tone dropping to a playful whisper.

Anthony's eyebrows raised slightly, curiosity flashing across his face. "Oh yeah? What's that?"

"You," I replied softly, a teasing smile spreading across my lips as I straddled his lap. Leaning in, I pressed a lingering kiss to his neck, letting my lips trail just enough to make him shiver. His hands instinctively found my waist, his fingers tightening slightly as his breath hitched.

"Let's go to bed," I whispered, my lips grazing his ear, my voice dripping with intent.

He exhaled sharply, his smirk growing wider. Without hesitation, he stood up, lifting me effortlessly as I wrapped my legs around his waist. The bedroom door clicked shut behind us, the quiet hum of the Christmas lights in the hallway fading as Anthony placed me gently on the bed.

"You're trouble, you know that?" he teased, his voice low as he leaned over me.

"Yeah but I'm *your* trouble," I shot back, pulling him down for a kiss. His lips were warm and insistent, and I melted into him, my fingers tangling in his hair as his hands roamed down my sides. The weight of him pressed against me, his body fitting perfectly against mine. My hands slipped under his shirt, tracing the hard lines of his stomach. He pulled the shirt off in one smooth motion, and I let my hands explore the warmth of his skin, loving the way his muscles tensed under my touch. Anthony's lips found their way to my neck, trailing soft kisses down to my collarbone. I couldn't help but let out a soft moan.

"Shh," he hushed, though his grin told me he knew just how impossible that was about to be.

I bit my lip, trying to stifle another moan as his hands slid under my shirt, caressing my bare skin. He paused to pull it over my head, his eyes lingering on me for a moment before he leaned down, capturing my lips in another deep kiss. His hands slid lower, slipping beneath the waistband of my leggings, his fingers grazing the warmth between my thighs. A sharp gasp caught in my throat as his touch found just the right spot, sending a jolt of pleasure through me. With the wetness already pooling, he skillfully circled my clit, using it as natural lubrication to heighten the sensation.

My body arched instinctively, and my grip on his shoulders tightened as his fingers moved in perfect motions, teasing and coaxing me closer to the edge.

"You're not making this easy," I whispered, my voice shaky but teasing.

I couldn't hold back the soft whimper that escaped me, and Anthony silenced me with his mouth, swallowing the sound as his tongue teased mine. The room felt electric, the quiet punctuated by our muffled breaths and the rustle of sheets as he slid my leggings off, followed by his own pants. He positioned himself above me, his eyes locked on mine as he pushed inside me slowly, filling me completely. My fingers dug into his back, and I bit down on his shoulder to keep from crying out.

"Patricia," he whispered, his voice rough and laced with restraint. "You have to stay quiet."

I nodded, but my body betrayed me as he began to move, each thrust deliberate and deep. I pressed my face into his neck, muffling the soft cries I couldn't hold back as he picked up the pace. The bed creaked faintly, and we both froze, glancing toward the door like guilty teenagers. Anthony chuckled softly, his lips brushing against my ear. "I told you," he whispered. I

"Keep going," I hissed back, my nails dragging down his back.

He obliged, his movements slower but no less intense. The quiet tension only heightened the sensations, making every touch, every kiss, every thrust feel more exhilarating. I clung to him as the pressure built, my breath coming in shallow gasps against his shoulder. His hand slipped between us, finding my clit and sending a jolt of pleasure through me.

"Anthony," I whimpered, my voice barely above a whisper.

"Let it go," he murmured, his lips brushing against mine.

And I did. My body arched beneath him, waves of pleasure crashing over me as I buried my face in his neck to muffle my cries. Anthony followed moments later, his body tensing as he let out a quiet groan, his release sending aftershocks through both of us. We stayed like that for a moment, tangled together in the aftermath, the quiet of the room settling over us like a blanket.

"You definitely woke someone up," he whispered finally, his voice tinged with amusement as he kissed the top of my head.

"You're the one who couldn't stay quiet," I teased, grinning against his chest.

He laughed softly, pulling me closer. "Whatever you say"

"You see, you're already learning how to be a good husband." I joked, sending us both into laughter.

| 22 |

Dreams Without Boundaries

The holidays had come and gone, leaving behind a mixture of exhaustion and bittersweet relief. The house was quieter now, the wrapping paper cleaned up, and the kids were back to school. The chaos of Christmas had given way to the more familiar rhythm of life, but the weight of everything still lingered. The engagement ring on my finger sparkled faintly in the morning light, a reminder of the joy and love I had amidst the stress. But even that couldn't fully quiet the thoughts that churned in my head. James was still out there, his presence lingering like a shadow, and Anthony's frustrations with our current arrangement weren't exactly hidden. I sighed as I sipped my tea, the warmth of the mug grounding me for a moment. Monday was here, and with it, my first post-holiday therapy session. Dr. Monroe had become an anchor for me over the last few weeks, helping me unpack the tangled mess of emotions that had come with James's stalking, my career uncertainty, and navigating my deepening relationship with Anthony. The house was silent as I grabbed my coat and bag, preparing to leave. For the first time in days, I felt like I could breathe. The holiday buzz had been a welcome distraction, but now it was time to dive back into the work of figuring out my next steps. By the time I arrived at Dr. Monroe's office, I was ready to let it all out.

"So, I started taking writing more seriously," I said, shifting in my seat during my therapy session, trying to keep my tone casual but unable to fully mask the vulnerability behind my words.

Dr. Monroe, ever calm and collected, nodded with a soft, encouraging smile. "That's great. Writing can be a wonderful resource for releasing feelings and processing emotions."

I shrugged, playing with the hem of my sleeve, avoiding her gaze for a moment. "I guess. It's just... the only time when things feel quiet, you know? Like everything else just fades, and it's just me and my thoughts."

She tilted her head slightly, her eyes thoughtful as she leaned forward. "What are your goals with writing?"

The question caught me off guard. Goals? That felt so formal, so structured. Writing had always been this organic thing for me, not something I'd ever tied to expectations.

"I don't know," I admitted, leaning back in my chair. "I just like it. It's not about getting published or anything. It's just... mine. Something that's completely mine."

"I see," Dr. Monroe replied, her pen gliding across her notebook as she jotted something down.

Her sessions always left me feeling lighter, like the weight I carried was being redistributed in a way that made it manageable—if only for a little while. Therapy had become my safe haven, the one place where I could be completely honest about my fears and frustrations without worrying about how it might burden Anthony or anyone else. Dr. Monroe looked up from her notes, her expression as steady and kind as ever. "Why don't you think about that tonight when you go home?"

"Think about what?" I asked, raising an eyebrow.

She smiled, sitting back in her chair. "Get a pen and a piece of paper and write down your potential goals for your future in writing. If you had no limitations—no financial constraints, no time constraints—what would you want your life to look like as a writer? Don't think about what's realistic. Just let yourself imagine."

I blinked, caught off guard by the thought. "That's... not something I've ever done before."

"Exactly," she said, her smile widening slightly. "Sometimes, we get so caught up in surviving the day-to-day that we don't allow ourselves the space to dream. Writing is already a tool for you to process. Why not use it as a way to envision the life you want for yourself?"

I sat with her words for a moment, letting them sink in. It was true—I hadn't thought about anything long-term, not in a real way. Writing had always been a passion, but I'd never considered what it could actually look like as a future, as something bigger than just the quiet moments it gave me.

"I'll try," I said finally, a small smile tugging at my lips.

"That's all I ask," she said, her voice warm.

As I left her office, I felt a strange mix of nervousness and excitement. The idea of dreaming without boundaries felt foreign but intriguing. Maybe it was time to start thinking about what I really wanted—what *could* be, not just what *was*. I hadn't considered it before, but maybe there was more to this writing thing than I'd let myself believe. Maybe, just maybe, it could be the key to the life I'd been too afraid to imagine.

That afternoon, I met Anthony at the kids' school to pick up Mia and Christian. It had become part of my new routine now that I wasn't working, and I cherished these small, grounding moments. James was reckless, but even I knew he wasn't crazy enough to pull something at a school. This gave us a sense of security, however small, and allowed me to feel connected to Anthony and the kids in a way that mattered. Mia came bounding out of the school doors, her backpack swinging wildly behind her.

"Mom, guess what?" Christian said from the backseat of the car. The word *Mom* still gave me a warm jolt every time he said it.

"What's up?" I asked, smiling at him through the rearview mirror.

"I did my homework!" he announced proudly, holding up a piece of paper with scribbles on it.

"That's amazing! High five!" I reached back awkwardly, laughing as he smacked my hand enthusiastically as Mia swiveled her way in the car. Anthony gave him a fist bump before starting the car, but I could see the subtle tension in his shoulders. Something was definitely on his mind. Anthony wasn't the type to keep his thoughts bottled up for long. I knew it would only be a matter of minutes after walking into his house before his words started spilling out like an overflowing sink. We pulled up to the house, and the kids darted out of the car, dashing upstairs to their rooms with their usual burst of energy. Within seconds, Anthony finally let it out.

"You know, I don't like this," he said as we made our way to the living room, his tone measured but firm.

"What don't you like?" I asked, glancing over my shoulder as I plopped down on the sofa.

"This whole... you staying at your house thing. Us not seeing each other as much. It doesn't sit right with me. I don't like it," he admitted, running a hand through his hair. His voice wasn't angry, just laced with frustration.

"Anthony," I said gently, leaning back into the cushions. "I'm not doing anything at home anyway. I'm literally just submitting writing gigs and seeing what's out there."

"Yeah, but you can do that here," he countered, crossing his arms and standing over me, his jaw set.

"Not yet," I said softly but firmly. "I just need things to die down first. You know how crazy he's been lately."

His jaw tightened, and I could see the unspoken words swirling in his head. He wasn't the type to blow up unnecessarily, but I could tell he was holding something back, his frustration barely contained.

"You're my fiancée," he said finally, his voice quieter but weighted with meaning.

"I know," I replied, standing up and stepping closer to him. I reached up, cupping his face in my hands. "And I'm trying to make sure we have the best, safest, and most loving life together."

I kissed him softly, letting my lips linger against his. When I pulled back slightly, I whispered, "I promise, this is just temporary."

I kissed him again, my lips brushing over his gently. "I love you," I said, punctuating the words with another kiss.

"And again," I added with a grin, kissing him once more. "Always and forever, babe."

By the time I fully pulled back, the tension in his shoulders had eased, his features softening, though a reluctant smile tugged at the corners of his mouth.

"I love you too," he said, shaking his head. "But this is ass."

I laughed, my grin widening. "I'll make it up to you," I teased.

"You better," he said, his grin finally breaking through fully, the frustration fading into something lighter.

| 23 |

The Patterns of a Predator

The strain was starting to show.

Anthony was a rock—strong, steady, and dependable. But even rocks can crack under enough pressure, and lately, the pressure was relentless. The distance I'd insisted on was wearing on both of us, and the cracks were becoming more obvious with every passing day.

"You're still acting like you're dealing with this alone," Anthony said one evening, his voice low but firm.

We were sitting at his dining table, the tension between us thick enough to cut with a knife.

"I'm not," I argued, though my tone lacked conviction.

"You are," he shot back, leaning forward, his hands clasped tightly in front of him. "Every time you insist on staying at your house, every time you handle this 'your way,' you're shutting me out. And I'm not okay with it."

I opened my mouth to respond, but he held up a hand, cutting me off.

"I know you're trying to protect me, Patricia. But you don't get to make that call. We're in this together—whether you like it or not."

His words hung in the air, and I felt a pang of guilt. He was right. As much as I wanted to shield him from the chaos, my actions were making him feel like an outsider in his own fight. Anthony's frustration wasn't just with me, though. The legal system's sluggish response was gnawing at him, making him feel powerless. Every call to the lawyer seemed to end with the same response: *"We're working on it. These things take time."* Time we didn't feel we had.

One evening, after yet another disappointing update from the lawyer, Anthony made a decision.

"That's it," he said, pacing the living room with his phone in hand. "I'm hiring a private investigator."

I blinked, caught off guard. "A private investigator?"

"Yes," Anthony said firmly, pulling out his phone and scrolling through his contacts. "If the system won't move fast enough, I'll get the evidence myself."

The decision felt sudden, but not impulsive. Anthony wasn't the type to let things fester for long, especially when it came to protecting the people he cared about. Within hours, he had scheduled a meeting with Carla, a no-nonsense investigator highly recommended by one of his colleagues. The meeting took place two days later at a small, private office tucked away in the business district. It was the kind of place you wouldn't notice unless you were looking for it—a small brass plaque by the door was the only indicator of its purpose. The office itself was sleek and efficient, with neutral tones, clean lines, and a faint scent of coffee lingering in the air. Carla herself matched the vibe perfectly: sharp-eyed, confident, and clearly in control. She wasted no time getting down to business. "I've reviewed the details Anthony provided," she said, flipping through a crisp folder filled with notes. "Let's start with what you've experienced so far and what specific concerns you have moving forward."

The process was straightforward but emotionally draining. Carla asked about James's recent actions—his texts, the vandalism, the unsettling deliveries—and then expanded her scope, digging into past patterns and any potential connections. She took detailed notes, occasionally pausing to ask clarifying questions.

"How soon can we expect results?" Anthony asked, his voice calm but with an undercurrent of urgency.

Carla didn't sugarcoat her response. "It depends. Gathering evidence takes time, but given what you've described, I'll prioritize this case. I'll start by looking into his history, his financials, and any recent activity that might give us a clearer picture of what we're dealing with. You'll have an update from me within the week."

True to her word, Carla got to work immediately. Just four days later, she called us back for an update. The second meeting was in the same office, but this time, Carla's expression carried a weight that made my stomach churn before she even said a word.

"James has a pattern," she began, laying out the files on the table. "And it's worse than I initially thought."

What followed was a harrowing deep dive into James's past and present—a web of troubling behavior that left no doubt about the seriousness of the situation. The air in the room felt heavy, almost suffocating, as if all the oxygen had been sucked out.

"What do you mean?" Anthony asked, his voice tight and steady, though I could see the tension rippling through him.

Carla spread the files across the table, her expression a mix of professionalism and concern. "There's a pattern of behavior here," she said, her voice measured but grim. "James has done this before—harassing and stalking women who tried to leave him. There's even a breaking and entering charge that looks like it was expunged. I found it through some deep digging."

I swallowed hard, my stomach twisting as her words sank in.

"In at least two other cases," Carla continued, her voice steady, "the victims had to move out of state to escape him. This isn't new territory for him."

Two other cases? My thoughts spiraled, each one louder than the last. I had been with this man for four years. Four years. How did I not know? How did I miss the signs? The realization hit me like a punch to the gut, leaving me breathless. Had I been so blinded by love, or was it denial? The version of James I thought I knew felt like a cruel illusion. The nagging thought crept in: Was I just another name on a growing list of people trying to outrun the damage he caused? The weight of it settled in my chest, suffocating and relentless. Anthony's hand tightened around mine under the table, his grip firm and grounding, though his jaw was clenched so tightly I thought he might shatter a tooth.

He didn't say anything, his eyes locked on the files in front of him.

"And that's not all," Carla added, flipping to another page in her neatly organized folder. "He's been making some... questionable purchases recently. Surveillance equipment, burner phones—things that suggest he's been planning this for a while."

My breath hitched, the words hitting me like a cold slap. Planning. That word echoed in my mind, conjuring images I didn't want to entertain. Anthony leaned forward, his voice low and edged with controlled fury. "What kind of planning are we talking about?"

"Enough to make it clear he's not acting on impulse," Carla replied. The room fell into an eerie silence, punctuated only by the faint sound of the heating system humming in the background. I glanced at Anthony, whose gaze was still fixed on the files. His knuckles were white, his anger and frustration barely concealed beneath his calm exterior.

"This isn't just about protecting Patricia anymore," Carla said, her voice softer now but no less serious. "It's about everyone in her life—your kids, your family. He's fixated and he's dangerous."

I squeezed Anthony's hand, trying to ground myself as much as him. His other hand ran through his hair, a gesture I'd come to recognize as his way of holding himself together.

"We need to end this," he finally said, his voice quiet but resolute. "Whatever it takes."

In that moment I felt the gravity of how far this had gone. James wasn't just someone from my past anymore—he was a clear and present threat. And now, we had to figure out how to stop him before it was too late. That night Anthony stood by the living room window, peering out into the darkness. "You're going to drive yourself crazy." I said softly.

He turned to me, his eyes tired but determined. "I can't help it. I can't let my guard down, not with him out there."

I couldn't blame him. James's behavior was escalating, and the knowledge of his past only added fuel to the fire. But seeing Anthony like this—on edge, constantly on high alert—made my heart ache.

"Am I the one losing it now?" he asked quietly, his voice breaking through my thoughts.

"No," I said firmly, wrapping my arms around him. "You're not losing it. You're just... under pressure."

The phrase triggered a fleeting thought of the song, the lyrics running through my head. Looking at him with a grin I began singing—*"Pressure, pushing down on me, pressing down on you..."*

Anthony burst into laughter, " I can't stand you!" He yelled out. It was the laugh he needed. But there was nothing funny about this. Anthony was carrying the weight of protecting all of us, and I knew I had to find a way to ease his burden. For now, though, I held him tighter, hoping my presence would be enough to keep him grounded—even if just for a moment.

| 24 |

Freelance Freedom

I don't know what caused it—whether it was my distance from Anthony, the holiday blues finally melting away, or something completely unrelated to me, like the snow on the ground being a literal barrier—but James seemed to tire himself out. It was odd, really. Days passed without any cryptic texts, drive-bys, or surprise gifts. Then weeks. It was like he'd disappeared off the face of the earth.

"Maybe it's his New Year's resolution," I joked to Anthony one evening. "You know, 'Be less of a stalker this year.'"

Anthony smirked, his arm draped around me on the couch. "Or maybe he just got bored. He's got the attention span of a toddler, anyway."

"Whatever the reason, I'm not complaining," I said, snuggling closer to him.

The relief was palpable, especially for Anthony. The tension that had gripped him for weeks seemed to ease. He wasn't checking the cameras every five minutes or pacing by the windows. Instead, he was fully present, laughing with the kids, teasing me about my terrible aim in the kitchen (*one misplaced spoon and suddenly I'm a hazard*), and even planning little date nights at his place. After our meeting with Carla, the private investigator, Anthony had decided that keeping his distance was no longer an option.

"If James is watching," he'd said, "I want him to know I'm here—and I'm not going anywhere."

True to his word, Anthony made his presence at my house unpredictable. He'd pop by at random times during the day or night, never sticking to a pattern. If James was watching, he couldn't plan around it. We also kept the kids away from my home, just to be safe, blaming it on everything from work schedules to "Daddy's house has better snacks." It wasn't ideal, but it gave me peace of mind. In return, I made sure to be present for all their after-school activities. Anthony and I knew James took pride in his position as a chief EMT. He wasn't going to risk his career by pulling something in public, where witnesses could jeopardize his spotless reputation. Honestly, I thought the restraining order would have done the job but he happened to find ways around it.

One early morning, I received a spontaneous text from Anthony. I had just finished my cup of homemade tea and was going through some writing prompts when my phone buzzed on the counter.

Anthony: *What are you doing today?*
Me: *The usual. Pretending to be productive until we pick up the kids.*
Anthony: *Wrong answer. Let's go on a date.*

I blinked at the screen, a smile creeping across my face. Anthony wasn't usually the "let's plan a spontaneous date" type. He was the acts-of-service guy, the "I fixed the leaky faucet" kind of romantic. So, this was unexpected.

Me: *A date? Don't you have like... a million things to do?*

Anthony: *Nope. Not today. Kids are at school, work can wait, and you're the boss of your schedule now. So, pick something cute to wear. I'll pick you up at 11.*

Rolling my eyes, I typed back, *Cute?*

His reply came instantly: *Cute.*

By the time he pulled up to my house later that morning, I was waiting on the porch, dressed in a casual but flattering outfit that said, "I tried, but not too hard." He leaned out the car window with a grin.

"Look at you, dressing up for me," he teased as I slid into the passenger seat.

"Don't get used to it," I shot back. "You caught me on a good day."

He laughed as he pulled away from the curb. "Well, buckle up. I'm taking you to the finest dining establishment in town."

"Please tell me it's not the drive-thru where the guy knows your order by heart," I said, raising an eyebrow.

"Better," he said confidently. "Our favorite sushi place."

Now, *that* caught my attention. "Oh yay!, okay, you get points for that."

By the time we settled at our table, the familiar warmth of the little sushi restaurant put me at ease. The gentle hum of lunchtime conversations, the soft clinking of chopsticks on plates, and the faint scent of soy sauce created the perfect atmosphere. It wasn't extravagant, but it was ours.

Anthony popped a piece of sashimi into his mouth and looked at me with a grin. "You know, I've been thinking..."

"Uh-oh," I teased. "This sounds serious."

"Not serious. Just... I kind of feel like a spy these days," he said, gesturing dramatically. "All this unpredictability, showing up at random hours. I should've bought a trench coat and sunglasses for the full effect."

I burst out laughing, nearly choking on my sushi. "I can see it now: Anthony Garcia, PI. Sneaking around in broad daylight with your Costco sneakers and dad jeans. Truly intimidating."

"Hey," he said with mock indignation. "At least I'd be a *good* stalker. None of this sending-flowers-and-creepy-messages nonsense. I'd be the guy who leaves snacks on your doorstep and shovels your driveway."

"Now *that's* the kind of stalker I'd sign up for," I said, shaking my head but grinning all the same.

His smile softened as he leaned across the table to take my hand. "Jokes aside, I just want you to feel safe. Always."

I felt my chest tighten, the warmth of his words settling over me. "I do," I said, squeezing his hand. "I really do."

As we finished the last of our sushi, I couldn't help but feel a mix of excitement and nervous energy. Freelance writing had taken off far more than I'd anticipated. What started as a creative outlet during my leave of absence had quickly turned into a viable career path. The realization that I could make the same income from home as I did in neurology had opened a door I wasn't sure I'd ever walk through. Anthony raised his hand to signal the waitress, letting her know we were ready for the check. My heart raced. Why did this feel like I was a little kid mustering up the courage to ask my parents if my favorite cousin could sleep over? Except now, there was no one to play middleman for me. It was all on me. The waitress returned with the checkbook, and Anthony, ever quick on the draw, slid his card inside and handed it back to her with a polite smile. This was my moment. I took a steadying breath and decided it was time to pitch the idea.

"I've been thinking about something," I said cautiously, sneaking a glance at him out of the corner of my eye.

He raised an eyebrow, pausing mid-scroll on his phone. "Uh-oh. What now?"

"I'm thinking about leaving the hospital," I said, the words hanging in the air like a challenge.

Anthony's brow furrowed, his focus shifting entirely to me. "Leaving? Like, for good?"

I nodded. "Freelance writing is going really well. If I keep up the pace, I can make the same amount as I do in neurology. And I'd be working from home."

He leaned back, considering this. "What about benefits?"

"I can pay for insurance on my own," I replied, trying to sound more confident than I felt. "It's not ideal, but it's manageable."

Anthony rubbed his beard, his expression thoughtful. "Okay, but it's risky."

"I know it is," I admitted, taking his hand. "But I think it's worth the risk. I've outgrown the hospital, Anthony. It's a great place, and the staff is amazing, but I don't feel passionate about the work anymore. I just... don't."

He studied me for a long moment before finally nodding. "Alright. If it's what you want, I'll support you. But," he added with a teasing smirk, "don't think this means you're off the hook for paying some bills."

I laughed, leaning against him. "Deal."

That night, I sat at my desk, the glow of my laptop illuminating the room as I typed up my resignation letter. I thought I'd feel emotional writing it—some sense of loss or nostalgia—but as my fingers moved across the keyboard, I felt... nothing. The hospital had been a huge part of my life, and I respected the work I'd done there. But as I reflected on my time in neurology, I realized how disconnected I'd been. I remembered listening to other surgical techs speak passionately about their work, their faces lighting up as they described procedures or new advancements in the field. And I remembered thinking how I wasn't like that. At all.

This wasn't a loss; it was a shift. I was stepping into something that actually excited me, something that felt like mine. Writing articles for magazines, ghostwriting for other authors, and even taking on random projects to pay the bills—it was all a challenge I was ready to embrace. I stared at the screen for a moment after finishing the letter, letting the magnitude of the decision sink in. And then, with a deep breath, I hit send.

It was time to turn the page. Literally.

| 25 |

Rewriting the Narrative

Time. It moves so quickly, almost too quickly. Days turned into weeks, and weeks into months. James's absence lingered in the air like a question unanswered. Was he truly gone, or simply biding his time? The thought crept into my mind now and then, but life, relentless as always, carried me forward.

The decision to leave the hospital was one of the hardest I'd ever made. When I submitted my 30-day notice, I braced myself for skepticism, disappointment, or even judgment. Instead, I was met with an outpouring of encouragement. My colleagues, people who had seen me at my best and worst, celebrated my decision to pursue new goals—even if those goals led me away from the medical field entirely. Their support was unexpected and overwhelming, leaving me both humbled and bittersweet. And now, here I was—on my last day as a surgical tech. The last day working in the medical field. I never thought I'd say those words, let alone mean them.

The thought stirred something deep within me, a mixture of nostalgia and anticipation. Working in healthcare had been my entire adult life. From my early days as a live-in caregiver, where I learned the weight of true responsibility, to the long shifts at assisted living facilities, where patience was tested and rewarded in equal measure. From traveling across the country for organ recovery, witnessing life and loss in the most profound ways, to finding my OR family at the hospital—a group of people who became more than just colleagues, but a second home. Each phase had shaped me, challenged me, and taught me more about life, resilience, and humanity than I could have ever imagined. But as I walked through the hospital halls for the last time, my thoughts turned to what lay ahead. The flowers outside the windows began to bloom, their delicate petals braving the crisp morning air before opening beautifully under the afternoon sun. They seemed to mirror my own journey—a symbol of change, growth, and the unknown.

I stopped for a moment to take it all in. The familiar hum of monitors, the echo of hurried footsteps, the quiet murmurs of care teams strategizing over patients. This was a world I knew inside and out, a rhythm that had become second nature. And yet, for the first time in years, it no longer felt like mine.

"Promise me you'll stay in touch," the nurse manager said, pulling me into a warm hug as my shift wound down.

"I will," I said, the words catching slightly in my throat. "Thank you—for everything."

"You always have a place here if you ever change your mind," she added, her tone genuine.

Throughout the day, my colleagues surprised me with kindness at every turn. A celebratory lunch, shared memories, hugs that lingered a little longer. I had always assumed my departure would barely register—turnover was high, and life moved fast. But they didn't let me feel like just another name on the "another one bites the dust" list. Instead, they reminded me of the impact I had made—not just on patients, but on them. As the clock ticked closer to the end of my shift, I took one last walk through the OR. The sterile halls, the bustling nurses' station, the breakroom where we exchanged tired laughs over lukewarm coffee. Each space held years of memories. Each space felt like a farewell. Finally, I approached the time clock, badge in hand. Swiping it for the last time, I watched the screen blink back at me with a familiar *Logged Out*. The finality of it hit me harder than I'd expected. I took a deep breath, feeling a swell of emotion—gratitude, pride, a touch of sadness—but no regret.

"That's it," I whispered to myself, a small smile tugging at my lips.

As I stepped out into the crisp air, the sun warming my face, I felt lighter somehow. The flowers lining the walkway seemed brighter, their petals fully open as if to remind me that the most beautiful things often bloom after seasons of uncertainty.

As I walked to my car, I felt my mind already racing ahead, slipping into planning mode. If I was truly going to treat writing as a career, I needed to give it the respect and structure it deserved. No more fitting it into spare moments or treating it like a casual hobby. This was my new chapter, my new profession, and I was determined to step into it with purpose. I decided to model my writing schedule after the aspect I loved most about my hospital shifts—the "working three days and being off four" routine. However, this time, there would be no grueling twelve-hour days. Instead, I planned for manageable six- to eight-hour blocks of focused work. It was a balance that allowed me to stay productive and creative while leaving room for the things that truly mattered—my family, my health, and my happiness.

When I finally settled into my new office, a wave of calm washed over me. The space was mine—free of the chaos that had defined so much of my past year. It was simple but intentional: a clean desk, a corkboard for brainstorming, and a shelf filled with books that inspired me. I added little touches of personality—pictures of the kids, a motivational quote taped to my monitor, and a small plant that reminded me of growth. The transition wasn't seamless. The first few days were a learning curve, filled with moments of doubt. Could I stay disciplined? Could I balance everything? But with each passing day, I found my rhythm. I felt like I had been teetering on the edge of losing my mind. Life had started to feel like it was happening to me, not for me—a relentless current dragging me along with no time to catch my breath. The chaos, the constant demands, the feeling of being stuck in a cycle I didn't know how to break—it was all too much. I realized if I wanted a different outcome, I needed a different strategy.

So, I took a leap of faith.

Writing became more than just an escape; it became my anchor. For the first time in a long while, I wasn't just reacting to life—I was shaping it. The structure and purpose

I brought to my writing gave me something I had been desperately craving—a sense of autonomy. Every carefully planned hour, every word I typed, felt like a step toward reclaiming the narrative of my own life. It wasn't just about the career change. It was about the realization that I had the power to create the life I wanted. Writing was my outlet, my passion, and now my profession, but more importantly, it was my way of proving to myself that I could take control again.

One afternoon, after finishing a particularly satisfying batch of submissions, I leaned back in my chair, stretching my arms over my head. The quiet hum of the house surrounded me—a peacefulness I hadn't felt in so long, I almost didn't recognize it. I turned toward the window, drawn by the sound of laughter, and there they were: the kids playing in the yard, their energy contagious even from behind the glass. Anthony stood nearby, his tall frame a comforting presence as he guided Christian through soccer kicks. Christian's determination was written all over his face, his little legs working hard to mimic Anthony's instructions. Mia sat cross-legged on the grass a few feet away, her sketchpad balanced on her knees, her pencil moving furiously across the page. Her lips curled in concentration, and I could almost hear her thoughts as she lost herself in her art. The scene was so simple, so ordinary, yet it was everything I had been yearning for. The laughter drifting through the open window was like a balm for my soul, soothing wounds I wasn't even fully aware I still carried. I let myself sink into the chair, just watching, absorbing the love and light radiating from the yard.

As the sun dipped lower in the sky, casting a warm golden hue over everything, Anthony looked up. His eyes found mine through the window, and he waved, a grin spreading across his face. It was a smile that said everything—comfort, ease, love. He looked so relaxed, so completely himself, and it made my heart ache in the best way. I waved back, smiling so wide my cheeks hurt. This moment was perfect. He was perfect. We were perfect. I stayed there for a few minutes longer, my chin resting on my hand, just watching them. I felt a wave of gratitude wash over me—not just for Anthony and the kids, but for the journey that had brought us here. It hadn't been easy. It had been painful, messy, and terrifying at times. But somehow, we were finding our way.

And yet, as much as I wanted to lose myself in the serenity of this moment, a faint shadow lingered in the back of my mind. James. He had been quiet—eerily so. The lack of any sign from him should have been a relief, but it only left me feeling uneasy, like waiting for the other shoe to drop. My chest tightened briefly, the what-ifs creeping in, threatening to pull me out of my peace. But I shook my head, exhaling slowly. I couldn't—no, I *wouldn't*—let the uncertainty of James's silence rob me of the joy and progress I had worked so hard to reclaim. I owed it to myself, to Anthony, and to the kids to stay present, to embrace what was good and beautiful in front of me. Life felt...manageable. Balanced. Mine. I didn't feel like a passenger in an airplane seconds from crashing, desperately trying to grab a hold of the oxygen mask. I was in control, steering my own ship. Maybe, finally, the worst was over.

| 26 |

Shadows in the Moonlight

The house was still, cloaked in the kind of silence only the dead of night could bring—the kind that makes every creak of the floorboards and hum of the fridge sound unnervingly loud. Then, the dogs erupted into a frenzy, shattering the stillness like glass.

Having dogs is a lot like having kids. You learn their different barks and cries, deciphering their meanings like a second language. There's the *I heard a squirrel* bark, the *feed me now* bark, and then there's this bark—the *someone's-here-who-doesn't-belong* bark. It was sharp, urgent, and relentless, a sound that struck right to my core. The hairs on the back of my neck stood on end, my instincts kicking in before my body fully caught up. I didn't even have to move to know what this meant. My stomach churned as I sat up slowly, the faint moonlight spilling through the blinds, casting long shadows across the room.

Anthony, sprawled out beside me, was dead to the world, snoring softly. His arm was draped over the edge of the bed, his face turned into the pillow, blissfully unaware of the chaos unfolding just outside. Unless the house was collapsing or the kids screamed his name directly into his ear, this man wasn't waking up. I envied him for a moment, the ease with which he could sleep through anything. Meanwhile, my brain was already spiraling into overdrive. My heart pounded in my chest, each thump echoing in my ears.

Before I could even reach for my phone, it buzzed with security camera alerts. "Activity detected." My heart pounded as I grabbed it, already dreading what I might see. Anthony stirred beside me, mumbling something unintelligible, but he didn't fully wake. I opened the app, scrolling through the live feeds from the cameras. My hands shook slightly as I flipped through the angles—front yard, backyard, side gate. But nothing. No movement. No shadows. Just still, quiet night.

Anthony groaned beside me, finally cracking an eye open. "What's going on?" he asked, his voice thick with sleep.

"The dogs are going crazy," I whispered. "And the cameras sent alerts."

He rubbed his face, sitting up. "Let me see."

I handed him the phone, and he squinted at the screen, flipping through the feeds. "Nothing," he said after a moment. "Probably just an animal. Go back to sleep."

I stared at him, incredulous. "It's not an animal, Anthony. I know my dogs."

"Mmhm," he groaned, already turning over to go back to sleep. "If it's something, they'll keep barking."

My jaw clenched. I knew it wasn't an animal. The way the dogs barked was different—urgent, protective. My gut

told me something wasn't right. Ignoring Anthony's suggestion, I slid out of bed, my bare feet hitting the cool floor. As
I reached for the door, I heard a soft creak behind me. Turning, I saw the kids' doors cracking open, their sleepy faces
peeking out into the dim hallway. Christian looked scared,
his small hands gripping the doorframe, while Mia's wide
eyes were calm but alert.

"Back to your rooms," I whispered firmly, my voice low
but steady. "Lock the doors and don't come out unless I say
so."

Christian hesitated, his lower lip trembling, but Mia
grabbed his hand, pulling him close. She nodded at me, her
quiet strength shining through as she gently guided him
back into the room and shut the door. The soft *click* of the
lock made my chest tighten, but I forced myself to refocus.
The dogs' barking grew louder, echoing through the house.
They were at the front door now, their nails scratching fran-
tically at the hardwood. My phone buzzed again in my hand.
"Activity detected." The words on the screen sent another
jolt of adrenaline through me.

Moving as quietly as I could, I crept downstairs, keeping
the lights off. My heart pounded in my chest as I tried to
peer out through the windows. The moonlight barely illuminated the yard, and from what I could see, it looked
empty. But the dogs wouldn't stop. Their growls were deep,
guttural, primal. I took another step closer to the front door,
my eyes scanning every shadow outside. My grip tightened
on the phone as another alert came through. "Activity detected." Still nothing visible on the cameras. It didn't make
sense. The hairs on the back of my neck stood on end.

Whatever—or whoever—was out there, the dogs knew. And I knew better than to ignore their instincts.

Then a loud bang echoed from the back of the house.

The sound sent a chill racing down my spine as I spun around, my heart hammering in my chest. The dogs bolted to the back door, their barking now frantic and relentless. My phone vibrated in my hand, but it wasn't a notification this time—it was a call. The name on the screen read *Security Alarm Company*.

I swiped to answer, whispering, "Hello?" But before I could say anything else, I froze.

James was standing in the dining room.

His figure was partially illuminated by the faint glow of the porch light filtering through the windows. He was dressed entirely in black, from his hoodie to his boots, and his eyes glinted with a chilling calmness. A knife gleamed in his hand, catching the faint light.

"I missed you, sweet pea," he said, his voice low and steady, as if this were some casual reunion instead of a nightmare come to life.

My stomach churned, and I fought the urge to scream. My phone was still in my hand, but I slowly set it on the table as discreetly as possible, hoping it would capture the audio. The security company was still on the line. *Stay calm. Stay calm.* James's gaze flickered toward the barking dogs, who were now standing just feet away from him, their growls deep and unrelenting.

"Might want to get control of your dogs," he said, his tone almost mocking. "Seems like they don't remember me."

He crouched slightly, addressing them in a cooing voice. "Come here, boys."

The dogs didn't move. They stood their ground, their bodies tense, growling louder, their teeth bared.

"Boys, crate!" I yelled, my voice firm and authoritative.

The dogs hesitated, their loyalty battling their instincts. "Now!" I barked, more forceful this time. Reluctantly, they retreated, their growls echoing as they padded to their crates. I latched the doors behind them, my hands trembling. *I'm not about to let this lunatic hurt one of my dogs.*

From behind me, I heard the unmistakable sound of Anthony barreling down the stairs. His footsteps were heavy, deliberate, and fast. Within seconds, he was in the room, a bat clutched tightly in his hands, his face a mix of fury and determination.

"Oh, now he wants to get up," I thought dryly, a flicker of sarcasm cutting through my terror.

"Get the fuck out!" Anthony bellowed, his voice reverberating through the house like thunder, shaking me out of my momentary distraction.

James didn't flinch. Instead, he tilted his head slightly, his calm demeanor unshaken, as though he had anticipated this reaction. His lips curled into a twisted smile. "Still haven't gotten rid of him, I see," he said, his voice dripping with disdain.

My breath caught as I saw James's grip on the knife tighten. The metallic sheen of the blade gleamed under the dim light, and a wave of nausea rolled over me. So many thoughts raced through my head. *This can't be happening.* Everything felt like it was happening in slow motion, but at the same time, it was all moving too fast. My pulse pounded in my ears as I positioned myself between Anthony and the table where my phone lay recording.

"Hello? Hello? Can you hear me?" the voice from the phone crackled faintly. It sounded so distant, like a ghost of reality trying to break through the chaos.

Anthony took a step closer, positioning himself between me and James. His grip on the bat was so tight that his knuckles had turned white. James shifted slightly, his dark eyes narrowing. The tension in the room was suffocating, the air thick with unspoken threats.

"Put the knife down," Anthony said, his voice low and commanding.

James smirked, taking a slow step forward. "What, you gonna play hero? Do you even know what she's been keeping from you? Hm?"

My stomach dropped. *Keeping from him? What the hell was this guy talking about?*

Anthony's grip on the bat tightened, his knuckles white, but I caught the briefest flicker of doubt in his eyes. It was gone as quickly as it appeared. He wasn't taking the bait.

"I'm not playing anything," Anthony said, his voice steady, low, and full of warning. "Drop the knife and leave. Now."

The seconds stretched out painfully, each one a coil tightening around my chest. James didn't respond. Instead, he looked at me, his smile fading into something darker. The way his eyes bore into mine sent a fresh wave of terror through me. I couldn't move. Couldn't breathe. And then, all at once, everything erupted into chaos. James's face twisted into something almost unrecognizable—an unsettling combination of desperation and anger. "I've been patient," he began, his voice trembling with barely contained rage. "I've waited and waited, Patricia. All I wanted was to give you the family we always dreamed of, but no. No matter what I did, all you ever did was reject me. For *him*."

He spat the last word, glaring at Anthony like he was the embodiment of every failure James had ever endured. His eyes burned with a mix of fury and desperation.

"You don't understand, do you?" James continued, taking another step closer. "I was ready to forgive you. To give you everything. And yet here you are, shoving me aside like trash."

Forgive me?! Oh, this man has really lost it, I thought, disbelief mixing with the fear twisting in my gut.

"Stop," I said, my voice cracking as I stepped slightly forward. "Just stop, James. This isn't going to fix anything." My words hung in the air, trembling under the weight of the moment, but I doubted they would reach him. He wasn't hearing anyone but the chaos in his own head. Anthony stepped forward, the bat in his hand rising slightly. "She said stop. Now get the hell out of here before this gets worse for you."

James snapped his head toward Anthony, his face contorting in fury. "You," he hissed. "You ruined everything."

It all happened so fast, a blur of chaos and panic that left no time to think. James lunged at Anthony, the knife in his hand catching the dim light of the room like a beacon of danger. Anthony swung the bat with all his might, but

James anticipated the move, dodging just enough to close the gap and tackle him to the ground.

The sound of their bodies colliding with the hardwood floor was deafening, a sickening thud that reverberated through the house. Grunts and shouts filled the air as they wrestled, each vying for control. Anthony's face was a mix of fury and determination, but James's deranged strength was unsettling.

"Stop it!" I screamed, my voice breaking with desperation. I ran toward them, reaching for James's arm in an attempt to pull him off Anthony, but his reaction was immediate. He shoved me with such force that I stumbled backward, slamming into the wall. Pain shot through my shoulder, but it was nothing compared to the dread consuming me.

Anthony's grip on the bat slipped in the struggle, and James's eyes gleamed with triumph as he saw his opening. He raised the knife high, the glint of the blade terrifying in its intent.

"No!" I screamed, my voice raw and full of terror.

Adrenaline coursed through me, overriding fear. Without a second thought, I darted across the room, my eyes locking onto the bat where it had rolled under the dining table. I grabbed it, my hands trembling but resolute. With every ounce of strength I could summon, I swung it, the heavy wood connecting with James's side in a resounding crack. He let out a guttural cry, toppling off Anthony and clutching his ribs. The knife slipped momentarily from his grasp, clattering against the floor. My heart pounded in my ears, drowning out the chaos as I turned to Anthony, who was scrambling to sit up, his face pale and strained. The sound of sirens pierced the air, their wailing growing louder with every passing second. Red and blue lights flashed through the windows, painting the walls in eerie, alternating hues. Relief mixed with dread as I realized help was just moments away, but the danger wasn't over. James, clutching his side, managed to grab the knife once more. His face was a mask of desperation and rage as he looked at Anthony, his expression a twisted cocktail of hatred and resignation.

"James, no!" I screamed, my voice cracking as I lunged toward them again.

But I was too late. James drove the knife into Anthony's stomach, the blade sinking deep. Time seemed to slow as Anthony's body jerked in response, a strangled gasp escaping his lips. His hand instinctively pressed against the wound, blood staining his shirt in an instant.

"No!" My scream tore through the air, a sound of pure anguish.

James removed the knife and raised it again, but before he could strike, the front door burst open with a resounding crash. Officers stormed in, their shouts commanding and authoritative.

"Drop the weapon! Get on the ground!"

James hesitated for a split second, his eyes wild, before two officers tackled him. The knife skittered across the floor, out of reach, as they pinned him down. His cries of protest were drowned out by the chaos of commands and the weight of justice finally catching up to him. I dropped the bat, rushing to Anthony's side as tears streamed down my face. "Anthony, hold on. Please hold on," I whispered, pressing my hands against his wound in an attempt to stem the bleeding. His eyes met mine, filled with both pain and reassurance. Blood seeped through my fingers, warm and terrifying. "I need a medic!" I shouted, my voice breaking. Anthony's eyes met mine, glassy with pain but still focused. "The kids," he whispered.

"They're okay," I said, my voice thick with emotion. "They're in their rooms. They're safe. Everything's going to be okay."

A faint smile tugged at the corners of his lips despite the agony etched on his face. "You owe me," he said, his voice barely above a whisper.

I choked out a laugh through my tears, shaking my head. "How can you make jokes right now?"

"Good timing," he teased, his eyelids fluttering as his body slackened.

"Stay with me," I begged, pressing harder on his wound. "Help is coming. Just stay with me."

The room was chaos—officers shouting, paramedics rushing in—but all I could focus on was Anthony. My Anthony. And I wasn't going to let him slip away. "Mam! We've got him," a paramedic called out as they carefully placed Anthony onto a stretcher. I stood frozen, my heart racing as the flurry of medical professionals worked around him. From the corner of the room, a cry pierced through the chaos.

"Daddy!" Mia and Christian came rushing toward us, their faces pale with fear. I caught them in my arms before they could get too close.

"He's going to be okay," I whispered, holding them tightly. "Everything is going to be okay."

The paramedic turned to me. "We're taking him to the nearest hospital. Are you coming with us?"

I hesitated. Every fiber of my being wanted to jump into that ambulance, to be by Anthony's side. But the kids needed me too, and his mother's house was only minutes away from the hospital. I had to think clearly for all of us.

"I'll meet you there," I said, my voice steady despite the storm inside me.

As the ambulance pulled away, its lights casting an eerie glow on the street, I loaded the kids into the car. We followed closely behind for most of the way until it was time to turn onto Anthony's street. My heart ached as I watched the ambulance continue without us. On the drive, I called his mother to explain what had happened. The panic in her voice was immediate.

"Is he okay? What do you mean he was stabbed?!" she exclaimed, her words rapid and frantic.

"He's stable, and they're taking him to the hospital now," I said, trying to sound calmer than I felt. "I'll update you as soon as I know something. But for now, I need you to stay with the kids."

Her voice wavered, but she agreed. "Okay, okay. I'll keep them with me. Just let me know what's happening."

When we arrived, I walked the kids to the door, crouching down to their level. "You two go to bed, okay? Grandma's going to stay with you, and I'm going to check on Daddy."

Mia sniffled, holding tightly to Christian's hand. "Is he really going to be okay?"

I swallowed hard, forcing a smile. "He's strong, remember? Daddy's going to be just fine."

As I hugged them goodbye, I could see their small faces pressed against the window, watching me leave. I resisted the urge to run to my car, knowing they'd be watching my every move. But as soon as I was out of sight, I sprinted to the driver's seat, adrenaline pushing me forward.

The drive to the hospital felt like an eternity. My hands gripped the steering wheel so tightly my knuckles turned white. The sound of Anthony's pained voice replayed in my mind over and over again. *The kids.* Even in his most vulnerable moment, his first thought was about them. That's who he was—selfless, protective, and unshakable. As I pulled into the hospital parking lot, the weight of everything hit me like a tidal wave. I took a deep breath, steadying myself. This wasn't over yet, but Anthony was alive. And as long as he was alive, I would do everything in my power to keep it that way.

| 27 |

The Breaking Point

The sterile white walls of the waiting room seemed to press in on me as I sat hunched in the corner chair, my knees pulled tightly to my chest. The hard plastic of the seat dug into my back, but I barely noticed. Anxiety had wrapped itself around me, squeezing tighter with every passing second. The faint smell of antiseptic, the murmur of hushed voices, and the distant chime of monitors all blended into a cacophony of dread.

The ER staff wouldn't let me go back to see him. I knew the drill from my own time working in the ER, and that knowledge only made the waiting worse. If they weren't letting me in, it could mean any number of things. Maybe Anthony was unstable, and the doctors didn't want to give me false reassurance only for him to crash minutes later. Or maybe they didn't even have a room yet, treating him in the hallway while they scrambled for space. Worst of all, the terrifying thought crossed my mind that he might still be in the ambulance, too critical to be moved.

Every possibility churned in my head, making my stomach twist painfully.

Old coworkers filtered through the waiting area, their familiar faces offering small doses of comfort. One handed me a bottle of water, her hand briefly resting on my shoulder. "We'll get you back there as soon as we can," she assured me, her voice soft. I nodded absently, my gaze fixed on the door that led to the trauma bays. I wanted to believe them, but the unknown loomed too large.

My mind replayed every second of the night: the look in Anthony's eyes, his pained gasp as he clutched his stomach, the flash of red and blue lights reflecting off the windows. I shivered involuntarily, wrapping my arms around myself for comfort. The minutes dragged on like hours until finally, the door swung open. A doctor entered, her expression calm but serious. My heart clenched, and I shot up from the chair, my knees weak as I braced myself for whatever she was about to say.

"Anthony is stable," the doctor said, her voice steady and calm. I exhaled a breath I hadn't realized I'd been holding, the weight of those words hitting me like a tidal wave. "We've taken him back for imaging to ensure there's no damage to his internal organs. The scans should be back soon, but so far, he's responding well."

"Thank you," I managed to say, though my voice cracked. Relief coursed through me, but it was tangled with the residual fear that still gripped my chest.

"We can take you back to his room," she continued gently. "You can wait there while he's in imaging. I'm sure he'll love to see you when he comes back."

I nodded quickly and made my way to the security desk to get a visitor badge. Room 19. I didn't need directions—I knew exactly where it was. The security guard buzzed the door open, and I stepped into the hallway, the familiar scent of antiseptic filling my lungs. Walking through the emergency room halls, I felt like I had tunnel vision. The sounds of beeping monitors and hurried footsteps faded into the background as I zeroed in on the room. Room 19. My heart raced as I stepped inside and took a seat, my hands trembling slightly as I rested them on my lap. Moments later, I heard the faint whir of wheels approaching the room door. Transport was bringing Anthony back. My breath caught when they wheeled him into the room. His eyes flicked open, finding mine immediately. Relief washed over his face, softening the tension in his expression.

"Hey you," he whispered, his voice hoarse but steady. His lips curved into a faint smile, one that barely masked the exhaustion etched into his features.

"Hey," I said, choking back tears. "You scared me." I stepped closer to the bed and took his hand. The warmth of his skin grounded me in a way nothing else could.

"I'm okay," he said, his voice more confident. "I'm not going anywhere."

But I couldn't hold it in anymore. The tears came in a flood as I buried my face in his shoulder. "This is my fault," I sobbed. "All of it. If I hadn't—"

"Stop," he interrupted, his voice firm despite his weakened state. "This is not your fault."

"Anthony—"

"Patricia," he said, squeezing my hand with more strength than I expected. "You didn't ask for any of this. You didn't make James do what he did. This isn't on you."

I shook my head, tears streaming down my cheeks. "But if it weren't for me—"

"Then he'd have found some other excuse," Anthony said. "That's what people like him do. They don't need a reason. They create one."

His words hung in the air as I tried to absorb them. He was right, of course, but the guilt still lingered like a heavy weight on my chest. A knock on the door pulled me from my thoughts. Two uniformed officers stepped inside, their presence commanding but not intrusive.

"Mrs. Garcia?" one of them asked.

I blinked, caught off guard for a moment before nodding. "Not yet," I corrected softly. "But soon."

"We're here to get a statement about the incident," the other officer said, pulling out a notepad. "We're glad we got there in time."

"Yeah," I said, glancing at Anthony. "So are we."

The next hour was a blur of recounting the events, from the moment I heard the dogs barking to the terrifying confrontation in the dining room. Anthony chimed in where he could, his voice steady as he described his fight with James.

"You showed a lot of courage," one of the officers said as they finished up. "It's not easy to face someone like that."

"I didn't have a choice," I replied, my voice trembling. "It was him or us."

The officers nodded, offering reassurances before stepping out, leaving the room quiet again. I let out a shaky breath, my chest tightening with the weight of everything that had just happened. Relief mixed with exhaustion as I leaned back, trying to steady myself. Seconds later, the door opened, and the doctor walked in, clipboard in hand.

"The scans are clear," she said, her voice calm but firm. "You're a lucky guy," she added, glancing at Anthony, who was beginning to stir on the bed. "The wound was just inches away from your spleen. A few more inches, and the outcome could have been much worse."

Her words slammed into me like a freight train. Inches. Just inches. My mind reeled with the possibilities—how close we had come to a very different ending. If that knife had gone just a little deeper or at a different angle... My stomach churned at the thought. My legs suddenly felt weak, and I sank back into the chair, gripping the armrests to steady myself.

"We'd like to keep him for a couple of days for observation," the doctor continued, her tone gentle but professional. "Complications can sometimes arise with stab wounds, and we want to make sure nothing unexpected develops."

I nodded, unable to find the words to respond. My eyes darted to Anthony as his eyelids fluttered open, his gaze slowly focusing. Relief poured over me in waves as I saw him—groggy, pale, but alive. A sight I hadn't dared to let myself hope for in those harrowing moments earlier. As the doctor left the room, I moved to Anthony's bedside, grabbing his hand and holding it tightly as if letting go might somehow undo this fragile miracle. His eyes met mine, tired but warm, and a faint smile curved his lips.

"We finally got our proof" he teased, his lips twitching into a smirk despite his obvious discomfort.

"You're damn right we did," I replied, my voice thick with emotion. I couldn't help but let out a small, choked laugh, tears welling in my eyes.

As the night wore on, Anthony's color returned, and his strength seemed to grow with each passing hour. I stayed by his side, holding his hand and watching his chest rise and fall.

"Get some sleep," he urged softly, his thumb brushing over my knuckles.

"I'm not leaving you," I replied, my voice firm.

"I know," he said, a small smile tugging at his lips. "That's why I love you. But you need rest, too."

I leaned my head against the edge of the bed, the weight of the day finally catching up to me. Despite the chaos and fear, I felt a flicker of hope. Anthony was here, alive, and we were one step closer to putting James behind bars. The following morning, the familiar sound of small feet pattering down the hall brought a smile to my face. Anthony's mom had brought the kids to visit, and their arrival filled the sterile hospital room with an energy that was impossible to ignore.

"Daddy!" Christian exclaimed as he darted into the room, climbing up on Anthony's bed before anyone could stop him.

"Careful, Christian," Mia said, more cautious as she followed, but her smile betrayed how happy she was to see her dad awake and alert.

Anthony laughed, wincing slightly as he adjusted himself on the bed. "It's okay, buddy. I'm fine."

Christian wrapped his arms around Anthony, squeezing him tightly before looking up with wide eyes. "You scared us, Dad."

Anthony cupped his son's face gently. "I'm sorry, buddy. But I'm okay now, I promise."

Mia lingered near the bed, her expression a mix of happiness and worry. I reached out and pulled her into a hug. "He's going to be okay," I whispered.

"I know," she replied softly. "He always is."

Anthony's mom stood by the doorway, holding a bag that I knew was full of homemade food. "I brought you something to eat, mijo," she said, stepping inside. "You need real food, not this hospital nonsense."

"Thanks, Mom," Anthony said, his voice warm. "I was starting to think they were trying to starve me here."

The room erupted in laughter, the tension that had hung over us the past few days momentarily lifting. Seeing Anthony interact with his kids and mom reminded me just how much he meant to all of us. He wasn't just the glue that held this family together—he was the foundation. As the kids played quietly in the corner with a deck of cards Anthony's mom had brought, a knock on the door signaled the arrival of two detectives. Their serious expressions sobered the mood instantly, and I stepped out into the hallway with them to talk.

"Ms. Ramirez," one of them began, his tone professional but kind, "we wanted to give you an update on James. He's being held without bail and will remain in custody until his trial. The evidence from the incident, as well as the history we've gathered, makes him a significant threat. He won't be able to bother you or your family for the foreseeable future."

Relief flooded through me, though I knew this was just one step in a long process. "Thank you," I said quietly. "That's... that's good to hear."

The detective nodded. "You've been through a lot. If there's anything else you need, don't hesitate to reach out."

I returned to the room, my mind still processing the information. James was locked away, at least for now. Anthony must've sensed my mood when I stepped back inside because he tilted his head slightly, studying me. "What's the verdict?" he asked.

I offered a small smile, sitting back down beside him. "He's staying in custody until the trial."

"Good," Anthony said firmly, his hand reaching for mine. "That's one less thing to worry about."

I nodded, my fingers intertwining with his. For the first time in days, I felt like I could breathe. That evening, after Anthony's mom had taken the kids home, I sat beside his bed, watching him sleep. His steady breathing was a comforting sound, a reminder that he was still here. Feeling the weight of the past few hours pressing down on me, I decided to stretch my legs and take a walk. My steps were aimless at first, wandering the quiet hospital corridors until a small sign caught my eye: **Chapel** →. The arrow pointed toward a tucked-away hallway I'd never noticed before. It felt like the Universe was giving me a nudge, so I followed.

The hospital chapel was serene, a stark contrast to the bustling chaos of the floors above and below. Its wooden pews were simple, polished, and bathed in the soft glow of flickering candles. Stained-glass windows lined one wall, casting colorful patterns across the floor. The faint scent of wax and the quiet hum of silence wrapped around me, offering a kind of solace I didn't know I needed. I slipped inside, closing the door softly behind me, and found a seat near the middle. For a moment, I just sat there, letting the stillness settle over me. My hands rested in my lap as I stared at the unadorned cross at the front of the room, my thoughts swirling.

Anthony was stable. The doctors said the wound had missed his spleen by mere inches. If it hadn't... I shook the thought from my head. No use going down that road now. Still, the realization of how close I had come to losing him weighed heavy on my chest. I leaned forward, resting my elbows on my knees. "Hey, Universe," I began softly, my voice barely audible in the quiet. "I don't have my notebook with me, but I figured this situation called for a face-to-face with the big man upstairs."

I let out a shaky laugh, though there was no humor in it. "First off... Thank you. Thank you for keeping Anthony safe. I don't know what I'd do without him. He's everything to me."

The words caught in my throat, choking me as I tried to force them out. My breaths were shallow and unsteady, each one more ragged than the last. My hands trembled as they pressed together, my body leaning forward as if it might collapse under the weight of what I was feeling.

"But... why?" The question escaped in a broken, guttural whisper, my voice splintering under the strain. My chest tightened painfully, like a vice was squeezing the air out of me. "Why did all of this have to happen? What lesson am I supposed to be learning here? Why does it feel like the universe is punishing us? Why did Anthony have to suffer? Why couldn't it have been me?"

The last word shattered as I gasped for air, my vision blurring with tears that came faster than I could wipe them away. My entire body shook as sobs erupted from deep within, uncontrollable and raw. My chest ached so badly I thought I might be having a heart attack, the pain radiating up to my throat and making it hard to breathe. My knees buckled, and I slid off the pew onto the cold, hard floor, my body folding in on itself as the flood of emotions poured out.

"He doesn't deserve this," I choked out, my voice almost inaudible over the sound of my own cries. "He's good, and kind, and selfless, and strong. And me?" My hands clawed at the floor as I hunched over, my forehead nearly touching the ground. "I don't even deserve him. I don't deserve any of this."

My sobs turned into gasps, my body heaving uncontrollably as I fought to catch my breath. I pressed my hands to my chest, desperate to steady the erratic rhythm of my heart, but the panic had already taken hold. Each breath felt like I was trying to inhale through a straw, the overwhelming pain and despair coursing through me in waves.

"I can't—" I cried out, my voice breaking completely. "Please... please make it stop. Just let this be over. Let us have peace. I can't take it anymore. Please, I'm begging you."

The room seemed to spin as my body trembled violently, every muscle tight with the strain of holding everything inside for so long. My tears dripped onto the polished floor, puddling beneath me, but I couldn't stop. The sobs kept coming, pulling me under like a riptide, and for a moment, I thought I might drown in them. I stayed on the floor, clutching at my chest, my fingers digging into my skin as if I could physically claw the pain away. My cries echoed through the small chapel, bouncing off the walls and filling the air with a grief I couldn't contain.

"Please," I whispered hoarsely, my voice barely audible. "Please just let him be okay. Let us have peace. I don't need anything else. Just him. Please."

The silence of the chapel enveloped me like a heavy blanket, the only sound my ragged breathing and the faint hum of fluorescent lights above. Slowly, agonizingly, the storm inside me began to calm. My chest still ached, my body still trembled, but the tears slowed, leaving me drained and hollow. I stayed kneeling on the floor for a long time, my head bowed, my hands limp at my sides. When I finally sat back, leaning against the pew, my eyes were swollen and my throat raw, but after days of suffocating under the weight of it all, I could finally draw a shallow, steady breath.

| 28 |

A Warm Welcome

The jingle of keys at the front door made my heart leap, the sound pulling me out of my anxious thoughts. The door creaked open, and there he was—Anthony, standing tall, though the cane he leaned on served as a reminder of everything we'd just endured. His mother followed close behind, carrying a bag of clothes over her shoulder. She had insisted on being the one to bring him home, which worked perfectly. It gave us the time we needed to set up the house for his surprise.

Relief washed over me as I took him in. He looked worn—his steps slower, the lines on his face etched deeper—but his eyes were warm, filled with a familiar light that instantly made my chest ache with gratitude. He was here. He was home. That was all that mattered. The exhaustion in his features seemed to evaporate the moment he spotted the kids. Christian let out an excited shout, and Mia's face lit up as she rushed forward. Anthony's expression transformed, his entire face softening as though the mere sight of them had reignited a fire that had momentarily flickered out.

"Surprise!" Mia and Christian yelled, practically vibrating with excitement. Mia held up a handmade sign that said *Welcome Home, Dad!* in bright, messy letters, while Christian carried a huge bouquet of balloons that swayed with every step. Anthony's smile was soft, the kind of smile that made you feel like everything would be okay. "You guys are amazing. You didn't have to do all this," he said, his voice thick with emotion.

"Yes we did," Christian replied matter-of-factly. "We missed you."

Mia chimed in, "We worked really hard on all this!" She handed Anthony a scrapbook she'd been making—a collection of pictures, ticket stubs, and little drawings from family moments over the past year. "So you have something to look at while you're, you know, stuck on the couch."

Anthony chuckled, taking it from her carefully. "I love it, sweetheart. Thank you."

I stepped closer, wrapping an arm around his waist. "And now," I said, raising an eyebrow at him, "you get to sit down and relax while we take care of you for once."

He looked at me with mock suspicion. "You sure this isn't a trick?"

"Positive. Now sit," I said, playfully pushing him toward the couch.

The days that followed were an odd mix of peace and adjustment. Anthony wasn't one to sit still for long, so watching him fidget through his recovery was both endearing and frustrating.

"Anthony," I warned one evening as he tried to carry a laundry basket upstairs. "You're not supposed to be lifting anything heavier than a remote control."

He gave me a mischievous grin. "What if I carry it *really* slowly?"

I crossed my arms and blocked his path. "Put it down."

He laughed but gave in, setting the basket down. "Fine."

Freelance writing had become my new focus, and honestly, I was thriving. I treated it like a real job, complete with a set schedule. Three eight-hour days a week felt like the perfect balance—structured enough to keep me productive, yet flexible enough to be there for Anthony and the kids when they needed me. Writing gave me the life I always dreamed of—a life where I had a sense of purpose, but still had the freedom to prioritize my family above all else. It was a delicate balance, one I never quite managed to find while working in the medical field. As much as you want to put your family first, the harsh reality is that in healthcare, someone's life is always at stake. Patients come first. They have to.

Working in the OR was like living on a constant adrenaline rush. There's a unique rhythm to the chaos—a pulse that keeps you sharp, focused, and completely absorbed in the moment. You form bonds with your coworkers that are hard to describe. They become a second family, forged in the fire of life-or-death situations and long, grueling hours. You laugh together, cry together, and hold each other up through the toughest days. It's beautiful in its way, but what they don't tell you is that the reason you create a second family is because you're away from your first one so much.

There were days when I would leave before the kids woke up and return long after they'd gone to bed. Missed dinners, missed school plays, missed bedtime stories. I'd tell myself it was worth it because I was making a difference, saving lives. And while that's true, it doesn't make up for the missed moments—the ones you can never get back. I just couldn't imagine living the rest of my life that way. Then there's the emotional toll. You're expected to move seamlessly from one patient to the next, even when the outcome isn't what you hoped for. You're supposed to put aside your own feelings and focus on the task at hand. And you do, because that's the job. But those feelings don't just disappear. They follow you home, slipping into the quiet moments when you're supposed to be present with your family. Sometimes, they're so loud, they drown out everything else.

Writing changed that for me. It allowed me to slow down, to be fully present in a way I hadn't been able to in years. It didn't have the same adrenaline rush, but it gave me something even better: peace. Now, when Mia wanders into my office to ask about current projects, or Christian suggests new ideas based off of his favorite show, I'm there able to fully engage. I'm not distracted or rushing to get to the next task. I'm with them, in the moment, soaking it all in. The transition wasn't easy. Letting go of something that had been such a big part of my identity felt like losing a piece of myself. But what I gained was so much more. Writing has given me the ability to live the life I always wanted—a life where my family comes first, and I no longer have to choose between being present and pursuing my passion. For the first time, I have both. And it's everything.

One afternoon, as I typed away in my little writing corner, Mia wandered over, leaning against the desk with her curious eyes peering over my shoulder. "What are you working on?" she asked, tilting her head.

"Nothing too exciting," I replied, chuckling. "Just some tips to help average people like us manage stress."

From the doorway, Christian's voice chimed in, full of seriousness and conviction. "Write about superheroes!"

I paused dramatically, pretending to mull it over. "You know what? That's... actually not a bad idea. Should the first superhero be your dad?"

"Yeah!" Christian practically yelled, his entire face lighting up as if he'd just been handed the most exciting assignment of his life.

I laughed, grabbing a pen and scribbling down the idea with a playful wink. Both kids beamed, clearly proud of their contribution, as if they'd just unlocked a secret to success. These small moments filled me with a warmth I hadn't realized I'd been missing. It wasn't about the big, grand gestures; it was these tiny, everyday interactions that reminded me why I'd fought so hard for this family. They were my reason for everything, and for the first time in a long while, I felt like I was truly present to enjoy them.

Although life wasn't perfect, it was starting to feel normal again. James had been arrested and would remain in custody until the trial. Knowing he was behind bars brought a sense of relief that I hadn't felt in months. There was still the looming stress of court dates and testimonies, but for now, I could focus on my family without the constant shadow of fear. As I typed away at my desk, crafting stories and articles that felt like pieces of myself, I realized something. I wasn't just surviving anymore. I was rebuilding, reclaiming the parts of my life that had been stolen. Anthony had fully embraced being doted on during his recovery, and let me tell you, the man was *milking it.*

"You know, I could get used to this," he said one afternoon, lounging on the couch with a blanket draped over him like he was royalty. "You bring me snacks, fluff my pillows... I feel like a king."

I raised an eyebrow, hands on my hips. "A king who can't go two minutes without whining about needing more ice for his water?"

He grinned. "Hey, I'm injured. You're supposed to spoil me."

I couldn't help but laugh. "You big baby"

"Better than being a stubborn nurse," he quipped, sticking his tongue out at me.

"Oh, you're funny now," I shot back, grabbing a throw pillow and lightly smacking him with it. "Just wait until you're fully healed. I'll remember this."

The teasing was a constant in our home, a way to bring lightness to what had been a dark and heavy time. Even the kids got in on it, offering to "help Daddy recover" by stealing his snacks or "testing" his pain meds. We were finding joy in the little moments, and it felt good—*really* good. One evening, after the kids had gone to bed, I sat at my desk, reflecting on everything we'd been through. The trauma James had brought into our lives was still there, like a scar that would never fully fade. But it no longer consumed us. We were moving forward, together. I glanced over at An thony, who was scrolling through his phone on the couch. He caught my eye and smiled—a real, genuine smile that made my heart swell. We had come so far, and while the road had been brutal, it had also brought us closer in ways I never expected.

Later that night, once the house had gone quiet, I decided to surprise Anthony. It had been a while since we'd had any real intimacy, and I wanted to remind him just how much I appreciated everything he'd done—not just for me, but for our family. I stepped into the bedroom wearing a white button-up shirt—one of his favorites—paired with thigh-high stockings and a stethoscope around my neck. His head snapped up as soon as I entered the room.

"What's this?" he asked, his eyebrows lifting.

"Nurse Patricia reporting for duty," I said, my voice sultry as I closed the door behind me. "I heard someone needed some extra attention."

He smirked, leaning back against the pillows. "Oh, I definitely do. I think I pulled something earlier, reaching for the remote."

I laughed, climbing onto the bed and straddling his lap. "Well, I'm here to make sure you recover fully."

Sliding my hands up his chest, I kissed him slowly, letting my fingers trail down his torso. His breathing hitched as I began undoing the buttons on his shirt, one by one.

"What's the prognosis, Nurse?" he murmured, his voice low and teasing.

"You're definitely going to need some hands-on treatment," I replied, my hands slipping lower.

Without another word, I slid down the bed, trailing slow, deliberate kisses along his stomach. Each one left a small gasp on his lips, and by the time I reached the waistband of his sweatpants, I could feel his anticipation thrumming in the air between us. Tugging them down, I glanced up at him, locking eyes as I let my tongue dart out to wet my lips, my movements teasingly slow.

"Let me take care of you," I whispered, my voice low and dripping with intent.

The moment my lips wrapped around him, a sharp hiss escaped from between his teeth, followed by a low groan. I started slowly, my tongue tracing lazy circles around the sensitive head, tasting the faint saltiness of him. Each flick of my tongue sent a shiver through his body, his fingers flexing against the sheets. I alternated between long, languid licks along his length and soft, warm sucks at the tip, making sure to keep him guessing. A soft slurp filled the air as I drew him deeper, hollowing my cheeks and letting a low hum vibrate around him. His hips bucked slightly, and his hand found its way into my hair, not to guide me, but simply to anchor himself.

"Fuck," he gasped, barely letting the word come out. I could feel him pulsing against my tongue, the faint throb telling me exactly when I'd done something he liked.

Pausing, I let my tongue slide down to his balls, gently sucking one into my mouth and rolling it with care. He let out a guttural moan, his free hand gripping the blanket tightly. "Oh my God," he groaned, his voice low and rough. I smirked, licking a slow path back up his shaft, letting my lips leave wet, glistening trails along his skin. My hand joined the action, stroking him with a firm but smooth grip as I kissed my way back to the tip. Looking up at him through my lashes, I wrapped my lips around him again, my tongue flicking against the sensitive underside of his head. His eyes locked with mine, the intensity making the heat pool low in my belly.

Each movement became more deliberate as I picked up the pace—fast, slow, deep, shallow. I wanted to feel him unravel. I wanted to hear him lose control. I took him deeper, my throat tightening briefly around him before pulling back with an audible pop. His breathing hitched, and I could see the tension coiling in his body, his abs tightening as he struggled to hold on.

"Patricia," he panted, his voice barely above a whisper. I could feel him nearing the edge, his grip in my hair tightening slightly as his hips began to move with me.

Not yet. I slowed down, dragging my tongue along his shaft with excruciating precision, pausing to flick the tip while my hand stroked him with a twisting motion. His groan turned into a low, desperate growl.

"Please," he whispered, the strain in his voice clear.

I took him in again, deeper this time, until my nose brushed against his skin. The wet, lewd sounds filled the room, accompanied by his ragged breaths. When I felt him twitch, I knew he was seconds away. I doubled my efforts, stroking him with my hand while my lips and tongue worked together. With a guttural cry, he came, hot and salty against my tongue. I swallowed without hesitation, letting a bit spill out and trail down his length. Slowly, I licked him clean, savoring every moment of his shuddering breaths and the way his body finally relaxed beneath me.

As I moved back up, he pulled me into his arms, his fingers brushing hair out of my face. "You're too good at that," he murmured, his voice low and sated.

I smirked, brushing a kiss against his jaw. "It's my duty as your fiancée...and your nurse."

His laugh rumbled against my cheek, warm and full of satisfaction. "I feel much better now. Remind me to thank you properly later."

"I'll hold you to that," I teased, snuggling into his chest.

| 29 |

All In

L ife was finally starting to feel normal again—or as close to normal as it could be after everything we'd been through. The echoes of chaos were fading, leaving room for something we hadn't dared to consider in a long time: the future. Over dinner one evening, Anthony cleared his throat dramatically. I raised an eyebrow, suspicious of whatever was coming next.

"So," he began, his voice taking on that faux-serious tone he used when he was about to say something ridiculous. "I've been thinking..."

"That's always dangerous," I teased, spearing a roasted potato with my fork.

He ignored the jab, leaning back in his chair with a smug grin. "Periwinkle roses?"

I froze mid-chew, glaring at him as he burst into laughter. "Not funny," I deadpanned, pointing my fork at him.

"Come on, you have to admit—"

"No. Absolutely not. Try again."

The nerve. The *nerve* of him to even joke about periwinkle roses after everything. As if that disaster of a conversation hadn't been one of the most mortifying moments of my life. Sure, I was glad that he could joke about it now—his laughter was one of my favorite sounds, after all—but I was not there yet. Not even close. Growth, healing, forgiveness? Yeah, I was working on all that. But laughing about periwinkle roses? That was a level of enlightenment I hadn't reached. I stabbed another potato with just a little more force than necessary, shooting him a pointed look. His smug grin only widened, as if he could see the inner monologue playing out in my head. "You're lucky I love you," I muttered, shaking my head.

"And you're lucky I'm funny," he shot back, still chuckling.

"Debatable," I replied, but even as I rolled my eyes, I couldn't stop the small smile tugging at the corner of my lips. Damn him and his ridiculous jokes.

He chuckled, reaching across the table to squeeze my hand. "Okay, no periwinkle roses. But seriously, I think we should start planning again."

The smile I'd been trying to suppress finally broke through. "You really want to dive back into all of that?"

"Why not?" he asked, shrugging. "We've been through hell and back. We deserve to celebrate."

I couldn't argue with that. For the first time in forever, the idea of planning a wedding didn't feel overwhelming or overshadowed by fear. It felt... hopeful.

"Alright," I said, setting my fork down and leaning forward. "No periwinkle roses. But I'm open to ideas."

He grinned, clearly pleased with himself. "How about a date? June 26, 2026. 6/26/26. Easy to remember, right?"

I rolled my eyes but couldn't help laughing. "You just want an excuse to have a date you'll never forget."

"Exactly," he said, unashamed. "So, what do you think?"

"I think it's perfect," I said softly, feeling a flicker of excitement spark to life.

As we brainstormed over dinner, the pieces started falling into place. I leaned back in my chair, an idea forming in my mind.

"Do you remember the first time we ever hung out outside of work?" I asked, a playful smile tugging at my lips.

Anthony tilted his head, thinking for a moment before grinning. "Yeah. We went to the casino at like 9AM. after our overnight shift. That was a terrible idea."

"Terrible?" I laughed. "I think it was great. We spent half our paycheck on penny slots and ate those questionable breakfast burritos. We even ran into one of my friends, remember? That was weird. So maybe the drive back home was terrible because we were so tired but the day itself was great." I ranted.

He chuckled, shaking his head. "Okay, fine. It was fun. Exhausting, but fun."

"What if we make that the theme of our wedding?" I asked, sitting up straighter.

Anthony frowned in confusion. "What?"

I leaned in, excitement bubbling in my voice. "We put all our chips in on each other. A Las Vegas theme—red, white, and black. It's symbolic. It represents the risk we took on each other, the gamble of falling in love."

His expression shifted as the idea clicked. "That's... actually perfect. It's us. It's fun, it's bold, it's meaningful, it's weird, I like it."

"It is," I agreed, already imagining how the colors and theme would come together. "And it's something that's ours—completely unique and has a special meaning behind it."

Anthony reached across the table, grabbing my hand. "Alright. Let's do it. Vegas without the plane tickets."

We laughed as we started throwing out ideas: custom poker chips as wedding favors, a blackjack table for the reception, a dessert bar styled like a casino buffet. Each detail felt like a celebration of not just our love, but everything we'd endured to get to this point. It was like we risked it all and hit the jackpot.

As the conversation about wedding plans carried on, I felt an odd mixture of emotions—joy for what lay ahead and a lingering tension I couldn't quite shake. While the thought of a Vegas-themed wedding filled with laughter and love was thrilling, it was hard to ignore the weight of everything else looming over us. Every joke about poker chips and desserts seemed to coexist with an unspoken undercurrent of dread.

It was inescapable. No matter how much fun we had planning our future, the reality of the looming trial crept back into focus like a dark cloud on the horizon. No matter how much progress we'd made as a family, or how much I tried to shift my energy toward the future, the upcoming court date demanded my attention.

The night before our meeting with the new lawyer, Anthony and I sat on the couch after tucking the kids into bed. The television played in the background, but neither of us was paying attention. My legs were draped over his lap as I fiddled with my phone, scrolling aimlessly.

"So, tomorrow's the big day," Anthony said, breaking the silence.

"Yeah," I sighed, setting my phone down. "Elise Carter. She's supposed to be the best, right?"

"Damn straight," he replied with a small smile. "She'll help us get through this, take all the weight off your shoulders. One step closer to walking down the aisle in peace."

I smiled at that, but the anxiety still lingered. "What if it's not enough?"

Anthony reached for my hand, lacing his fingers with mine. "It will be. We've done everything right—statements, evidence, working with the investigator. This meeting is just the next step. And if Elise Carter is half as tough as her reputation, she's not going to let anything slide."

His confidence helped, even if only a little. I nodded and leaned against him, letting myself imagine, just for a moment, what life might look like after all of this was behind us.

The next morning, the drive to Elise's office felt like heading into battle. Anthony drove while I stared out the window, the city blurring past as I replayed everything in my mind—the evidence, the testimony, the sheer weight of what was coming.

"You okay?" Anthony asked, glancing over at me during a stoplight.

"Yeah," I said, offering him a faint smile. "Just... ready to get this part over with."

"Same here," he said, squeezing my hand briefly before turning his focus back to the road.

We pulled into the lot and walked into Elise Carter's building. The air-conditioned lobby was quiet, and the receptionist greeted us warmly before showing us to her office.

Anthony and I sat across from Elise Carter, whose reputation for handling high-stakes cases was unmatched. Her office reflected her sharp personality—sleek, modern furniture, files meticulously organized, and a coffee mug on her desk that read "I object!" It was oddly comforting, like she could bulldoze through anything in our path.

"Thank you both for coming," Elise began, her gaze shifting between us. "This is an important step in preparing for trial. Since both of you are victims, we'll be focusing on coordinating your testimonies while ensuring you're ready for cross-examination."

She slid two identical folders across the desk, one for each of us. "Inside, you'll find the evidence we're presenting—witness statements, the timeline of events, photos, and your own recorded accounts. I need you to review these thoroughly."

I opened my folder, and the sight of James's name staring back at me felt like a punch to the gut. Anthony leaned back in his chair, his face stoic but his jaw tight. I knew he was struggling to keep his emotions in check.

"Patricia, we'll start with you," Elise continued, flipping through her notes. "We'll rehearse your testimony today.

The defense will likely attempt to paint this as a situation you could have avoided, so we need to be clear and direct about your experience. The truth is your strongest weapon."

I nodded, trying to push down the lump forming in my throat. Elise fired off a series of rapid questions, each one designed to simulate the grilling I'd face on the stand.

"What did James say to you that night?"

"How did you feel when you saw him with the knife?"

"Why didn't you report his behavior to the police sooner?"

Each question cut like a knife, dredging up memories I'd been trying to bury. Anthony's hand brushed mine under the table, his silent way of grounding me. By the end of my session, I felt raw but slightly more prepared.

"You did well," Elise said, her tone reassuring but firm. "Now, Anthony, let's shift to you. Your perspective as both a victim and witness is critical to this case."

Anthony straightened in his seat, exhaling deeply. "Alright, let's do it."

Elise started with the basics, asking him to recount the events of that night. His responses were clear and measured, but when she pressed him to describe how he felt in the moment James attacked him, his voice faltered for the first time.

"I thought I was going to die," he admitted, his eyes fixed on the table. "When I saw the knife coming at me... all I could think about were the kids. Mia and Christian. I kept picturing their faces, and it hit me—I might not get to see them grow up. I might not be there for their first heartbreaks, their graduations, or their weddings."

My chest tightened as I listened to him, tears welling in my eyes. He had always been so strong, so steady, and hearing him speak with such vulnerability broke something in me.

"And Patricia," he continued, his voice cracking slightly. "I kept thinking about how she'd blame herself. How she'd carry the weight of this forever, even though it wasn't her fault."

I reached over and grabbed his hand, squeezing it tightly. "Stop," I whispered, my voice trembling. "Don't do this to yourself."

Elise allowed the silence to linger for a moment before speaking. "Anthony, that honesty—that raw emotion—is exactly what the jury needs to hear. Your testimony isn't just about recounting events; it's about showing them the impact James's actions have had on your lives."

Anthony nodded, taking another deep breath. "I'll do whatever it takes."

As we wrapped up the session, Elise gave us both encouraging smiles. "You're both stronger than you realize. This trial will be difficult, but it's also your chance to take back control."

On the way home, the weight of the day hung between us. Anthony broke the silence first.

"You okay?" he asked, glancing over at me as he drove.

"I hate this," I admitted. "I hate seeing you like this. I hate that we even have to go through it."

"I know," he said, his voice soft. "But we're going to get through it. Together."

His words, as always, were a lifeline. And while I couldn't shake the fear of what the trial might bring, I clung to the hope that this would finally be the end of James's grip on our lives.

That evening, Anthony found me sitting at the kitchen table, staring blankly at the stack of notes Elise had given me.

"Hey," he said, placing a mug of tea in front of me. "You okay?"

I sighed, rubbing my temples. "Just... overwhelmed."

Anthony pulled out a chair and sat down across from me. "Look, I know this is hard. And I know you're scared. But you've already survived the worst of it. This trial? It's just the final step to putting it all behind us."

"I don't know if I can do this. How will I be up there and say everything while he just stares at me with a dumbass smirk on his face? He's going to try to trigger us and we're supposed to just act like he doesn't exist and tell our story?" I admitted, my voice barely above a whisper.

"You can and you will," he said firmly, reaching across the table to take my hand. "You've been ready since the moment you decided not to let him control your life anymore years ago. This is just the last step. He will try to trigger you but you're not doing this alone. *We* are sending his ass to jail."

His words brought tears to my eyes and gave me the confidence boost I needed.

Despite Anthony's reassurances, a quiet tension lingered in the days leading up to the trial. I couldn't shake the nagging fear of being in the same room as James again, of having to relive every terrifying moment in front of a courtroom full of strangers. Late one night, as I lay in bed staring at the ceiling, I found myself whispering to the universe once more.

"Please let this be the end," I sighed. "Let us finally have the peace we deserve."

Though the thought of the trial loomed like a storm on the horizon, I reminded myself that storms eventually pass. This was just one more hurdle to clear before I could fully reclaim my life. And with Anthony by my side, I knew I could face whatever was coming.

| 30 |

The Testimony

The courtroom felt colder than it should have, the sterile air chilling my skin as I sat in the witness chair. My hands gripped the edges of the wooden armrests, knuckles white, as I glanced at the faces around me. Anthony sat in the gallery, his gaze unwavering, his presence a silent reassurance. The judge called the room to order, and my lawyer, Elise Carter, approached with her usual calm authority. She gave me a brief nod, signaling that it was time. Taking a deep breath, I straightened my posture and faced the courtroom.

"Patricia," Elise began, her tone gentle but firm, "can you please recount the events that led to this trial?"

I swallowed hard, my voice trembling as I started. "It began with small things—texts, friend requests on social media. At first, I ignored them, thinking he would eventually give up. But he didn't."

I paused, gathering the strength to continue. "Then he started leaving flowers at my door. At first, it was just a bouquet, but the colors... they were the exact ones I told him I wanted for a wedding we never had. Then there were notes left on my car at work, at home, and even at the grocery store. It was like he always knew where I was."

Elise nodded encouragingly. "What did you do to address this behavior?"

"I tried to resolve things peacefully," I said, my voice firmer now. "I agreed to meet him at a diner to hear him out and put an end to it. I thought... maybe if he could say what he needed to say, it would stop." I took a shaky breath. "It didn't stop. It got worse."

The memories came flooding back—the vandalized mailbox, the late-night sirens that startled me awake, the feeling of being watched everywhere I went. "He sent teenagers to vandalize my mailbox. He called my work pretending to be my uncle, trying to get information about me. I couldn't escape him. I couldn't even feel safe in my own home."

My voice cracked as I continued, "and It wasn't just me anymore. It was Anthony, the kids, our whole family. He put us all in danger. Living like that... it wasn't living. It was surviving, every single day."

Elise placed a hand on the corner of the stand, her presence steadying me. "And how has this affected you personally, Patricia?"

I hesitated but knew this was my chance to speak my truth. "It's taken everything from me. I'm in therapy now, trying to process the trauma and rebuild some sense of security, but it's hard. I jump at every noise. I check the cameras constantly. I feel like I'm always waiting for something bad to happen. It's exhausting."

Tears blurred my vision as I looked toward Anthony and the kids sitting quietly behind him. "They're the only reason I've been able to keep going. Anthony and the kids—they've been my anchors, my strength."

Elise's voice softened. "Thank you, Patricia." She turned to the judge. "Your Honor, I'd like to present evidence gathered by a private investigator, showing Mr. Sterling's premeditated actions."

She clicked a remote, and the screen at the front of the courtroom displayed a list of purchases—burner phones, surveillance equipment, weapons. My stomach churned as Elise highlighted each item.

"Ladies and gentlemen of the jury," Elise said, addressing them directly, "this isn't just a case of obsession. This is premeditation. These purchases were made with the intent to terrorize and harm my client and her family. James planned this."

The defense attorney stood next, his expression neutral as he approached the stand. "Miss Ramirez," he said, his voice smooth, "Would you agree that meeting Mr. Sterling at the diner could be seen as leading him on? Perhaps giving him false hope?"

I bristled but held my ground. "No," I said firmly. "I met with him to give him closure. To make it clear that there was no future between us. I wanted peace, not this."

The attorney didn't flinch. "You said you didn't involve the police right away. Why not?"

I glanced at Elise, who gave a subtle nod. Turning back to the attorney, I answered, "Because I didn't think it would get this bad. I didn't think he would go this far. I was wrong."

The attorney shifted his weight, readying another question, but Elise objected, her tone sharp. "Your Honor, this line of questioning serves no purpose other than to victim-blame."

"Objection sustained," the judge said, and the defense attorney retreated with a small, calculated smile.

Anthony's name was called next, and he walked to the stand with a quiet determination. As he settled into the chair, Elise began. "Anthony, can you tell us what happened the night of the attack?"

He took a deep breath, his eyes briefly meeting mine before he spoke. "It was late. We were asleep, and the dogs started barking. That's when Patricia saw him—James—standing in the dining room. He had a knife."

His voice tightened as he continued. "I ran down with a bat. I didn't think. I just acted. My only thought was to protect Patricia and the kids. But then..." He paused, his jaw clenching. "He stabbed me. Right in front of her."

Elise nodded, her voice steady. "What went through your mind at that moment?"

Anthony hesitated, his voice dropping. "I thought I was going to die. I thought about my kids—how I might not see them grow up, how they might not have a father anymore. And Patricia... I kept thinking about her. About how she'd blame herself for all of this."

My heart ached as I listened, tears slipping down my cheeks. Anthony's strength had always been my rock, but hearing the depth of his fear broke something inside me.

Elise gave him a moment before continuing. "Anthony, how has this affected your family?"

"It's changed everything," he said, his voice steady but laced with emotion. "Our lives have revolved around fear. Fear of what he might do next, fear of letting our guard down. But we've fought through it because that's what we do. We fight, and we protect what matters."

He glanced at me again, his eyes filled with quiet resolve. "And we'll keep fighting if we have to. Together."

The courtroom was silent as Elise finished questioning Anthony. The defense attorney, a sharp-dressed man with an overly polished demeanor, adjusted his tie as he approached Anthony on the stand. His tone was calm but calculated, each word dripping with an intent to undermine the gravity of what had happened.

"Mr. Garcia," he began, his voice smooth, "I understand that you and Miss Ramirez recently got engaged. Congratulations."

Anthony nodded, his face impassive. "Thank you."

The attorney tilted his head, a faint smirk playing at the corners of his mouth. "But tell me, Mr. Garcia, how can you claim that this situation has brought such emotional distress to your lives when you're actively planning a wedding? Doesn't that suggest you're both moving on quite easily?"

I tensed in my seat, anger bubbling just below the surface. Anthony, however, remained composed. He leaned forward slightly, his tone firm but calm.

"James kept us stuck for so long," Anthony replied, his eyes locking with the attorney's. "The wedding is one thing we could actually look forward to. We are not pretending everything's fine or ignoring what happened in the slightest bit. We are trying to move forward in a healthy way. Trying to hold on to something to keep us sane. It's a way to remind ourselves that his actions don't define our lives."

The attorney blinked, clearly unprepared for Anthony's straightforward response. "So, you're saying the wedding is more about... coping?"

"It's about healing," Anthony corrected. "It's about re-claiming our lives and showing our kids that love and hope can still exist even after everything we've been through. If you want to paint that as a weakness, go ahead, but I see it as strength."

Whispers rippled through the courtroom, the jury ex-changing subtle glances as Anthony's words hung in the air. Even the judge seemed to take a moment to absorb his response. The defense attorney faltered briefly but quickly composed himself. "Thank you for your answer, Mr. Garcia. No further questions."

Anthony stepped down from the stand, his movements steady and purposeful as he returned to his seat beside me. I reached for his hand, squeezing it tightly. He didn't look at me, but I could see the tension in his jaw easing slightly.

"Perfect answer," I whispered, leaning closer to him.

He smirked, finally glancing my way. "You didn't think I'd let him win, did you?"

I squeezed his hand again, a small smile breaking through the storm of emotions swirling inside me.

| 31 |

The Defense

James sat on the stand, and I couldn't believe the show he was putting on. His face was painted with a mix of remorse and defiance, as though he were the one who had been wronged. He let out this dramatic sigh, like he was carrying some great burden, and started speaking in this shaky voice that almost sounded sincere. Almost.

"I never meant to hurt anyone," he said. His voice cracked for effect, but all I felt was anger. "I was desperate. I just wanted a chance to talk, to explain myself. That's all."

I couldn't stop my fists from clenching in my lap. My nails bit into my palms as I glanced at Anthony. He looked as stunned as I felt, his jaw tightening with every word James spewed. James's attorney stepped up, all polished and smug. "Mr. Sterling, the prosecution claims that you purchased surveillance equipment, burner phones, and even a weapon as part of some... sinister plan. How do you respond to that?"

James nodded solemnly, playing his part perfectly. "I bought those things because I was afraid for my safety," he said, glancing in Anthony's direction. "He hired a private investigator to dig into my life. It felt like *he* was obsessed with me. I didn't know what he was capable of, so I took precautions."

The audacity of it all nearly made me lose it. I bit the inside of my cheek to keep myself from yelling. Anthony, sitting next to me, tensed even more. I could practically feel the anger radiating off him. Elise must've sensed our reactions, because she gave us a quick glance and shook her head, silently reminding us to stay calm. Easier said than done. Their attorney kept going, twisting everything like a master manipulator. "So, you're saying that these actions—actions the prosecution calls calculated—were in fact just self-preservation?"

"Yes," James replied, his voice dripping with fake sincerity. "I was scared. I didn't know what else to do. I felt cornered."

I couldn't believe what I was hearing. It was like he was living in an alternate reality where he wasn't the one stalking us, breaking into our home, and stabbing Anthony. My hands started shaking, and I focused on breathing, trying to keep my composure. This was exactly what Elise had warned me about. When the defense finally rested, Elise stood up with a confidence that instantly steadied me. She walked to the center of the courtroom, her heels clicking against the floor, and turned to face the jury.

"Ladies and gentlemen of the jury," she began, her voice calm but commanding, "what you've just witnessed is an attempt to rewrite reality. James wants you to believe that he's the victim here—that his actions were driven by fear and desperation. But let's examine the facts."

Her words hung in the air, sharp and deliberate. She didn't need theatrics; the truth was powerful enough on its own.

"This man was warned," she said, her voice growing stronger. "He was told—repeatedly—to stay away. There was a restraining order in place, a clear legal boundary, and yet he chose to cross it. He didn't just show up uninvited; he entered their home armed with a deadly weapon. That's not desperation. That's premeditation."

Elise gestured to the evidence table, where all the damning proof sat in plain sight. "You've seen the receipts, the surveillance footage, the private investigator's findings. These are not the actions of a man trying to protect himself. These are the actions of a man determined to control, intimidate, and harm."

My chest tightened as she spoke, every word cutting through the lies James had tried to spin.

"Desperation is one thing," Elise continued, her voice unwavering. "But planning? Calculating? Continuing to escalate even after being told to stop? That's not innocence. That's guilt. And that's exactly what James is—guilty."

She turned to the jury, her expression softer but no less resolute. "Patricia and Anthony have been living in fear. Their sense of safety was stolen by this man's deliberate choices. It's time to send a clear message: this ends here."

She walked back to her seat, her head held high, and I let out a shaky breath I hadn't realized I was holding. I reached for Anthony's hand, gripping it tightly. Whatever happened next, I knew we had done everything we could to fight for our lives and reclaim our peace.

| 32 |

The Verdict

"We will take an intermission while the jury concludes a verdict."

The judge's words hung in the air, reverberating in my mind like an echo in an empty cavern. As the jury filed out of the courtroom, Anthony and I were ushered into a waiting room with Elise. The small, sterile space felt suffocating, its white walls closing in as my mind raced with a thousand what-ifs. What if our statements weren't convincing enough? What if we didn't come across as sincere or were seen as too emotional? Could our engagement—our attempt to find joy amidst chaos—be misconstrued as us moving on too easily, as if what James had done hadn't left lasting scars? My thoughts spiraled, each one making my chest feel tighter and my breathing more shallow. Anthony sat next to me, unusually quiet. His fingers were interlocked and resting against his chin, his leg bouncing slightly—a telltale sign of his nerves. Anthony rarely showed his anxiety; he was always the calm in the storm, the steady rock I leaned on. But now, even he seemed unmoored. Elise, ever composed, offered a reassuring smile. "The evidence speaks for itself," she said softly, her voice calm and steady. "Take a moment, both of you. The verdict will come soon enough."

I nodded, though her words felt like a faint comfort against the roar of my inner fears. Anthony glanced at me, his eyes meeting mine briefly before returning to the floor. The silence between us wasn't strained, but it was heavy—weighted down by everything we'd already said and everything we feared we'd hear. We decided to step out for lunch, though calling it "lunch" felt almost comical. Food was the last thing on my mind, but the thought of sitting still in that waiting room for another minute made my skin crawl. We walked to a small diner just down the block from the courthouse, the cold air biting at my cheeks and hands.

Once inside, we slid into a booth near the back, away from the few other patrons. A waitress brought over menus, but I barely glanced at mine before ordering something simple—whatever would come out the fastest. Anthony did the same. When the food arrived, we ate quickly, almost robotically. The hunger we didn't realize we had collided with the nerves knotting in our stomachs, creating an odd urgency. We didn't talk. Not about James, the trial, or even the kids. The silence wasn't awkward, but it was thick, like the weight of everything we were carrying had muted us. Halfway through the meal, Anthony reached across the table and squeezed my hand. His touch was warm, grounding, and I glanced up at him. He gave me a small smile—not forced, but faint, like it was all he could muster. I squeezed back, hoping he could feel how much his presence meant to me, how much I needed him to keep holding on just a little longer.

The buzzing of my phone shattered the stillness between us. I snatched it up, my heart hammering as I saw Elise's name flash across the screen. "They've reached a verdict," she said simply. "Report back to the courtroom."

My stomach dropped like a stone. I nodded, swallowing hard as I looked at Anthony. "It's time," I whispered.

He nodded back, sliding out of the booth and offering me his hand. I took it, and together, we walked back toward the courthouse, the weight of the moment pressing down on us with each step. The next few minutes were a blur. The cold air nipped at my skin as we walked, but I barely felt it. My thoughts churned: Would this finally be the closure we needed? Would justice be served, or would James find some way to wriggle free, as he always seemed to do? As we stepped into the courthouse and walked toward the courtroom doors, Anthony stopped and pulled me close. "No matter what happens in there," he said softly, his hand resting on the back of my neck, "we're going to be okay. You hear me? We're okay."

I nodded, unable to speak, and he kissed my forehead before we entered the room. It was time. The courtroom felt colder than before, the air thick with tension. I clung to Anthony's hand as the jury filed in, their faces unreadable. My pulse pounded in my ears as the foreperson stood, holding the verdict in their hands.

"In the matter of State vs. James Sterling, we find the defendant guilty on all charges: stalking, harassment, breaking and entering, and assault."

The words hit me like a wave. Relief, disbelief, sadness—they all came crashing in at once. James barely flinched as the verdict was read, his face a mask of indifference. I couldn't tell if he was in shock or if he truly felt nothing.

The judge's voice cut through the room. "James Sterling is hereby sentenced to 15 years in prison without the possibility of bail."

Fifteen years. The number echoed in my mind. It wasn't forever, but it was enough. Enough time for us to rebuild, to heal, to finally live without looking over our shoulders.

I glanced at Anthony, who gave me a faint, reassuring smile. His grip on my hand tightened as if to say, *We're okay now.*

As we walked out of the courthouse, the weight on my chest began to lift. The cold air hit my face, and I paused, inhaling deeply. For the first time in what felt like months, I could breathe without the heaviness of fear pressing down on me.

"And that's our story," I whispered, my breath visible in the crisp air. Saying it aloud felt like closing a chapter of my life that had been written in chaos and pain.

Anthony stopped, turning to me with a small smile. "No, babe," he said, his voice warm and steady. "This is our beginning."

ONE YEAR LATER

O*6/26/26*

Dear Universe,

Holy shit. We finally made it.

I can't believe I'm writing this right now. Today is my wedding day. My actual wedding day. You know, the thing I used to daydream about while simultaneously convincing myself I'd be eating ice cream alone forever? Well, Universe, jokes on me, because here I am. Dressed in white, about to walk down the aisle—I finally got my Prince Charming.

Let's take a moment to reflect, shall we? Because, wow, what a wild ride this has been. Honestly, I feel like I deserve a medal. Forget the "Bride of the Year" title—I want something shiny for surviving stalkers, restraining orders, courtrooms, and enough emotional whiplash to last a lifetime. With James behind bars, life feels... possible again. And not just the "barely scraping by" kind of possible, but the "I can actually breathe" kind. The weight is gone. The shadows have lifted. And I'm finally standing here, not just surviving but thriving. If I could've seen myself a year ago, I wouldn't have believed it. But enough about him.

Let's focus on the real MVP here—Anthony. This man is something else. My partner, my best friend, my rock, and the only person who can put up with my sarcasm 24/7 without filing a complaint. He's been my light through the darkest times, and now, he's my forever. I mean, let's be real, Universe, how many people get to say, "Yeah, my fi-

ancé fought off a literal psychopath for me and still proposed"? Not many.

Also, let's talk about this wedding for a second. I swore I wasn't going to cry today, but the second I saw the cake (yes, I said the cake), it was game over. Anthony suggested we get matching dice for the cake topper as a nod to the casino where we had our first real hangout—and because, apparently, we've been gambling on each other ever since. Romantic and slightly risky? That's so us.

Now, about this book I'm writing. Yep, I'm officially doing it. Because if my life has taught me anything, it's that the craziest stories make for the best material. It's not just about what happened, though—it's about the lessons. Mental health, self-love, resilience... all the stuff people say but don't really talk about. This is my chance to put it all out there, to remind people that even when life feels like a dumpster fire, you can still rise from the ashes. (And look fabulous while doing it, by the way.)

But today? Today is about celebration. About love, family, and the fact that we didn't just survive—we freaking thrived. Anthony likes to joke that I saved him, but the truth is, we saved each other. Definitely him more than me, I must admit. Together, we turned chaos into something beautiful. So, Universe, thank you. Thank you for every challenge, every heartbreak, and every tiny miracle along the way. Because somehow, all those twists and turns led me here—to the happiest day of my life.

Over and out,
Patricia

| 33 |

Mrs. Garcia

The day was here. The day I once thought was only a pipe dream, tucked away behind the chaos and challenges of life. But as I stood there in my white gown, the sunlight filtering through the trees, catching the gentle ripples of the water behind me, it felt surreal. The ceremony was set in a whimsical outdoor paradise, surrounded by greenery and overlooking the water. White chairs were arranged in perfect rows, their edges adorned with garlands of eucalyptus and tiny fairy lights. The timing couldn't have been more perfect—the ceremony was planned so that the sunset would cast a golden glow over everything as we said our vows. Mia stood beside me as my maid of honor, radiating confidence in her elegant dress that matched the deep red accents of the decor. She carried herself like she'd been preparing for this role her entire life, and honestly, she probably had. Christian, on the other hand, was determined to be the most responsible ring carrier ever. He walked down the aisle with a level of focus and determination that made the guests chuckle.

Anthony, waiting for me at the altar, looked so effort-lessly handsome in his black suit, the crisp lines of the jacket complemented by the single white rose pinned to his lapel. When our eyes locked, my breath hitched. His face lit up with a smile so warm it could have melted glaciers. As if we were the only two people in the world, he mouthed, "You're stunning." The simple gesture sent heat rushing to my cheeks, despite the cool breeze swirling around us. I couldn't help but let my gaze drift briefly to his mother, seated in the front row, her face glowing with pride. The real MVP, the queen who had every reason to tell her son to run for the hills years ago, had stood by our side through everything. Anthony's unwavering support might have held me up, but it was her quiet strength that gave me the confi-dence to believe I deserved it. As the music swelled, I walked down the aisle with my arm wrapped tightly around my fa-ther's. His steps were steady but slow, and when I glanced at him, I saw tears pooling in his eyes. My heart squeezed at the sight—it wasn't often I saw my father emotional, but this moment seemed to crack open something deep inside him.

"Who here wishes to give Patricia to Anthony?" the offi-ciant's voice echoed gently.

With a deep breath, my father answered, his voice thick with emotion. "I do."

He stopped just before the altar, turning to Anthony with a nod of approval that said more than words ever could. Anthony, ever the man of quiet strength, returned the gesture, his expression full of assurance. In that ex-change, they seemed to say everything: I'll take care of her.

You're making the right choice. My father leaned in, giving me a brief kiss on the forehead before stepping aside. He turned to Anthony's mother, offering her a warm smile as he joined my mother in the front row. Anthony's mom returned the gesture with a slight nod, her eyes darting toward us with a mixture of pride and, perhaps, just a hint of nervousness. This was her son, after all, and he was making one of the most important commitments of his life.

Their shared glance felt like a silent acknowledgment between parents—relief, pride, and maybe a touch of *Finally, they made it.*

When it was time to say our vows, I barely made it through without breaking down entirely. My voice wavered as I spoke, the weight of every word settling deep in my chest. Anthony, my steady rock, held my hands tightly, but for the first time, he wasn't the calm, composed man I was used to. His eyes glistened with unshed tears, and as I finished my vows, a single tear slipped down his cheek. When it was his turn, his voice trembled, and for a moment, he paused, swallowing hard as the emotions overtook him. "I told myself I wouldn't cry," he said with a shaky laugh, causing a soft ripple of chuckles from the guests. But as he continued, his voice broke slightly. He spoke about how we'd fought for this moment, how every obstacle had tested us but only made us stronger.

"I'm standing here because of you," he said, his gaze locked on mine. "Because no matter how hard it got, you never gave up on us. And I promise, I'll never give up on us either."

By the time he finished, there wasn't a dry eye in the crowd—including mine. I squeezed his hands tighter, silently thanking the universe for the man standing in front of me.

The reception was a dazzling shift from the dreamy serenity of the ceremony. Inside, bold and lavish decor brought the Vegas theme to life with striking reds, whites, and blacks. Chandeliers shimmered overhead, casting a warm glow over tables adorned with crisp linens and playful casino-themed centerpieces featuring lush arrangements of red roses. The transformation from the whimsical, ethereal outdoor ceremony to this vibrant and lively setting made guests feel as if they'd stepped into another world. It was the perfect blend of both of us—romantic yet daring, serene yet bold—capturing the essence of our journey together.

Anthony and I walked in as newlyweds to thunderous applause, but the real show began with the dances. Anthony's mother-son dance was a tearjerker. They swayed to Boyz II Men's *Mama,* and there wasn't a dry eye in the house. The way she looked at him, pride and love etched into her face, made me fall in love with him all over again. Then it was my turn. My father, beaming with pride, took my hand for our father-daughter dance. Marc Anthony's *My Baby You* filled the room, and as we swayed, I could feel years of emotion welling up. And, of course, we couldn't resist adding a little fun. Anthony and I, along with Mia and Christian, surprised everyone with a family dance to *We Are Family.* It was a burst of joy and energy that had the crowd clapping along and laughing. Seeing the kids so happy, so carefree—it was everything I'd ever wanted for them, for us.

The night was filled with laughter, incredible food, and heartfelt speeches that kept everyone entertained. My parents took the opportunity to share some embarrassing stories from my childhood, much to my chagrin but everyone else's delight. The reception reached an emotional high point when Mia took the mic. She stood with a calm confidence far beyond her years, her petite figure poised under the soft glow of the chandelier. Clearing her throat, she glanced at me, then at Anthony, and then out to the crowd.

"Okay, so, first of all," she started, "I'm not, like, a professional speech-giver or anything, so if this is bad, just... pretend it's good, okay?"

Laughter rippled through the crowd, and she relaxed a little, glancing at Anthony and me before continuing.

"But today is too important not to try."

Her eyes swept the room before landing back on me, and her expression softened. "I've known Patricia almost my whole life. I don't remember the first time we met—but it feels like she's always been there in some way. What I do remember is that for a long time, even though our family was great, it always felt like something was missing. Like a piece of the puzzle wasn't there yet."

Anthony's hand tightened around mine, and I felt my throat constrict as I fought back tears.

"My dad," Mia continued, her voice faltering just slightly as her gaze shifted to Anthony, "he's always been the best. The kind of dad who shows up for every game, every project, every tear. But even as a kid, I could see something wasn't right. He wasn't happy. Except..." She paused, her voice trembling as she looked directly at me. "Except when he was with you."

The room fell utterly silent, everyone captivated by the raw honesty of her words.

"I'll never forget the day we saw you at the ice cream shop," Mia said, her tone taking on a softer, almost reverent quality. "That day, something changed. I saw something in my dad's eyes that I hadn't seen in a long time. Hope. I knew that's what it was because it was the same thing I felt when I saw you."

I couldn't hold back my tears any longer. They slipped down my cheeks as Mia's words pierced straight to my heart.

"And I remember thinking, maybe you weren't just another one of his friends. Maybe you were something... more." She paused for a second, her cheeks flushing, but she kept going

"And I was right. You brought something into our lives that we didn't even know we needed." She paused, her fingers gripping the mic stand as she looked directly at me.

"Mama—my grandma—she helped raise me and Christian. She's been there for us through everything, and I love her so much for that. But I always wanted a mom—someone who was here, with me and Christian, so we could have a family like everyone else."

The crowd was completely silent, hanging on every word, and I was doing everything I could not to full-on sob.

"You gave us a real family. You make my dad really happy. And you make me and Christian feel really loved. You're the mom I always wanted."

Her voice broke completely now, and she wiped at her eyes, laughing through her tears. "I'm gonna stop before I start bawling, but I just wanted to say thank you. For loving my dad. For loving us. And for being the best stepmom anyone could ask for."

She hesitated for a second before adding with a teasing grin, "Even if you are a little strict sometimes."

The room burst into laughter, giving Mia the perfect way to step down from the mic. As she stepped down, the room erupted into applause. There wasn't a dry eye in sight, including Anthony, who wiped his face with the sleeve of his jacket as he pulled Mia into a hug. She grinned up at him, and then at me, before joining Christian at their table.

The mood lightened when Anthony's best man took the mic. "Alright," he began with a sly grin, "let's get back to what this day is really about: roasting Anthony."

Laughter rippled through the room, and he continued, "Now, don't get me wrong—Anthony is a catch. He's charming, he's smart, he's loyal. But when it came to dating? Oh, man. He was awkward. So awkward. Honestly, he made me, as his wing man, work twice as hard just to keep his chances alive."

The crowd laughed harder, and even Anthony shook his head, a wide grin on his face.

"But thank goodness for Patricia," the best man added, his tone softening slightly. "She saw something in him the rest of us were starting to question." The laughter returned, followed by a warm wave of applause as he raised his glass. "To Anthony and Patricia—the perfect example of how even the awkward ones can find love!"

As the night wound down, I found a moment to step outside. The water shimmered under the moonlight, and the distant sound of music and laughter carried through the air. The cool breeze kissed my cheeks as I stared out over the lake, my heart full.

Anthony found me there, wrapping his arms around my waist from behind. His warmth was grounding, and I leaned back into him with a contented sigh.

"You okay, Mrs. Garcia?" he whispered, his lips brushing against my ear.

"More than okay," I replied, smiling as I turned to face him. "I'm perfect."

He cupped my face in his hands, his thumbs brushing lightly over my cheeks as he gazed into my eyes. "This is just the beginning, you know."

I smiled, my heart swelling. "I wouldn't have it any other way."

We stood there for a while, wrapped in each other's arms, letting the reality of everything sink in.

This moment was everything. It was the life we had fought for, the family we had built, and the future we were ready to embrace together.

| 34 |

The Price of Peace

WELCOME TO PUERTO RICO
    In bold red, white, and blue letters, the banner hung above the arrival gate at the airport. It greeted Anthony and me as we stepped off the plane, bags in tow and hearts full of excitement. Puerto Rico was everything I imagined and more. The sun was warm, the ocean breeze salty and refreshing, and the island's rhythm seemed to whisper, *Relax. You deserve this.*

Our first two days were pure bliss. We indulged in fresh mofongo and piña coladas, explored the cobblestone streets of Old San Juan, and let the stress of the past year melt away under the Caribbean sun. By the third day, we'd settled into the slower pace, waking late and lounging on the balcony of our resort with coffee in hand.

Anthony stretched beside me, his bare chest catching the golden morning light. He glanced at me, his eyes warm and full of contentment. "I'm going to get us some breakfast," he said, his voice soft but firm, the way it always was when he was determined to take care of me.

Before I could respond, he leaned in, gently cupping my face with both hands. His lips pressed against mine in a slow, lingering kiss that made my heart flutter. When he pulled back, his gaze stayed locked on mine, his thumb brushing lightly across my cheek.

"I love you," he said, his voice a quiet promise.

"I love you too," I replied, my voice barely a whisper, but I knew he heard me.

With a grin, he grabbed his wallet and headed toward the door. I watched him leave, the slight bounce in his step a reflection of how light and carefree the last few days had been.

That's when the texts started pouring in. My phone buzzed insistently, the screen lighting up with a string of messages. Multiple notifications from old EMT and hospital co workers appeared in rapid succession, each with the same cryptic tone.

"Hey! Not sure if you have service out there but have you been online lately?"

"Hey girl, you go check your socials."

"Patricia there's something you'll want to see."

No one told me exactly what I should be looking for—just that I needed to go online and see for myself. I assumed it must be wedding pictures or videos that had started making the rounds. These days, everyone captures every moment on their phones. I couldn't help but wonder what embarrassing or unexpected moments had been caught on camera that were apparently so urgent for me to check out. I sighed, half-annoyed that they couldn't just *tell me* what it was, and opened my phone's browser to check my social media feed. It took less than a minute for my breath to catch in my throat.

"R.I.P. James Sterling."

The words stared back at me, stark and unfeeling. My stomach flipped, and my heart dropped. A chill ran through me, the sunny morning suddenly feeling far too bright. I froze, unable to process what I was reading. What had happened? How did this happen? My fingers fumbled as I clicked on the post, scanning for details. The caption offered no clarity—just a flood of condolences and memories from those who once knew him. My heart pounded as I scrolled furiously, trying to make sense of it. *Did they attack him? Did he... do it to himself?* My thoughts raced as I searched for answers. And then, I found it. A post from his wife.

Her words hit me like a freight train:

"I loved him deeply, but I never had his heart. He was haunted, torn between two worlds he created. We found a letter in his cell, one that tried to make sense of the pain he carried."

The letter was attached, and as much as I didn't want to read it, I couldn't stop myself.

"To those I've hurt,

Client satisfaction is my top priority. I will do my best to adapt my writing to your preference as you provide feedback during the weekly updates and final revision.

What the fuck? I read the letter over and over, each word pulling me deeper into a vortex of emotions—confusion, anger, sadness, guilt. Why would she post this for everyone to see? Was it a cry for help? A way to process her own pain publicly? Or was it her way of ensuring I saw it? Maybe she wanted to share the hurt, to make me feel some of what she was feeling. Or perhaps it was simply to notify me of the money he'd left. Whatever her reasons, it felt strange—jarring, even.

I didn't want his money. I didn't want anything from him. All I'd ever wanted was peace. And even in death, James managed to find a way to disrupt it. My hands trembled as I closed my phone, the weight of the letter pressing heavily on my chest.

The door opened, and Anthony walked into the room, holding two plates of breakfast from the resort buffet. His smile, so warm and full of life just moments before, faltered the second he saw my face.

"Hey," he said gently, setting the plates down and sitting beside me. "What's wrong?"

I wanted to tell him, but the words wouldn't come. Instead, I shook my head, forcing a weak smile. "Nothing. I just... got lost scrolling through wedding pictures. I think I need some fresh air."

Anthony didn't press, sensing my need for space. "Okay," he said, leaning over to kiss my temple. "Take your time."

I quickly composed myself, shoving the whirlwind of emotions to the back of my mind. I couldn't let James ruin this moment—or this trip. Forcing a bright smile, I turned toward Anthony.

"What's for breakfast?" I asked, trying to keep my voice upbeat.

Anthony smiled as he stepped forward, carrying a tray with two plates of food. "Pan sobao—your favorite," he said, setting the tray on the small balcony table. Pan sobao, the soft and slightly sweet bread from Puerto Rico. Its fluffy texture and faint sweetness paired perfectly with butter or café con leche. Just seeing it on the plate felt like a warm hug from the island itself.

"You know me so well," I said, grinning widely.

"I was hoping I'd come back to you naked," he teased, a playful smirk lighting up his face.

I laughed, feeling some of the tension in my chest ease. "I'm beach ready—that's close enough," I shot back, leaning in to kiss him as he set the tray down. Anthony pulled out one of the chairs and gestured for me to sit. "Beach ready or not, you're beautiful...just more beautiful when you're naked," he said, his tone playful but sincere. I rolled my eyes, but I couldn't hide the blush creeping up my cheeks as I took my seat. As he settled across from me, the scent of the warm bread mingling with the salty ocean breeze, I let myself soak in the moment.

The days in Puerto Rico flew by in a whirlwind of sun, laughter, and adventure. Anthony and I had vowed to make the most of every moment, and we held true to that promise. The day after our leisurely breakfast on the balcony, we dove headfirst into all the island had to offer. From kayaking in the glowing bioluminescent bay at Fajardo to strolling the colorful streets of San Juan, we embraced our inner tourists. The vibrant murals, and historic forts were straight out of a postcard, and Anthony couldn't stop snapping pictures—of me, of us, of anything that caught his eye.

"You're like a kid with his first camera," I teased, watching him squat to get the perfect angle of the Cathedral of San Juan Bautista.

"Hey, these are memories," he replied with a grin. "Plus, one day, I'll be old and need something to remind me how gorgeous my wife was back in the day."

I rolled my eyes, though I couldn't hide the smile tugging at my lips. "Nice save."

By midweek, we tackled one of the activities I'd been looking forward to the most—an excursion to El Yunque National Rainforest. The lush greenery and cascading waterfalls felt like stepping into another world. We joined a small group and hiked along winding trails, surrounded by towering trees and the symphony of coquí frogs. At one point, Anthony decided to climb onto a large rock by the waterfall for a photo.

"Be careful!" I called, watching as he struck a triumphant pose, arms raised like he'd just conquered Mount Everest.

"Relax, babe! I've got cat-like reflexes," he shouted back before promptly losing his footing and sliding down into the shallow pool below.

The group burst into laughter, myself included. Anthony emerged, soaked but grinning. "Okay, maybe not cat-like," he admitted, wringing out his shirt.

The cool, refreshing swim at La Mina Falls made up for any mishaps, and as we floated together in the clear water, I found myself momentarily free of the weight of James. The rainforest had a way of silencing everything else, letting me just exist in the moment with Anthony. By the fifth day, the exhaustion had caught up with us. Between snorkeling, hiking, and a seemingly endless supply of delicious Puerto Rican food, we were ready to see the kids and share our adventures with them. Our last night on the island was spent packing up our bags for the morning flight. The villa was quiet except for the rhythmic sound of the waves outside and the occasional rustling of clothes as we folded and zipped up suitcases.

"I can't believe it's almost over," Anthony said, glancing at me as he stuffed his sneakers into his bag. "This trip went by too fast."

"Doesn't it always?" I replied, sitting on the edge of the bed as I folded one of my sundresses. "But I think I'm ready to see the little ones. I miss them."

He nodded, smiling. "Me too. This has been amazing, though. Just us."

"Yeah," I said softly, looking around the room. "It's exactly what we needed."

As much as I tried to focus on the beauty of our time together, James's name still lingered at the edge of my mind. I'd successfully avoided thinking too much about him during our adventures, but the silence of the evening brought everything back. Still, I refused to let him take this moment from us.

"Hey," Anthony said, breaking my thoughts as he zipped up his suitcase. "What do you say we take a walk on the beach before calling it a night?"

I smiled, nodding. "Sounds perfect."

Hand in hand, we stepped out onto the moonlit sand, letting the waves lap at our feet. The stars above seemed brighter here, their light reflecting on the water. As we walked, I made a silent promise to myself: to hold onto this peace, this love, and this life we were building. James was a part of our past, but our future was ours to claim.

| 35 |

The Final Goodbye

"Now Boarding Zone 1 to Philadelphia"

That was our cue. As we got in line to show our boarding passes, a nagging feeling churned in my stomach. I needed to tell Anthony. Keeping it bottled up any longer felt unbearable, but I decided to wait until we were settled in our seats. I'd paid for an extra seat so we could have the row to ourselves, something Anthony initially wasn't thrilled about because of his frugal tendencies.

"Okay, not going to lie, the extra leg space and extra seat are really nice," he admitted, stretching out as we settled in.

"I told you," I replied, laughing.

The plane began to ascend, and I stared out the window, watching the golden glow of the sun bathe the clouds below us. Anthony was flipping through an in-flight magazine, his attention divided between the articles and the snack menu. The hum of the engines created an odd calm, but my chest felt tight.

Now or never, Patricia, I told myself.

"Anthony," I said, my voice softer than usual.

He glanced up, his brow furrowing slightly. "What's up?"

I shifted in my seat, my hands fidgeting with the hem of my sweater. "There's something I need to tell you."

His face immediately grew serious. "Yeah, I've been waiting for you to tell me what's on your mind. What is it?"

I should have known he'd already sensed something. Apparently, we were on the same wavelength—both of us choosing not to ruin our honeymoon by bringing it up sooner.

I took a deep breath, trying to steady myself. "It's James. He's... gone."

"What do you mean, gone?"

"I mean dead. He... committed suicide," I said carefully, gauging his reaction.

Anthony's eyes widened slightly, and his lips pressed into a thin line. "Jesus. Are you okay?" His concern was genuine, and his hand reached over to cover mine.

"Yeah, but... there's more," I admitted, biting my lip.

"Of course there is," he said, rolling his eyes slightly in exasperation.

"He left behind a letter. In it, he apologized for everything and..." I hesitated, unsure of how to phrase the next part.

"And?" Anthony prompted gently, though his posture had tensed.

"And he left me money. Fifty thousand dollars," I said quickly, bracing for his reaction.

Anthony blinked, his expression caught somewhere between shock and disbelief. Then, to my surprise, a faint smile tugged at the corner of his mouth. "So he left us a wedding gift? Well, the least he could do was leave you some money for pain and suffering."

"Anthony!" I gave him a sharp look.

"What? I'm just saying," he replied, shrugging and trying to look innocent.

I shook my head, though a small laugh escaped despite myself. Leave it to Anthony to lighten the mood without dismissing the weight of the situation entirely.

"No, but seriously. That's horrible. Are you really okay, though?" he asked again, his teasing giving way to genuine concern.

"I think so," I said after a moment. "It's just... strange. I don't want his money. It feels wrong."

I handed him my phone, showing him the screenshot of the letter. He read it, his eyebrows climbing higher with each line.

"What the fuck? His poor wife," Anthony said, equal parts amazed and disgusted.

"I know, that's exactly what I said! And like, did I kill this man? I don't want this money. This is just fucking crazy."

"Let's not get carried away now. We'll accept the money," he joked, deadpan.

"Anthony!"

He couldn't hold back his laughter anymore. "You didn't kill anyone. This was his way of manipulating you one last time. Honestly, how did you keep this to yourself for days? You might be just as crazy."

"You are *literally* the worst," I said, shaking my head but unable to suppress a small smile.

He shrugged, his expression softening as he squeezed my hand. "Whatever you decide, I'm with you. I love your crazy ass."

And just like that, the weight on my chest lightened.

We arrived back at Anthony's house to the kids' excitement bubbling over, their faces lighting up the moment we walked through the door. Christian launched himself at Anthony, wrapping his little arms around his dad's legs with a shriek of pure joy. "You're back!" he yelled, his voice echoing through the house. Mia hung back slightly, her usual calm demeanor on display, but the wide grin on her face betrayed just how excited she was to see us. She stepped forward to give me a tight hug. "How was it? Did you guys eat any weird food?" she asked, her curiosity bubbling over.

Anthony scooped up Christian, spinning him in a playful circle before setting him down. "We missed you guys," he said, his voice warm.

"We brought you something," I said, reaching into my carry-on bag to pull out souvenirs—small trinkets, colorful bracelets, and a stuffed coquí frog that immediately caught Christian's attention. "This little guy is all yours," I said, handing it to him.

He clutched it tightly, his eyes wide. "I love him! I'm going to name him… Coquí!" he announced, as if the decision had been life-changing.

The house was filled with laughter as we shared stories from our trip over dinner, the kids hanging on to every word. For a brief moment, it felt like life had settled into a perfect rhythm. The honeymoon glow followed us into our daily lives, and everything felt brighter, lighter, as if the weight of the past had finally lifted.

The kids moved into my home shortly after we returned, making it feel like our family was truly becoming one. Their rooms were decorated to their liking—Mia's filled with twinkling fairy lights and a cozy reading nook, while Christian's was all superheroes and soccer posters. Hearing their laughter echoing through the house as they adjusted to their new space brought a joy I hadn't anticipated. Family dinners became our favorite tradition, the table filled with stories, jokes, and the occasional sibling squabble over the last piece of garlic bread. It was chaotic, but it was ours.

But life, as always, had other plans.

One month later, I found myself staring at a pregnancy test in the bathroom, the two unmistakable lines staring right back at me. My heart pounded as reality sank in—Anthony and I were going to have a baby.

I didn't even try to play it cool when I told him. Standing in the kitchen, holding the test behind my back like a surprise gift, I blurted it out. "You're going to be a dad. Again."

Anthony, who had been mid-sip of his coffee, froze. For a second, I thought he might choke. Then his face lit up, his eyes wide with disbelief and joy. "Wait... seriously?" he asked, his voice brimming with excitement.

I nodded, unable to keep the grin off my face. "Seriously."

Without hesitation, he set down his mug and crossed the room, pulling me into one of those tight, warm hugs that made me feel like everything was right in the world. His reaction was everything I could have hoped for. His face lit up like a kid on Christmas morning, and he pulled me into one of those tight, warm hugs that made me feel like everything was right in the world. "We're having a baby!" he yelled, his voice brimming with excitement and love. If there was ever a sign to take the next step, this was it. It was time to find a home big enough to hold all of us, a space for new memories and a fresh start for our growing family. And, finally, I knew exactly what to do with the money James had left behind.

The house hunt began in earnest, our days consumed by scrolling through listings, attending endless showings, and coordinating with attorneys to finalize everything from James's will. It was a whirlwind, each step a mix of exhaustion and exhilaration. Despite the chaos, it was a hopeful reminder that life was moving forward, and we were building something new.

After three months of searching, we finally found it. A beautiful farm-style home with a wraparound porch overlooking the tranquil waters of a nearby river. It was as if the house had been waiting for us all along. Everything about it felt perfect: an in-law suite for Anthony's mom, a detached finished garage that would become my dream writing studio, and sprawling land where Mia and Christian could run free and create memories.

We stood on the porch together, the gentle sound of the river harmonizing with the soft rustling of leaves in the breeze. The sunset cast a golden glow over the property, making the white exterior of the house shimmer with warmth. Anthony slid his hand into mine, his thumb gently brushing over my knuckles.

"This is it," I said softly, my voice catching with emotion.

He nodded, his gaze fixed on the view before us, but his grip on my hand tightened. "Yeah, it is," he replied, a mixture of awe and certainty in his tone.

By the grace of God, everything fell into place. Within a few weeks, we were able to sell both of our homes. The funds from James's will and the profits from the sales made purchasing our dream home not just possible, but seamless. It felt like the universe was finally giving us a break—a chance to create the life we'd dreamed of for so long.

"Rocking chairs," I said as I looked around the porch, imagining it filled with laughter and peace. "We need rocking chairs. One for each of us, plus your mom. Red ones. They'll pop against the white."

Anthony smirked, shaking his head slightly. "Slow down there," he said, but then his expression softened. "I'm glad you said that, though, because six red rocking chairs are getting delivered tomorrow. Thought you'd like that."

"What?!" I squealed, throwing my arms around his neck. "How did I get so lucky?"

He smiled as I kissed him. "I ask myself the same thing."

The next afternoon, as promised, a delivery truck pulled into the driveway. The sight of the six bright red rocking chairs being unloaded made my heart skip a beat. Anthony stood on the porch with a satisfied grin, directing the delivery workers as they carefully arranged the chairs in a neat row. Each one was perfectly aligned, facing out toward the water.

Once the workers had left, I ran my hand over the smooth wood of the chair closest to the door. "They're perfect," I said softly, my eyes misting.

"Go ahead," Anthony urged. "Try it out."

I didn't need any more encouragement. I sank into the chair, the gentle creak of the wood beneath me feeling like a warm embrace. Anthony took the seat next to me, the two of us swaying slightly in unison as we gazed out at the river. The water shimmered under the late afternoon sun, and a soft breeze rustled through the trees.

"This is home," he said, reaching over to squeeze my hand.

Later that evening, I grabbed my laptop and returned to the porch. The rocking chairs were now my favorite spot in the house, a place where the noise of the world seemed to fade away, leaving only the sound of the river and the occasional chirp of a cricket. In the midst of all the chaos, I somehow managed to finish writing my book—a self-help guide that delved into the often-overwhelming struggles of managing mental health in the day-to-day world. It offered practical advice, heartfelt anecdotes, and hard-earned lessons I'd learned along the way. It was a deeply personal project, my way of turning pain into purpose, and creating a guide for anyone feeling lost in their own storms brewing within.

As I sat at my desk, reviewing the final draft, a deep sense of accomplishment settled over me. The words on the page felt like an extension of my soul—a raw and honest reflection of my journey. And yet, something felt incomplete, like a crucial piece was missing to truly bring it all together.

Then it hit me.

I leaned forward, my fingers poised over the keyboard, the words flowing effortlessly:

Beyond The Roses

In loving memory of James W. Sterling.

I sat back, exhaling deeply. "And that's my story," I whispered to myself, the words carrying a quiet finality. The book was ready, and so was I—for the next chapter, for our new life, and for everything that lay beyond the roses.

How To Continue Your Healing Journey

Book 3: Beyond The Roses

A self-care workbook for emotional healing and personal growth

Priscilla Salcedo is a multifaceted author and the visionary founder of Lunar House Publishing, a dynamic hybrid publishing company. With a background as a surgical technologist and a life-long passion for writing that began at the age of 14, Priscilla has dedicated her life to guiding others towards a healthier path.

As a self-published author, Priscilla seamlessly weaves themes of mind, body, and spirit into her writing while exploring new creative avenues. Recently, she has ventured into the realms of romance and erotic fiction, embracing the evolution of her personal and professional journey. She believes that as she grows, so does her voice as a writer, allowing her to explore diverse genres with authenticity and passion. Her latest work, The Rose-Colored Garden, marks an exciting new chapter in her career—a deeply personal foray into fiction that has ignited her love for storytelling.